RETURN TO HONOR

Knights Of Honor
Book Ten

Alexa Aston

Copyright © 2018 by Alexa Aston
Print Edition

Published by Dragonblade Publishing, an imprint of Kathryn Le Veque Novels, Inc

All rights reserved. No part of this book may be used or reproduced in any manner whatsoever without written permission, except in the case of brief quotations embodied in critical articles or reviews.

Books from Dragonblade Publishing

Dangerous Lords Series by Maggi Andersen
The Baron's Betrothal
Seducing the Earl
The Viscount's Widowed Lady

Also from Maggi Andersen
The Marquess Meets His Match

Knights of Honor Series by Alexa Aston
Word of Honor
Marked by Honor
Code of Honor
Journey to Honor
Heart of Honor
Bold in Honor
Love and Honor
Gift of Honor
Path to Honor
Return to Honor

Legends of Love Series by Avril Borthiry
The Wishing Well
Isolated Hearts
Sentinel

The Lost Lords Series by Chasity Bowlin
The Lost Lord of Castle Black
The Vanishing of Lord Vale
The Missing Marquess of Althorn
The Resurrection of Lady Ramsleigh
The Mystery of Miss Mason

By Elizabeth Ellen Carter
Captive of the Corsairs, *Heart of the Corsairs Series*
Revenge of the Corsairs, *Heart of the Corsairs Series*
Shadow of the Corsairs, *Heart of the Corsairs Series*
Dark Heart

Knight Everlasting Series by Cassidy Cayman
Endearing
Enchanted
Evermore

Midnight Meetings Series by Gina Conkle
Meet a Rogue at Midnight, book 4

Second Chance Series by Jessica Jefferson
Second Chance Marquess

Imperial Season Series by Mary Lancaster
Vienna Waltz
Vienna Woods
Vienna Dawn

Blackhaven Brides Series by Mary Lancaster
The Wicked Baron
The Wicked Lady
The Wicked Rebel
The Wicked Husband
The Wicked Marquis
The Wicked Governess
The Wicked Spy
The Wicked Gypsy
The Wicked Wife

Highland Loves Series by Melissa Limoges
My Reckless Love
My Steadfast Love
My Passionate Love

Clash of the Tartans Series by Anna Markland
Kilty Secrets
Kilted at the Altar
Kilty Pleasures

Queen of Thieves Series by Andy Peloquin
Child of the Night Guild
Thief of the Night Guild
Queen of the Night Guild

Dark Gardens Series by Meara Platt
Garden of Shadows
Garden of Light
Garden of Dragons
Garden of Destiny

Rulers of the Sky Series by Paula Quinn
Scorched
Ember
White Hot

Highlands Forever Series by Violetta Rand
Unbreakable
Undeniable

Viking's Fury Series by Violetta Rand
Love's Fury
Desire's Fury
Passion's Fury

Also from Violetta Rand
Viking Hearts

The Sons of Scotland Series by Victoria Vane
Virtue
Valor

Dry Bayou Brides Series by Lynn Winchester
The Shepherd's Daughter
The Seamstress
The Widow

Men of Blood Series by Rosamund Winchester
The Blood & The Bloom

Table of Contents

Prologue 1
Chapter 1 11
Chapter 2 20
Chapter 3 28
Chapter 4 37
Chapter 5 48
Chapter 6 57
Chapter 7 66
Chapter 8 76
Chapter 9 85
Chapter 10 94
Chapter 11 104
Chapter 12 114
Chapter 13 122
Chapter 14 132
Chapter 15 140
Chapter 16 148
Chapter 17 156
Chapter 18 163
Chapter 19 171
Chapter 20 180
Chapter 21 189
Chapter 22 196
Chapter 23 203
Chapter 24 211
Chapter 25 218
Chapter 26 225
Chapter 27 233
Epilogue 238
About the Author 242

Acknowledgments

My *Knights of Honor* series would never have been possible without the encouragement and support of Kathryn Le Veque, the Queen of All Things Medieval and a superb mentor. Kathryn believed in me and gave this series a place at Dragonblade Publishing. I'm so happy to be part of the Dragonblade family.

My editor, Scott Moreland, has left his mark on every page of this series, for which I am grateful. His guiding hand has challenged me to become a better writer and his eye for details is second to none. I wouldn't want to be on this journey without him.

Kris Newberger's organizational skills and friendship smoothed the way to publication every single time. She's a lady who knows how to get things done efficiently and quickly.

Aven Ellis provided invaluable feedback and suggestions and came to love all of my knights and their ladies as much as I did. She always has my back.

Last of all, to my husband—you are the hero of our love story. May it go on for many years to come.

PROLOGUE

London—July, 1376

GREGORY DE CHALLON felt the waves of disapproval coming off Sir Rodric Shelley as the two men traipsed silently through the empty streets of London. Today had proven hot and the heat seemed to linger into the night as the midnight hour approached. The streets stunk of waste that had been dumped from windows, reminding Gregory why so many of the nobility left London during the summer months. At least it wouldn't take long to reach the cottage he'd leased for Celia since the teeming crowds were now tucked into their beds for the night. He needed it that way because he didn't want to be seen visiting the girl, heavy with child.

His child.

It was her fault for being so damned beautiful. Gregory had been tempted beyond measure when he first spied Celia Achard at court. Only ten and six, she was small in height when compared to most women, but her full breasts and tiny waist had caught his attention, as did her glorious mane of golden hair. But it was her eye color that truly whetted his appetite. The sprite's eyes were amethyst in color, like two jewels set in a perfect face.

He'd had his share of women—and then some. Growing up, he'd bedded anyone in a skirt, be it a servant or local village wench. When his father brought him to the royal court in London, Gregory had plowed through a bevy of pretty widows before working his way through a dozen or more married lovers, both at court and in the city of London.

That was before Celia arrived. Why a naïve virgin had turned his very experienced head was something Gregory didn't understand, only that she made his blood sing. He had thought to steal only a kiss from her in a darkened alcove. Mayhap two. Then kisses had turned to touch and touch crashed out of control until she found herself with child. She hid it for as long as she could and then told her father she'd been asked to visit a friend at her family's country estate. Lord Americ Achard rarely saw his daughter and had only given her a cursory glance when she told him of her travel plans for the summer. Celia said her father seemed relieved that she had somewhere to go so that he wouldn't be responsible for her.

That had allowed Gregory to rent the tiny cottage in the heart of London while Celia's time to deliver drew near. He'd stolen away from the palace to visit her a few times, not nearly as much as either of them would have liked, but that had to end. Today.

When he broke her heart.

Oh, she wouldn't know right away. He would make gallant promises tonight and cover her in sweet kisses. She would deliver the child and Sir Rodric would take her back to Nesterfield. She had no mother and her two younger brothers had come to court for their summer break to spend time with their father, a man heavily involved in court politics and the royal treasury. Once he'd taken a few days to show his sons London, Americ and the boys left to join the court's summer progress. Because of that, Celia could recover from childbirth alone at home, with no one the wiser.

Except for the babe.

As they drew near their destination, Gregory paused. His companion halted and looked at him with wary eyes.

"Today is the last day I will see her," he promised the knight, who'd gotten Gregory out of more scrapes that anyone could imagine.

"And I'm to take her to Nesterfield after she gives birth. To your babe," Sir Rodric said, his tone even but accusing Gregory all the same.

"Aye. Offer to pay the midwife to take the child away."

"If she refuses?" the knight asked boldly.

Gregory swallowed. "Then get rid of it on the way."

Sir Rodric's brows rose. "You want me to kill it. A babe. *Your* babe."

He steeled himself. "Do whatever you have to do, Rodric. But Celia is not to arrive home with a child in her arms."

"What should I tell the lady happened to her babe?"

"Whatever you wish."

Gregory turned away and strode off, knowing the loyal knight would follow. He'd been in service to the de Challons his entire life and would do his duty, no matter how much he despised the outcome.

They reached the cottage and Gregory opened the door, leaving his soldier outside to make sure no one else entered behind him. A single candle glowed in the one room. Celia lay atop a pallet on the floor, fast asleep. He went and knelt beside her.

In sleep, she looked even younger but she still resembled an earthly angel. Her face had grown slightly fuller. He placed a palm against her rounded belly. A moment later, he felt a strong kick against it. He jerked his hand away, not wanting to think about the child they'd made together. Lowering his mouth to hers, he pressed a kiss against her soft lips.

She awakened and opened her mouth to him. He accepted the invitation, kissing her deeply, knowing it would be the last time their lips met. Breaking the kiss, he helped her sit up, her back supported against the wall behind her. Gregory pulled a small, velvet pouch from his pocket and handed it to her.

"A gift?" Celia's face lit up.

"A little something to remember me by," he said lightly.

She loosened the strings and reached inside, withdrawing an amethyst brooch. It had taken going to three jewelers until he found what he wanted but the smile that lit her face made his troubles worthwhile.

"'Tis the most beautiful thing I have ever seen," she swore.

"I thought the gems matched the color of your eyes. Here, let me pin it on you."

Gregory opened the clasp and slid the pin through the material of her nightdress. Celia fingered the brooch lovingly.

Cupping her face, he said, "I have to go away for a little while, love."

"To Egelina?" she asked, her mouth turning down.

"Aye. She is my betrothed and we are to wed in three days' time."

"But you will stop it, won't you, Gregory?" Her large eyes pleaded with him.

"I will do what I can, Celia," he said, knowing he would never dream of halting the marriage between him and the homely cow whose bridal price was large enough to ensure she would be taken off her parents' hands for good. "To do so, I must convince both her and her parents—as well as my father—that we should not marry."

"But you are so good with words, Gregory. You are intelligent. You will be able to reason with them. Make them see why you cannot marry Egelina." Her mouth set in determination.

He shrugged. "I cannot predict what will happen, love. A betrothal is as good as being wed. Persuading all parties involved will be difficult."

"But not impossible." She gave him a tender smile. "I believe you can do anything, Gregory. Even guarantee that we will always be together."

"Not for a while," he reminded her. "If they knew of you and the babe, that would not be reason enough to break our arrangement. I must find a way that appeals to all sides. Try not to worry. You and the child will be safe at Sturnwick. Your father and brothers will be gone for a few months and then most likely, Lord Achard will return them to where they foster before he arrives back at court. By then, I hope I will have worked out a solution to our problem."

Celia's eyes misted with tears. "You think of me—and the babe—as a problem?" Her lips trembled and he knew she was on the verge of breaking down.

"Nay, love. You misconstrued my meaning."

Tears leaked from her eyes. "I'm sorry. 'Tis being with child. I find myself so emotional." She paused. "I think my time draws near."

"Rodric has been tasked to take care of everything. He will bring a midwife for the delivery. Then he will wait a few days until you are strong enough to travel before he escorts you home."

"I wish I could go to your home. Our home," she said stubbornly.

Gregory knew he needed to leave before her demands became unreasonable. Brushing his lips against hers a last time, he then said, "I must go. Take care."

Celia threw her arms about his neck. "I love you, Gregory."

He felt the hot tears against his skin. Wrapping his arms around her, he inhaled one final time the sweet scent of her innocence. An innocence he'd ruined. Guilt flushed through him, knowing he would marry his betrothed and live a hundred leagues away from a woman who just might have captured his hard heart. Gregory told himself it was all for the best. There would be no child. Hopefully, it wouldn't live but if it did, Rodric would see that Celia Achard arrived home with only herself. Her body would heal. Eventually, her heart would, too.

Or so he told himself.

"Let me help you."

Gregory eased her back onto the pallet. On her back, her belly rose like a majestic mountain. A belly filled with his child. He shrugged off the thought and brushed back a lock of hair from her face.

"Go to sleep, Celia."

"I hope my dreams are of you," she said. Her eyes closed and within seconds, she appeared asleep.

Rising, he drank in one long, last look and left the cottage. Nodding at Rodric, who would remain behind, Gregory slipped back through the quiet, dark streets, regret rending his heart in two.

RODRIC'S ANGER AT his liege lord's oldest son rippled through him. The boy had played with fire his entire life, never being burned, thanks to always having someone to clean up his messes after him. Rodric could understand a boy seeking adventure but Gregory de Challon's attraction to danger would cost him dearly someday. The boy had become a man who knew no boundaries. He'd dallied with every eligible woman at the royal court without consequence and now he had walked away from any sense of duty to Lady Celia Achard. By now, the fool was wed to that ugly Egelina and either counting the money she'd brought or seducing some serving wench in the nearby village. Rodric knew Sir Gregory would never look back at the trouble he'd caused.

Fortunately, Lady Celia had lived through the delivery, though he thought her blood loss great. Rodric had worried at her small size, as had the midwife, but the young noblewoman had managed to give birth to a healthy girl after a day and half in agonizing labor. The child thrived—but her mother grew weaker by the minute. He wasn't certain the lady would live through the journey to her home. He'd bought a cart and had thought she would ride next to him in it on the way to Sturnwick but now determined she would need to lie in the back with the babe and conserve what little strength she had left.

The midwife refused to entertain the idea of accepting the child after its birth. The woman told Rodric no one wanted a newborn, least of all a nobleman's cast-off, and she'd be hard put to find the girl a home in London. Though no names had ever been exchanged, he knew there'd been no way to hide the fact that Lady Celia was nobility. Her speech, her dress, her very manner gave that way.

Now, Rodric was to take his two charges out of the city. The rent on the cottage had run out, so they would be leaving for Sturnwick in minutes. He'd already put a small trunk of Lady Celia's in the wagon bed and laid blankets out for her to rest upon. The midwife had left a basket behind for the child to sleep in. He'd bought a small blanket at a vendor's stall and placed the brown wool inside the basket for the child to sleep upon.

Returning inside, he saw a pale Lady Celia standing, wobbly on her feet.

"Come, my lady. Let me help you to the cart."

"But the—"

"I'll return for the babe. She's fast asleep in her basket. You needn't worry about her."

He led her to the wagon and gingerly lifted her into it.

"Lie down and settle yourself. I'll be back in a moment."

Rodric returned and glanced around the cottage one last time, making sure they left nothing behind, especially anything that might give a clue as to who had stayed here and what had occurred. He'd already paid the midwife enough to keep her lips from flapping. Turning to the basket, he lifted it by its handle, the sleeping child not stirring at the subtle movement.

Gazing down, he couldn't see anything of Sir Gregory in the babe. She had blond fuzz atop her head, which would grow out one day to be the same shade as her mother's. She also possessed the delicate nose and mouth of Lady Celia. He fought the bile rising in him.

How could he kill a babe?

Rodric didn't have it in him. He'd killed on the battlefield. Done things he wasn't particularly proud of—especially when cleaning up the multitude of troubles Sir Gregory left behind. But he had to draw the line at murdering an innocent child. His code as a knight prevented it. He'd vowed to protect the weak, including women and children.

Yet, he knew he couldn't go against Sir Gregory's wishes. Somehow, he would have to find a place for the babe along the way before they reached Sturnwick.

And lie to the mother about what happened to her child.

Returning outside, he climbed into the back of the cart. Lady Celia lay there, looking even more ashen than before. So far, she'd been able to nurse the babe but he worried that time might soon run out.

"Let me have her," the noblewoman begged.

"You are too weak, my lady," he warned. "I will place the basket next to you. She will be fine."

Rodric knew how ill Lady Celia must be for she didn't argue with him. He nestled the basket against her side and then covered the babe with a portion of the blanket and then her mother with another one.

"Call out if you need anything and I'll stop the cart right away," he said cheerfully, trying to placate her.

"All right." She gave him a sad smile. "Thank you, Sir Rodric. For everything. I know how much Gregory counts upon you."

"That he does, my lady. Don't you worry. I'll get you to Sturnwick, safe and sound," he promised.

"And my child."

He gave her a tight smile and a nod—but couldn't force himself to speak an untruth.

Rodric climbed into the driver's seat and steered the horse through the busy London streets. It would take almost a week to reach Sturnwick. That gave him time to decide what to do.

As the days passed, he realized Lady Celia would not reach her childhood home alive. She grew punier by the day and the babe had trouble nursing at her breast. He'd thought to tell the mother that her child had died and he'd stopped to bury it while she slept but realized he might not have to lie to her—for she would be the one who passed on.

He stopped in a village and bought some bread and cheese and a jug of ale at a tavern. While waiting for the maid to gather up what he'd purchased, Rodric listened to a conversation occurring next to him because he heard the name *de Montfort* mentioned. He had met a couple of the same name at court, Lord Geoffrey and Lady Merryn. He'd been impressed by the pair's intelligence and kindness and obvious affection toward one another. Others at court had nothing but good to say about the two and how devoted they were to each other and their children.

As he listened, he learned the very same couple's estate lay not far from this village, in the direction he now headed. A plan began to form in his mind.

Rodric thanked the maid and gave her a coin and returned to the wagon. He drove it through the village and down the road two leagues until he spied the castle on a hill up ahead. He stopped the cart and climbed in the back. Lady Celia had begged to hold her child when they'd stopped at the village. He'd taken the girl from her basket and handed her to the mother to nurse and allowed the babe to remain with her mother.

Glancing down, he saw the little one was wide awake, a small dribble of her mother's milk on her chin. Rodric wiped it away with his finger. The babe cooed at him. He lifted her and placed the girl in her basket. Turning to Lady Celia, his jaw dropped.

The lady looked at peace though her eyes stared up at the sky above. He touched his fingers to her throat and found no pulse beating within. Brushing his hand over her eyes, he closed the lids. Lady Celia seemed to wear a small smile of thanks.

Rodric jumped from the wagon and reached for the basket. He lifted it and walked to the edge of the woods near the road. His fervent prayer to the Virgin implored Her to intercede and have someone from these lands find the babe and take her in. Setting the basket on the ground, he saw the babe look up at him with her large eyes, as if she questioned his actions.

"'Tis the best I can do for you, my little lady," he said softly. "I hope you will find a home near here and happiness, as well. I will take your sweet mother to her own home to be laid to rest."

A thought occurred to him. Quickly, he strode to the cart and, with trembling fingers, removed the brooch that Sir Gregory had gifted to Lady Celia. She had worn it each day next to her heart, telling Rodric how that kept her love close to her.

Returning to the basket, he opened the blanket. Not trusting his fingers in fear of pricking the babe, he slipped the piece inside the blanket, pushing it to the bottom, then folded the blanket again so that it wrapped snuggly around the child. He pressed his lips to the babe's head.

"Godspeed, Child. May the Good Christ watch over you and bring you peace."

With a heavy heart, he returned to the cart and brought the blanket over Lady Celia's face, tucking it underneath her to secure it in place. Rodric climbed into the driver's seat and lifted the reins. He would see Lady Celia home.

And pray every day he lived for her daughter to be happy and safe.

CHAPTER 1

Suffolk—May, 1395

MARCUS DE HARTE tried to ignore the uneasy feeling rumbling inside him. He looked across at Sir Rand Trammel, his closest friend, who stood surveying the late spring evening. They had spent many nights on sentry duty together, from their days of fostering through the past couple of years as members of King Richard's army. The two men had been part of the force that had swept away rebellion in the north, and then traveled across the sea to Ireland to appease the Irish chieftains, who had many grievances against their absentee English landlords. The king had treated these so-called "High Kings" of Ireland with kindness and shown them respect, which awed the Irish leaders who'd trekked to Dublin for the series of meetings.

It hadn't hurt that Richard had brought along an army over eight thousand strong in a show of force. Marcus thought that had helped speed along the concessions made by the Irish as much as anything the monarch had discussed with them. Thankfully, the king had accomplished all of his objectives and the borders of English rule were firmly established once more.

Because of it, Marcus now led his men home to Hartefield. They had parted ways with what was left of the king's army, as various groups pulled away and headed toward their homes as the mass of soldiers journeyed across England. Only a core group would return to the Palace of Westminster with the king.

Marcus thought of the ten men who had accompanied him two years ago when they'd left Suffolk. Eight of them now returned and seven of those had bedded down for the night. He and Rand usually took the first watch, liking to see everything settled before they caught a few hours of sleep.

A restlessness came over Marcus. He looked to his companion, whose eyes swept across the area. Night had settled, though the full moon shone brightly.

"What have you missed most about home?" he asked his friend.

The corners of Rand's mouth turned up. "It's a toss-up," he declared. "Part of me says 'tis Cook's roasted boar that I've missed most, for it always makes my mouth water. No one can prepare a boar like Cook."

"I agree," Marcus said. "And the rest of you?"

Rand now grinned mischievously. "I am eager to see if your sainted mother has hired any new serving girls for the great hall. I will give them my famous tour of every nook and cranny found within Harte Castle and continue on to places along the way throughout the estate."

Marcus shook his head. Rand could charm the skirts off of any woman—and frequently had from the time the two had been strapping young lads on the cusp of manhood. While Marcus indulged his own appetite now and then with various women in the nearby village of Little Morrholm, Rand plowed his way through every female at Hartefield and beyond. Never one to commit to a single woman, Rand would die a happy, old man someday—one who'd never acquired a wife but had plenty of stories to tell about his many female conquests.

On the other hand, Marcus would need to wed to provide at heir. As an only son, he knew once he returned home that it would be expected. He'd been betrothed years before but the girl had died and his father hadn't found a suitable replacement before Marcus left to join the king's army. He already dreaded listening to his father discuss betrothal terms, much less the physical characteristics of women for Marcus to wed. While Lord Charles de Harte had never raised a hand against his wife, Lady Margaret—and those surrounding her—had listened to an earful of complaints made by her husband since she hadn't produced any more children after her son's birth.

At least any who lived.

Marcus knew of five miscarriages his mother had suffered although he suspected there might have been more. Of those Lady Margaret managed to bring to term, none survived. Three children, all females, had been stillborn. Two other girls had each lived less than a day, mewling softer than newborn kittens before they succumbed to death.

That had led Lord Charles to rage against his wife, sometimes for hours at a time. The baron complained about how delicate his wife was. How her narrow hips failed her when it came time to give birth. How even the children she did produce were dreaded girls. Lady Margaret always kept calm during these tirades and would finally point out that their firstborn was a magnificent male—tall, broad of shoulders, healthy, and strong.

With each birth, his mother had grown weaker and less animated, which concerned Marcus. Fortunately, his father turned his attentions elsewhere, deciding his wife would never produce another child—much less a son. Consequently, Marcus now had a smattering of half-siblings throughout the surrounding area.

All female.

He wondered if the fault lay in his father, but would never be bold enough to point that out to Lord Charles, nor would he voice that opinion and hurt his mother. Despite the bitter tirades the nobleman went on, his wife continued to love her husband beyond measure. Unfortunately, the love was one-sided. Marcus had seen how desperately his mother loved her husband, to the point he pitied her. He swore he would never love a woman. He wouldn't want to experience the desperation his mother did. Marcus would protect his heart above all else.

"And what have you missed most about home?" Rand asked him in return.

"My mother," he said without hesitation. "I long to see her. Next to you, she is my best friend. She has taught me much about managing an estate. In truth, I believe she knows more about it than my father does."

"We all have missed Lady Margaret's sweet smile and even disposition," Rand confirmed.

"I still worry because I haven't heard from her in so long," he shared.

"'Tis hard to get a missive through to an army on the march, Marcus. You know that."

"Still, I did receive one from her soon after we left. If Father cared enough, he would have sent a determined messenger who could have found me and delivered any missives Mother had written."

"Your father?" Rand snorted. "Don't get me wrong. You know I would do anything for you or your mother, just as I would defend the people of Hartefield with my life." He paused. "But though I am loyal to Lord Charles, I think little of him."

Marcus' eyes widened and Rand held up a hand.

"I know. 'Tis treasonous to speak in such a manner but if I cannot speak plainly to you, my closest friend, then when can I say it? No one likes your father, Marcus, least of all you. We all know our place, though, and would never utter our thoughts aloud. I only share them with you and I hope you will forget what I've said. Only know this—everyone awaits the day when you become the new baron."

Marcus knew his father would never be one to have the love of his people. Charles de Harte was much too harsh and unyielding. But despite his personal feelings, he would never wish for his father's demise. Still, the inklings within him had grown stronger as he and Rand talked. Marcus wanted to be home. No, *needed* to be home.

"I am leaving at once," he told his friend. "For Hartefield."

"What? Now?" Rand looked at him as if he'd gone mad. "Marcus, we're less than a day from reaching Hartefield. Wait until dawn breaks so that we may all ride together."

"Nay. I will ride ahead." He grinned. "And let Cook know that you and the other men are on their way."

Rand frowned in displeasure and merely said, "If you insist."

"Don't worry, old friend," Marcus said. He gripped Rand's forearms. "Just think. This time tomorrow we will be home in front of the fire in the great hall. Our bellies full. Our beds awaiting us." He grinned. "Mayhap, you will have a woman—or two—ready to share yours."

He went to where they'd hobbled the horses and found Storm. Freeing him, Marcus swung into the saddle. With a wave, he trotted away from the camp of sleeping men and hit the open road. Though he longed to gallop, he would not risk Storm in such a manner. At least the bright moon helped him keep a steady pace. As Marcus rode, he cherished this time alone. He'd always been someone who treasured privacy, which rarely came to a soldier. He couldn't think of a single time in the past couple of years when he'd truly been alone, with only himself for company. Everywhere he turned, other men had formed about him. He couldn't even relieve himself in solitude.

That's what made these last few hours before he reached Hartefield special. Tension had built in him for days after they'd parted from the king's troops and made their way toward Suffolk. Marcus fought the rising panic that seemed to ooze from every pore. Something seemed very wrong the closer he came toward home. He only prayed that these pricklings proved foolish. That he would arrive at Harte Castle and find nothing amiss.

The first pale streaks of pink tinged the sky as he rode up to the gates. The gatekeeper called out a cheery greeting, which Marcus returned. He informed the retainer that his men would follow later that day and to be on the lookout for them. Riding to the stables, he awakened a slumbering stable boy and asked him to give a double measure of food to Storm and rub the beast down thoroughly.

At last, he headed toward the keep. No one stirred yet but soon the castle and its inhabitants would spring to life. Marcus pushed open the door and climbed the stairs two at a time, hurrying along the dimly lit corridor toward the solar. Without bothering to knock, he slipped through the door. No candle burned in the outer room. That surprised him. His mother had a fear of the dark and always left a candle burning in the bedchamber and out in this room, as well.

He left the door open so he could see to reach the inner chamber. Opening the door, only darkness greeted him. His senses went on high alert.

Something was definitely wrong.

He slipped carefully into the room, pushing the door wide. Making out the large shape of the bed, he inched toward it, his father's loud snores reverberating throughout the chamber. He neared the bed and reached out his hand, only to find it brushed the bed curtain. Now, Marcus knew something was amiss. His mother never drew the curtains on her side of the bed, not as long as he could remember. She feared being trapped and always wanted a way to escape quickly should disaster strike in the middle of the night.

Easing his hand forward, he located a warm lump. He ran his hand up it and found a shoulder, which he gently shook.

"Mother?" he asked in a whisper, as he caught the smell of milk.

A piercing scream sounded in the darkness. It was quickly joined by the wail of a babe.

Had his mother finally given birth to a child who had survived? At her age?

Movement rippled in the bed as another child somewhere in the room began to cry.

Two children?

The snores finally ceased and his father began bellowing. Stunned, Marcus stumbled from the room into the solar's family room, his heart beating fast.

Then a tiny female toddled from the bedchamber, her dark hair askew. She came toward him and reached her hands out. Instinct took over and Marcus lifted the child in his arms.

"What's your name?" he asked gently.

"Livia," the girl said, promptly jamming her thumb in her mouth and sucking loudly on it.

Movement caught his eye and Marcus turned to the bedchamber door. A young woman barely a score old appeared, a squalling babe in her arms as she balanced a lit candle. She pushed it toward Marcus and he took it.

"Hush," she said, guiding the child's mouth to her bare breast. Greedily, the babe latched on to it and drank, immediately calming.

"Who are you?" the woman asked, her brow knit in confusion.

"I am Sir Marcus de Harte. Who are *you*?" Marcus demanded as he set the candle down on the nearby table.

The woman gasped. Her eyes widened, shock evident upon her face. Before she could reply, his father appeared in the doorway, his hair much sparser than it had been only two years ago and now totally gray.

"What is one of your whores doing in your bed? Where is Mother?" Marcus demanded.

"Your mother is dead," Lord Charles said, his voice flat. "She died a month after you left for the rebellion in the north."

Numbness shot through Marcus, followed by a searing anger. "Why didn't you get word to me?"

His father's eyes narrowed. "And why should I? You accompanied the king. You represented Hartefield. You and the men in your command had a mission to accomplish. Believe me, I agreed with most of those rebels in the north. The king should not be suing for peace with those French bastards. Not after all the time and effort and money that have been involved in this bloody war. But you answered the king's call. Even if you had known of her death, you wouldn't have been free to race home. Your mother would have already been in the ground, so what good could have come by you knowing she had died?"

Rage boiled within him. "And how long has this whore warmed your bed?"

His father's glare matched Marcus' own. "This is your stepmother, Lady Ailith. You will treat her with respect." Lord Charles shook his head. "I am tired and wish to sleep." He looked to his wife. "I don't wish to be disturbed. You can handle my son."

With that, the baron returned to his bedchamber and slammed the door.

"I am sorry about Lady Margaret, my lord," the young woman said. "I met her briefly when my father and I came to Harte Castle on business." Her lips trembled. "I was supposed to be... your bride. When your mother passed away suddenly, Lord Charles... well, he arranged with my father for me to wed him instead."

"He must have replaced Mother quickly since you've already had two children by him."

The child in his arms nestled closer to Marcus. She seemed so fragile as he held her.

"And do you hold a daughter or a son, my lady?" he asked.

Lady Ailith looked down at the babe who'd fallen asleep. She covered her breast. "This is Mary. You are holding Livia."

"Two girls."

"Aye. Other than you, it seems your father can only get girls."

His anger began to subside but hurt and emptiness filled Marcus.

"I must go." He handed Livia to her mother, her hands now full with both daughters.

"But you only returned, my lord," Lady Ailith protested.

"I came back to see my mother. With her dead..." His voice trailed off.

"Will you be gone long?" she asked softly.

He thought of how adrift he seemed in this moment and replied, "I don't know."

Marcus left the solar and returned downstairs to where servants had risen and started their day's work. He left the keep and collected his horse, riding out to where all de Hartes were buried. It was easy to find his mother. Marcus silently knelt beside her grave and stayed for several minutes before rising and returning to his horse.

As he rode away from Harte Castle, he came across Rand and his men. Rand must have awakened them soon after he'd left and urged them to mount their horses and ride home.

Marcus slowed his horse and the group joined him.

"Your mother?" Rand asked, instantly picking up on Marcus'

mood.

"Dead. For almost the entire time we have been away from Hartefield." Marcus paused, swallowing the hard lump in his throat. "Father has another wife—and two new daughters."

"Where will you go?" his friend asked.

"Anywhere except here." Marcus nudged Storm and galloped away.

CHAPTER 2

Kinwick Castle—mid-June

JESSIMOND DE MONTFORT awoke after a restless night of sleep. She no longer had to contain her excitement, which had grown over the past month. The faire would arrive at Kinwick today, full of peddlers erecting stalls of goods. More importantly, they would be accompanied by the mummers' troupe, which had come to Kinwick grounds for the past five years and stayed a week. In that time, she had come to know the proprietors, two brothers who had never married, as well as becoming familiar with many of the actors as she'd watched the plays unfold.

She'd especially enjoyed listening to Bartholomew, the troupe's troubadour, who had a wonderful, rich baritone and told the most marvelous stories through song, as did Beatrice, Cousin Raynor's wife. Some of Jessimond's happiest times in childhood had been spent at Ashcroft in Beatrice Le Roux's company, learning new songs as Beatrice taught Jessimond the words to sing and the music to play on her lute.

This time when the group left to continue to the next stop on their tour, Jessimond was determined to go with them. At least for this season.

All she had left to do was break the news to her unsuspecting parents.

Geoffrey and Merryn de Montfort had been the best parents in the world. Everyone thought highly of the pair, who had raised six children and were beloved by their tenants and servants and the knights who served them. To Jessimond, not only were they wonderful parents but shining examples of love. Outsiders thought the couple newly wedded, due to their tremendous affection toward one another. And that was what she wanted for herself.

Love.

If she were being honest, she would admit that love rarely played a role within the noble class. Arranged marriages brought strangers together. Most wedded couples hoped for respect—or possibly even friendship—to grow between them, though often, neither of those occurred. Thankfully, Jessimond didn't have to worry about marrying a stranger for, in a bold decision, her parents had not betrothed any of their children. Geoffrey and Merryn had been a love match and seeing how their love grew more deeply over the years, they wanted their children to have the same opportunity and wed only for love.

As their youngest child, Jessimond watched for years as, one by one, her brothers and sisters had found their soul mates. Wed them. Begun their own families, binding their children to them in a rich tapestry of love. She'd seen firsthand how love enriched the lives of not only her parents, but also her siblings. Alys and Kit. Ancel and Margery. Hal and Elinor. Edward and Rosalyne. Nan and Tristan. Each de Montfort child had found love and captured it, never letting it go.

Except for her.

Everywhere she went, Jessimond had looked for love. Wondered if this was the place she would find her special someone. She'd spent time at four of her siblings' estates, as well as making extended visits to various cousins. No matter how hard she'd looked, no one stood out. Not a single man appealed to her the way she had supposed he should.

Fear gripped her heart. Mayhap love would never come her way.

Because she wasn't a true de Montfort.

Jessimond dressed quickly and braided her thick waves of golden hair, so unlike any of the other seven de Montforts. Each of her siblings had variations of Geoffrey's dark, thick hair or Merryn's chestnut locks, though gray strands now wove through both of her parents' hair. Her eyes, too, were unusual in color, a deep violet, which no other de Montfort child possessed. Jessimond was short in stature, almost dwarfed by her three brothers and two sisters.

Would not being a blood de Montfort keep her from finding lasting happiness?

She pushed those thoughts aside and hurried from her bedchamber, down the stairs and out the doors. Racing across the bailey, she caught up with Elinor, her sister-in-law, and linked arms with her.

Elinor gave her a warm smile and squeezed Jessimond's arm as they entered the chapel for morning mass. Jessimond admired Elinor because Elinor knew exactly who she was—a falconer. Elinor's father abandoned her to the care of his estate's falconer. The man became a father to Elinor and taught his adopted daughter all he knew about raptors.

Now married to Hal de Montfort, Jessimond's middle brother and captain of the Kinwick guard, Elinor spent much of her days with Joseph, Kinwick's falconer, as they trained various peregrines for hunting. Besides falconry, she was a mother to three children and spent countless hours with them, as well. Elinor was defined by her devotion to her family—and her raptors. Jessimond admired her greatly and longed to discover who she was, in the same way Elinor had.

Mass ended and both women returned to Kinwick's great hall, allowing Hal to hand them up onto the dais in order to break their fast. He brushed a brotherly kiss against her cheek and a tender one against his wife's lips.

"You both look most beautiful today," he said.

Jessimond smiled fondly at her brother. "And you will continue to charm all females until you have one foot in your grave," she retorted in a friendly manner.

"If genuine compliments toward those I love and adore can be seen as charming, then aye—I will happily charm you until my dying day, Jess."

A servant brought bread and ale to them. She tore a piece from the small loaf and tried to chew it, but her nerves made swallowing hard. Seeing Elinor in conversation with Merryn, Jessimond touched Hal's arm.

"How did you know Elinor was the one for you?" she asked.

A smile lit her brother's face. "I just did. I don't know if I was aware of it when we first met but it crept upon me until it engulfed me. Soon, my every thought was consumed by Elinor's image. How I could spend more time with her. How I could make her smile. How I could—"

He broke off, his face flushed with embarrassment.

"Oh, go on, Hal," she teased. "It isn't as if I haven't noticed the heated looks that pass between you two for years now. And you do have three children, so I know you've been up to something in your bed."

He had the grace to ignore her teasing. "You will simply know, Jess." He paused. "Wait. Have you already found someone?" he asked eagerly. "When did you—"

"Nay. I have been thinking of it lately, though. Every day, I see your happiness. How Elinor completes you. How after decades together, Mother and Father still give each other that certain look and then disappear for hours."

Hal took her hand. "And you want that for yourself."

Frustrated, Jessimond nodded. "I do. More than anything, Hal."

He squeezed her hand and released it, taking another long draw from his cup. "You are of age. You will be ten and nine in less than a fortnight." Hal smiled. "Summer to me always means you coming into the de Montfort fold." He brushed another kiss against her cheek. "You will find the man you are meant to be with, Jess. Have faith. All de Montforts do, especially when we least expect it."

But I'm not a real de Montfort.

"You haven't eaten much," Hal pointed out.

"I find I am not very hungry. Besides, I need to speak to Mother and Father about something."

A gleam lit his eyes. "This sounds interesting. You have something up your sleeve."

"I may," she said cryptically.

He laughed. "If I can't get it out of you, then Elinor will. People seem to tell my wife anything and everything."

Jessimond's eyebrows rose in mock indignation. "And you think she would share a secret I told her with the likes of you?"

Hal shook his head. "Nay. If you confide in her and swear her to secrecy, Elinor would be as quiet as a tomb. But if you don't ask for her silence, then she would certainly talk it over with me." He studied her. "Should I be concerned?" A worried look crossed his face.

"Nay. I hope I will have your support, though, in what I plan." Quickly, she told him what she wished to do.

Hal whistled low, thankfully not the shrill whistle he'd taught her and Nan that could bring a room to a halt. "*If* they give you permission—and that is a big if, Jess—then I think it would be a promising adventure. Why, even I would like to go along with you."

She shook her head. "I want to be on my own. No protective brothers hovering over me, especially the captain of Kinwick's guard. You would frighten everyone away and then I would never get to make any new friends."

He squeezed her shoulder. "I wish you the best of luck when you speak to Mother and Father. You're going to need it."

Rising, he gave her an impish smile as he left the dais and made his way over to the group of soldiers gathered at several tables to their left. Jessimond watched Hal give instructions and the men rose as a group in order to head to the training yard. By now, Elinor also had come to her feet. Giving Jessimond a quick nod, she hopped to the floor. Most likely, she went to nurse her youngest one before meeting up with Joseph, as she was already dressed in pants and a man's tunic.

The time had come. Jessimond looked to her parents.

"Mother, Father, I would like a word with you."

Merryn's brow wrinkled in concern. "You sound serious, Jessimond. Is anything wrong?"

"I would prefer privacy while we speak."

Geoffrey rose and lifted his wife's elbow so she stood next to him. "Let's adjourn to the solar," he suggested.

As they went upstairs, Jessimond's heart beat rapidly. Her breath came in short, nervous spurts. She sent a prayer to the Virgin to guide her in the words to use in order to convince her parents to allow her to leave Kinwick with a band of strangers.

Her father ushered them into the solar and they all took a seat. Jessimond glanced from one to the other, knowing her words would probably hurt them both.

Drawing on the courage that her sister, Nan, always seemed to display, she decided not to ask but inform them of her intentions. "I plan to leave Kinwick for a few months," she began.

Merryn visibly relaxed. "I thought you were going to tell us something awful by the look on your face. Do you plan to visit some of your brothers or sisters? Or mayhap, will you spend time with Raynor and Beatrice? You know that would make them so happy."

"Neither." Jessimond swallowed and then plunged ahead. "I am going to travel with Elias and Moss when they leave Kinwick."

Geoffrey leaned forward, his forearms braced upon his knees, a puzzled look upon his face. "The men who own the mumming troupe?"

"Aye. They arrive today and will be at Kinwick for a week. When they leave for their next stop, I want to go with them."

"Do they know this?" asked Merryn pointedly, skepticism in her eyes.

"Nay," Jessimond admitted. "But I know there are many things I could help them with. I'm an excellent seamstress and they're forever damaging or needing new costumes. Though I have no talent for painting people like Rosalyne can, I could paint backdrops or even create props. And if Bartholomew, their troubadour, ever fell ill, I know enough songs so that I could take his place."

"You are talented in many areas," her mother began. "I'm sure you would prove useful in numerous ways to this troupe, but answer me this, Jessimond. Why?"

Her eyes misted with tears. "Because I need to do something for me. Find out who I am. You and Alys have taught me about the healing arts. Nan has drilled into me how to use a bow and arrow. Hal taught me swordplay and Edward how to ride. Elinor has allowed me to help her with the raptors some. I've known how to run a household for years and even set Nan's up for her when she and Tristan wed."

She sighed. "But in knowing all these things, I don't know exactly who I am."

"You're a de Montfort," declared Geoffrey, no doubt in his voice.

"Am I really?" she asked softly.

When she saw his face fall, she quickly added, "I know I'm loved, Father. Mayhap almost too much. You and Mother wrapped me in love, as did all of my siblings, from the moment you and Nan brought me home from the woods. I may not have come from Mother's womb but I will always be a de Montfort and know I am cherished.

"I think it's time, though, for me to explore who I am. Who I can be. Who I need to be."

"And to do that, you wish to be on your own," her mother said quietly, intuitive as always.

Jessimond nodded. "Aye. Joining the mummers will allow me to be on my own for the first time, with no family to rely upon. I will be able to make friends with others I might never have come in contact with. Travel and see places I haven't been. Learn to depend upon my skills and discover what I enjoy most."

And find love, she thought—but chose not to voice that.

Her father appeared so downcast that Jessimond almost changed her mind. She had to force herself to stay seated so that she wouldn't throw her arms around him and swear she wouldn't go. Then she looked at her mother. Their gazes met and Jessimond saw approval.

"This could be good for you, Jessimond," Merryn said.

Geoffrey opened his mouth to protest and then glanced from his wife to his daughter and back. "I see I am outvoted in this matter. As usual, 'tis the women who decide matters of importance in this family," he said lightly.

He stood and Jessimond did go to him then, embracing him tightly. "I love you so much, Father."

Kissing the top of her head, Geoffrey said, "Always know that I love you even more."

Merryn rose. "Once the mummers arrive, we will invite Elias and Moss to dine with us. We can discuss whether they will agree to take you on."

Jessimond smiled. "I'm a very hard worker. And I've decided I'll work for free. That should entice them."

"Nay," her mother said. "You will work many hours, but you will earn every pence they pay you. I think it's important for you to have coin of your own and decide how you wish to spend it."

She hugged Merryn. "Thank you for understanding, Mother."

Merryn sighed. "Understand that I will miss you every moment that you are gone. You are irreplaceable, Jessimond de Montfort. And when your grand adventure is over, I hope you will have new songs to write about these travels. I look forward to hearing you sing them in our great hall."

Jessimond left the solar, a weight lifted from her. Now, she had to speak to Elias and Moss Vawdry and win the two of them to her side.

CHAPTER 3

JESSIMOND ANSWERED THE knock on her door and saw one of the castle's young pages standing there, out of breath.

"They've arrived?" she asked.

The boy nodded. "Lots of wagons, my lady. Couldn't be anybody else but them."

"Thank you."

She closed her bedchamber door and removed her yellow, silk cotehardie and the chemise beneath it, folding both carefully and placing them inside the trunk at the foot of her bed. From the trunk, she withdrew some of the new clothing that she had sewn over the past few weeks after she had retired to her chamber each night. She hadn't wanted anyone asking what she worked on in the great hall, not wanting to explain what she had in mind unless it came to pass.

Being accepted by the mummers was important to her. Jessimond wanted their approval of her as an individual and not as a noblewoman who needed to be humored. That meant leaving her fine silks and satins behind and dressing as someone not of her class but those far beneath her status.

Pulling on the rough, hemp undertunic, she knew she would miss wearing a soft, silk chemise against her skin each day. The undyed undertunic had long sleeves and a low hemline that perched just above her ankles. She had already washed it several times, trying to soften the material, as well as the other undertunic she'd created.

Next, she pulled a blue wool tunic over her head and fastened the wide neck hole closed with cloth ties that she'd attached. Jessimond had crafted it with slits up the sides to afford her more freedom of movement. This tunic struck her mid-calf, unlike all of her cotehardies, which fell to the ground. She knew from observing Kinwick's servants and farmers that many of the woman shortened their tunics at times, based upon the chores they did. She'd learned she could tuck the ends of it up in her belt and had even watched one woman tuck and fold the excess fabric in order to create a pouch to carry chicken feed while another did the same to carry fruit.

Jessimond made sure that the wool she'd used was finely woven but lacked the quality of one a noblewoman would wear. She'd noticed blue was the most common color worn by peasants, who used woad to dye their cloth. Two of the three tunics she'd sewn were shades of blue, while the third was a dark green in color. She knew the dyes she'd used would cause the colors to fade over time since average laborers couldn't afford more expensive ones. To make hers look worn, she'd left the material out in the sun for several days.

Last, she slipped on a cheap, leather belt that she'd bought in the nearby village, cinching it so that her shapeless clothes now hugged her body better instead of hanging lifelessly around her.

The one thing she refused to compromise on was giving up her boots. She'd had the pair several years and they would last many more, thanks to their fine craftsmanship and her good care. Not only would her feet remain comfortable until she returned home in the autumn, but the boots also afforded her a place to hide her baselard. Her brothers always insisted she carry one for protection. All three of them at one point over the years had given her lessons in how to use the dagger, each sharing different ways of how she could not only protect herself but attack another who threatened her. Jessimond never left her chamber without the blade tucked into her boots. Leaving the safety of Kinwick made it even more important for her to have the small weapon with her at all times.

She'd wondered about how to explain the expensive boots if someone asked why she didn't wear shoes typical of a peasant, ones made of calfskin or goatskin, with leather shoelaces. She'd even practice her story until it sounded believable to her ears and she thought anyone asking would believe her.

Touching her hands to her hair, she knew the single, unadorned braid would suffice. She glanced down and, for a moment, felt naked. The amethyst brooch she always wore attached to her cotehardie had remained in place when she'd placed the gown inside her trunk. It wouldn't do for a poor country girl to go about flaunting a jewel of such value. Still, it seemed a part of her was missing with the brooch not in its usual place.

Smoothing down the skirts of her new, simple clothing, Jessimond left her room and hurried down the stone staircase, exiting the keep without running into anyone. She crossed through the inner bailey and then the outer one and went through the open gates. The vendors always set their booths up in the large meadow adjacent to the castle's walls and the mummers would construct a couple of stages for their plays in the same area. The troupe would pitch their tents on the far side of the meadow. Already, she saw the line of wagons in the road and dozens of people milling about like worker bees.

Jessimond shielded her eyes from the strong sun and skimmed the meadow and road but did not see either Vawdry brother. She decided to ask the two men unloading a wagon near her where the owners might be. As she approached, she noted both men were tall and stripped to the waist, their torsos gleaming with sweat from their endeavors.

The one on her left was lean and wiry, with dark blond hair on both his head and chest. His companion's shoulders were broad and his chest heavily muscled. A fine matting of dark hair on it matched the hair of raven's black atop his head. Both men slowed their activity, watching her with curiosity as she came toward them.

The blond greeted her with a charming smile that must have melted the hearts of most women who received it. "How can we help you?"

For a moment, it took her aback that his question hadn't ended with the inevitable *my lady*. She smiled, knowing at least that she looked the part. Now, she simply had to play it.

"I need to find Elias and Moss," she explained.

"And what would a pretty girl like you want with those two ugly brothers?" the dark-haired man asked casually as he eyed her appreciatively.

Coolly, she responded, "The earl and countess would like to speak with the Vawdrys before the faire opens tomorrow."

"So you work in the keep at Kinwick?" the blond man asked. The look in his eye told her that his interest was growing.

Jessimond did her fair share of work and so she honestly replied, "Aye."

"I'll show you where they are," the dark one volunteered. He lowered the trunk that had rested on his shoulder to the ground. "I'll be back soon," he told his fellow worker.

"I'm sure you will be," the man muttered and returned to unloading the wagon.

The dark-haired worker came to her and pointed. "The Vawdrys'll be this way."

Jessimond began walking in the direction the man indicated. He fell into step beside her. She kept a quick pace, as usual. Once she spotted the brothers, she would need to send this man on his way. She wanted to join the troupe without anyone other than the owners knowing who she was, hoping it would lead to enjoying her time more. If anyone knew she was a de Montfort, though, the word would spread like wildfire. She'd never have a chance at making friends on her own terms because others would hold her at a distance.

She thought she had a decent chance of remaining anonymous. Though the mummers had come to Kinwick five years in a row, Jessimond had been gone for the last three. One summer had been spent with her cousin, Cecily, who'd given birth to her last child, a most welcomed girl. Both Cecily and William had been grateful for Jessimond's help with their other five, all rambunctious boys who adored Jessimond. The other two summers she'd been away from Kinwick, first visiting Edward and Rosalyne at Shallowheart and then

Nan and Tristan at Leventhorpe.

That meant no one in the troupe had seen her for a while and hopefully, she wouldn't be recognized. She didn't know how much she'd changed in the four years since she'd seen the mummers, much less how much turnover had occurred within the troupe itself.

"I'm Marcus de Harte," her companion said. "What's your name?"

"Jess. Jess Vernon."

She'd decided Jessimond sounded too formal for a group such as this. A peddler by the name of Vernon used to call at Kinwick over the years until he passed a year ago. She liked his friendly face and his name and had decided to take it as her own for this summer of adventure.

"So, Jess Vernon, do you plan on attending our faire?"

She thought his gaze far too bold and curtly replied, "Mayhap."

"I would love to show you around the stalls." He gave her a lazy smile. "Why, I'd even buy you a sweet or two. What say you?"

This man was far too inquisitive—and far too attractive. Already, she felt her pulse quickening as he studied her with sideways glances while they walked. She needed to concentrate on what she would say to the Vawdrys and not worry about a flirtatious mummer.

When she didn't answer, his fingers grasped her upper arm and brought her to a halt. For the first time, Jessimond looked into his eyes, which she'd avoided.

For good reason.

They were a piercing blue in color—and seemed to see right through her. She swallowed and tugged hard, forcing him to release her arm. Even though his fingers were now absent, she still felt them searing her skin.

Moving quickly away, she saw a thatch of wild red hair and breathed a sigh of relief.

"I see Elias now," she said curtly. "You needn't accompany me further."

"I don't mind—"

"But I do," Jessimond said, her eyes narrowing. "Thank you for escorting me to his tent. Good day."

She turned and kept an even pace though, for some odd reason, she wished to run away. She wouldn't give this handsome stranger the satisfaction of knowing he'd flustered her. As Jessimond widened the distance between them, she sensed Marcus de Harte's eyes drilling into her spine.

Elias entered the tent. Jessimond saw the flap was opened and followed him inside. It took a moment for her eyes to adjust from the glare of the summer sun to the dim interior.

"Elias Vawdry?" she asked.

The tall, redheaded man turned, a puzzled look on his face. She also caught sight of his brother, Moss, who studied her a moment and then smiled.

"Lady Jessimond, I'll wager, though I wouldn't have guessed by your clothes," Moss said. "We haven't seen the likes of you in a few years. My, you have certainly grown up."

"I have been visiting various family members during your recent stops," she explained. "I'm sorry I missed the faires. 'Tis something I always looked forward to."

"We always enjoy coming to Kinwick," Elias said. "Lord Geoffrey and Lady Merryn are most generous to us and local support of our shows is strong."

"Mother and Father would like to have you come to their solar and dine now," she told them.

Elias said, "Why, we'd be delighted."

"Before we go, I have something to ask of you," she said.

Immediately, both men's faces shone with curiosity.

"Go ahead, my lady," Moss encouraged.

"I have a favor to ask. Nay, more than a favor. I have a proposition for you." She paused and then plunged ahead. "I would like to travel with your troupe the remainder of the season. Work for you as a member of your company."

Elias frowned. "Doing what?"

Quickly, Jessimond explained how she was skilled with a needle and could not only repair costumes that needed it, but whip up new ones.

"We haven't had a seamstress since last year," Moss pointed out to his brother. "We've been having to make do and patch when we can." He looked at her. "But why, my lady?"

"I want to see something of the world. In a different way than others do. Besides my needle, I know much about the healing arts and can minister to anyone who falls sick. I also am a fair shot with a bow and arrow and a crossbow and could run a booth where others demonstrate their skills. I promise that I could be a valuable member of your troupe.

"But I would ask one thing in return," she continued. "I don't want to be known as Lady Jessimond de Montfort. I will be plain Jess Vernon, one of your workers. Would you agree to hire me—and keep my secret?"

Moss scratched his chin in thought. After pondering it a few moments, he looked to his brother. "I don't see why not. Do you, Elias?"

The large man shrugged. "I can be happy with that arrangement. But are you sure, my lady?"

Jessimond frowned at him.

"Are you sure, Jess?" he corrected and gave her a sheepish grin.

"I am. I've always traveled well on the road and can cook a bit. I work hard and will do whatever you ask of me."

"Is this why Lord Geoffrey wishes to see us?"

She nodded. "He will probably scare you to death and demand that you keep me safe."

"Of course, you'll be safe," Moss proclaimed. "We take care of all our troupe members. We are a family." He gave her a smile. "I hope you will come to look upon us that way, Jess."

"Excellent. Can you accompany me to the keep now?"

"Lead the way," both brothers responded in unison.

They crossed the field. Already, several booths were taking shape, with wares being displayed. Elias, the more outgoing of the two, pointed out workers by name to her, while Moss merely waved a greeting to all. Reaching the end of the line of wagons, Elias noted the two men Jessimond had already encountered.

As they passed them and turned toward the gates, Elias said, "Those are our newest additions. Marcus de Harte and Rand Trammel. They joined with us almost two months ago."

"Are they mummers?"

"Sometimes. They're very strong and load and unload most of our wagons and set up the backdrops. Marcus has acted some, with a few lines here and there. Rand has only stood in the background of a few scenes. But they also know how to fight as well as knights do."

"How do you know this?" Jessimond asked.

"'Tis part of our shows this season," Moss said. "They duel with their swords before some of the plays or sometimes in a separate area. They also do a bit of jousting."

"Jousting!" she exclaimed. "That can be very dangerous."

"The crowds love them," Elias confirmed. "Especially the women."

Jessimond could understand that, especially having seen both men up close. In fact, she thought the two men *were* knights. Probably knights-errant, attached to no liege lord. Ones who traveled about, seeking adventure and ways to show off their prowess with weapons.

That didn't sit well with her. All three of her brothers had fostered for years, first becoming pages and then squires before they took their sacred oaths of knighthood. The knights at Kinwick were all loyal to the de Montforts, as well as the king. Jessimond didn't think she could trust men who refused to commit and swear allegiance to a single liege lord. It didn't speak well for their characters.

At least she wouldn't have much to do with them. More than likely, they both enjoyed swapping stories with the men in the company and spent time wooing the few women in the troupe until they stopped on an estate. She could see the two cozying up to local women, young and old alike, especially since they had both already vied for her attention. Let them concentrate on the females in the areas the mummers stopped. Jessimond had better things to do.

They reached the keep and she stopped a servant, asking her for a meal to be brought to the solar, and then accompanied the Vawdrys upstairs. She knocked upon the solar's door and was granted permission to enter by her father. Ushering in the two owners, Jessimond hoped by the time they left that her next few months would be settled.

Geoffrey de Montfort offered the men a seat, while Merryn de Montfort assessed both brothers as she poured wine for everyone.

"Thank you for coming," her father told them. Looking to her, Geoffrey said, "Jessimond, fetch Peter Gilpin at once."

When she hesitated, he smiled. "Don't worry. We won't talk of anything significant until the two of you return."

Jessimond left to find the blacksmith's son, who'd been a childhood playmate of hers.

Why on earth did her father wish for Peter to be present?

CHAPTER 4

Jessimond went to the blacksmith's shed and saw Peter and his father hard at work. Peter held a sword's blade in the fire and then lifted it out, placing it on an anvil. He pounded the heated metal, shaping it with his hammer and subtle turns. He raised it and frowned. Once more, he dipped the blade back into the flames and returned it to the iron block, slamming the hammer down several more times. After lifting it, Jessimond saw the satisfied smile touch his lips as he inspected the sword. Peter turned and plunged the hot steel into water.

She stepped into the shed and immediately felt the blast of heat hit her in a wave.

"Peter!" she called loudly since his father also hammered on the far side of the shed.

Peter turned and grinned. Jessimond motioned him to come away from the fire and moved back into the bailey. She inhaled deeply, drawing fresh, cooler air into her lungs.

Peter joined her, a rag in his hand. He wiped the sweat from his face and took a deep breath.

"I admire you for being able to work next to such heat," she said. "You seemed pleased with the sword you were working on."

He ran the cloth over his neck and bare chest. "It can get hot, I'll grant you that, my lady. But I love what I do." He paused. "What brings you here?"

"Father wants to see you. Now."

"Now? Hmm. Let me tell Father."

Peter returned to the shed and touched the older man's shoulder.

"The earl has need of me, Father."

"Then wash off, Son. And put on a clean tunic." The smithy saw Jessimond standing there and gave her a nod. "Good day to you, my lady."

She returned the greeting as Peter stepped to the trough just outside the shed. He plunged his head in and quickly withdrew it, shaking his head like a wet dog would.

"Be right back," he told her.

Moments later, Peter appeared in a new tunic, his face dry but his mop of brown curls still damp.

"Your hair is going every which way," she cautioned him. "Run your fingers through to tame it."

He did as she asked and then grinned. "'Tis more fun when one of the girls from the village combs their fingers through my hair."

Jessimond punched him hard in the shoulder and then began walking toward the keep. Peter fell into step beside her.

She glanced up at him, realizing that he must have his fair share of attention from women. At ten and eight, he was very tall and strong, thanks to the time spent swinging his hammer. He had a strong jaw and warm, brown eyes that forever seem to twinkle. His thick, curly hair would certainly be tempting to any female who caught sight of it. If Jessimond hadn't looked upon Peter as one of her brothers, she could see it would be easy to be attracted to his good looks.

"What do you think your father wants of me?"

In truth, she had already figured out Geoffrey de Montfort's plan. While Jessimond would have vetoed sending one of Kinwick's knights along with her, she could understand her father wanting to have Peter accompany her when she joined the mummers on the road. He would be useful to the Vawdrys in many ways and could still keep an eye on Jessimond. They had been playmates from an early age and Peter remained protective of her, even now.

"I have an idea but I think Father should explain it to you."

They returned to the keep and went straight to the solar. Opening the door, Jessimond saw that a meal had been brought in her absence and the four gathered now sat at the large table. She bit back a laugh as she heard Peter's stomach gurgle noisily.

"Come and have a seat," Merryn urged as she began piling food high on a plate, which she handed to Peter.

"Thank you, my lady." He looked at the plate and back at the countess.

"Go ahead, Peter. Eat," she urged.

As he dug in to his food, Geoffrey said, "These are the Vawdry brothers, Peter. Elias and Moss. Their mummers will be at Kinwick this week and then continue their travels during the rest of summer and into autumn."

Peter swallowed. "I go every year to the faire, my lord. I enjoy watching the plays."

"I have a special request, Peter," Geoffrey continued. "You may refuse me and remain at Kinwick without fear of reprisal, but I hope you'll look upon it as an opportunity."

Peter nodded. "I'll do whatever you wish, my lord," he replied and took a large bite from a roasted chicken leg.

"My daughter will be traveling with the mummers for the next few months. I would like you to accompany her on the road. You will remain in my employ and I will pay you but you will do as the brothers here bid—and watch over Jessimond at the same time."

Jessimond listened as her father explained to Peter how no one was to know about Jessimond's background. To his credit, her friend took it all in stride.

When Geoffrey finished, Peter said, "You know I am loyal to you, my lord, and I will be to Lady Jessimond, too. She is my lady—but she has also been a good friend to me. I would give my life for her."

Merryn said, "Let's hope it never comes to that, Peter. I do thank you for guarding Jessimond." She looked to her daughter. "Anything to add?"

"You'll need to start calling me Jess, Peter. Jessimond is very formal. I want the troupe to accept me as one of their members."

He nodded in understanding. "So no one will know you are a de

Montfort." Peter grinned. "Do you have a new last name?"

"Vernon."

"I have a better one. Gilpin," he suggested.

Jessimond frowned. "But that is your name."

"And yours as well." Peter's grin broadened. "Sister."

"An excellent idea," Geoffrey declared. "That will explain Peter's presence and why he would be interested in safeguarding you. The two of you are leaving service at Kinwick to seek your fortunes elsewhere. I quite like it."

Jessimond smiled. "It makes perfect sense." She looked to the Vawdrys. "Does everything meet your expectations?"

Elias took a swig of wine. "Aye. We are happy with the arrangements. We gain a strapping young man's labor for free and the troupe will have a new seamstress and healer."

"The Vawdrys will accompany you back to the blacksmith shed," Geoffrey said to Peter. "Gather your things and wait there for . . . Jess. Tell your parents farewell and that you'll see them come late autumn."

"Aye, my lord. And thank you for having faith in me. I will make sure Jess enjoys her time on the road and contributes to the troupe." Peter caught Jessimond's eye and winked at her.

The three left the solar and Jessimond rose. It was time to say her goodbyes. Her throat grew thick with unshed tears. Her mother embraced her.

"You won't be able to take quill and parchment on the road, I'm afraid. Jess Gilpin would not know how to read, much less write a missive to her family back at Kinwick." Merryn kissed both her cheeks. "Stick close to the truth, Jessimond. Make Peter's family your own so that you each tell the same stories. You will be in my prayers every day, my sweet."

Geoffrey enfolded her in his arms, the place Jessimond had always felt most protected from her earliest memories. He pressed a kiss to her brow. "The Vawdrys finish their season at an estate near Ancel's. You and Peter go to Bexley when the troupe disbands for the winter. Stay a week or so and then have Ancel send you home with an escort."

"I have a better idea, Geoffrey," Merryn interjected. "Jessimond can write to us once she arrives at Ancel's. Then we can go to claim her. I would love to see Ancel and Margery and we can all return to Kinwick together afterward."

Her father released her and wrapped his arms around his wife. "I knew I married you for good reason. Your ideas are always better than mine," he said huskily.

"Oh, I know that look in your eyes," Jessimond said, laughing. "I will go and gather my things and head to the blacksmith's to meet the others. And remember—if you two can break away long enough from one another and actually attend the faire—I am not your daughter. I am a former servant in the keep at Kinwick."

Her parents laughed, their arms now entwined around one another.

Jessimond left them and returned a last time to her bedchamber, quickly gathering her spare tunics, a comb, and her case full of medicinal herbs. Everything else would be left behind. She glanced around the room and changed her mind, retrieving her precious lute. It might come in handy. She then hurried to meet up with her employers and new brother.

MARCUS AND RAND finished unloading the wagons and began pitching the tents that the troupe would sleep in. The work was physical but allowed his mind to wander.

Unlike battle.

Part of Marcus experienced guilt at walking away from Hartefield. He'd trained to be a knight his entire life and then had led others on the battlefield. His knightly code of honor—dedicating himself to king, country, and family—had been rudely shoved aside when he rode away from Harte Castle six weeks ago. His emotions that day proved raw and uncompromising. Marcus knew that if he didn't leave the castle grounds he might kill his father.

No love had ever existed between the two men. Charles de Harte took every opportunity to belittle his son, claiming his harsh words and even harsher fists would toughen the boy up. Marcus had first feared his father and then grew to despise him as time unfolded. He couldn't remember a civil conversation between them in all his years. His father barked orders and Marcus obeyed them without flinching. For the most part, the two men avoided one another.

He had known unconditional love from his mother. Margaret de Harte was a wise woman from a young age, full of grace and dignity. Though she adored her only child, she never spoiled him. Her high expectations and calm demeanor brought a balance into his life. Marcus had learned what he needed to know about running Hartefield from her.

And now she was gone.

News of her death had set him off. Rage followed the numbness that first set in. That's when he knew he had to escape. Be on his own for a while. Falling in with the mummers only two days after he'd left Hartefield had proven to be a godsend. The Vawdrys needed someone suited to physical labor and Marcus needed an outlet for his immense anger.

It helped that Rand accompanied him as he searched for who he was without his mother. Marcus knew the kind of man she had raised him to become and, more than anything, he wanted to be that man. He promised himself he would be the best baron that Hartefield had ever seen once his time to lead it arrived.

But not now. Now, he wanted liberation from all responsibilities. For just a few months—a single season—he wanted to be selfish and think only of himself. Deep in his heart, he knew he would return and face his responsibilities. Be the good son, the good knight, the good heir that everyone expected.

In the meantime, he would sow a few wild oats and return home, ready to wed and begin his own family. Marcus planned to be a husband who showed respect to his wife. One who would love his children beyond measure. And in time, he would become the nobleman that others looked to in order to lead them to prosperity.

Marcus finished erecting his tent and glanced to where Rand labored on the last, largest tent, the one that would house the costumes and props of the plays the mummers put on for the crowds. When he returned to Hartefield, he would insist Rand come with him. Since the knight had not spoken to his liege lord, much less been granted permission to be away from the estate, Marcus knew his father would want to cut Rand loose, hacking his spurs from the knight's boots in a show of shame.

But Rand Trammel had been the closest thing Marcus had to a brother. He would insist Rand remained at Hartefield as if no disobedience had occurred, despite any misgivings from Charles de Harte. When Marcus became Baron of Harteley, Rand would serve as his right hand in all things. Even if he had to beat his father into submission, as Charles had done to him countless times, Marcus would make certain that Rand kept his place as a knight of Harte Castle.

His friend had definitely exposed Marcus to a different, lighter, and wilder side of life. Where Marcus had been all about war and serving his king and living up to his responsibilities, Rand—though a seasoned knight and the best swordsman Marcus had seen—enjoyed life to its fullest.

And that meant women. Lots and lots of women.

In their time on the road with the mummers, Marcus had followed Rand's lead and flirted with anything in a skirt. He'd coupled with more village women and servants in two months than he had in the previous half a score. At first, it had been in good fun. A different woman every night in the towns and estates they'd traveled to. Lately, though, Marcus grew tired of it. 'Tis why he knew the urge to settle down with one woman was real. Mayhap, he wanted to show his father what a good marriage entailed.

Marcus did worry about returning home and living in close quarters with his father again, though he wondered how many years Charles de Harte had left. The nobleman had looked ill in the brief time Marcus had seen him upon his return after two years at war. Also, Marcus would have to consider that caring for his stepmother and his half-sisters would become his responsibility once his father passed. How ironic that the very woman once meant to be his wife now served as his stepmother. More than likely, he would request that the king find a new husband for Lady Ailith. Since neither of her children had been sons, there would be no reason for the girls to remain behind at Hartefield when their mother left.

He joined Rand, picking up a stake to help secure the tent to the ground. The men worked in amiable silence until the tent stood tall and sturdy. Several of the mummers then helped them bring the many trunks inside as Agatha began organizing all of the costumes. At least she was better at this than cooking their meals. As the troupe's only woman, the cooking had fallen to her. Agatha came up short every time. He and Rand ate as often as they could from the various food booths set up at the faire so they wouldn't have to partake of Agatha's tasteless cooking.

Marcus returned to the outside. Though the air was fresher than inside the tent, the heat and exertion had sapped his strength.

"Would you like to wash?" Jopp asked. "There's a nearby brook the earl allows us to use. I can take you and Rand there."

"Rand!" called Marcus, motioning his friend over. To Jopp, he said, "Lead the way."

The boy hurried away, eager to show them the stream. Marcus had taken to the ten-year-old, whose father, Ralph, was the lead actor of the mummers. Jopp did a bit of everything around the camp and was a favorite of everyone.

As they followed the boy, Rand said, "You certainly staked your claim quickly to the prettiest girl we've yet seen. Nay, not the prettiest. A rare beauty, that one. Does the heavenly creature have a name?"

Marcus thought of the fresh-faced woman he'd accompanied earlier to the Vawdrys' tent. Her heart-shaped face and smooth, porcelain skin had called out to his fingers and he'd fought the urge to graze her cheeks with them. Eyes he'd never seen before had stared at him, a deep amethyst unlike any color he'd known in another. He'd been tempted to grab her long, golden braid so he could unwind it and loosen waves of hair the color of summer wheat.

But it was her lips that had entranced him. Plump and berry-colored. Begging to be kissed.

"Jess Vernon," he replied. "Though she's a prickly one."

"I'd thought one so petite would have a higher voice," Rand said, "but hers was deep and rich. Like honey." He waggled his brows. "And tasting just as sweet, I'm sure."

Marcus chuckled. "That's because you didn't hear how her tone could cut sharp as a knife."

"Ah. So the beautiful Jess wasn't willing to fall into your arms immediately. Good. I like to know that you'll have to actually work at this one."

He doubted Jess Vernon would couple easily with a man. As it was, he didn't know if she was married or had a sweetheart. That's where Marcus drew a firm line. He refused to encroach on another man's property and only engaged in love play with willing, unattached females.

"Here it is!" Jopp ran down the bank and into the water, splashing.

They followed him in once they'd shed their boots. Marcus cupped his hands and drank from the cold water before throwing a handful Jopp's way. Soon, all three of them were soaked from their impromptu water fight and climbed from the brook.

Marcus raked his fingers through his hair, pushing it back from his face. The water had revived his flagging strength. They headed back to the area where the tents stood, Jopp scurrying in front of them.

Then Marcus spied the Vawdrys, whom he'd seen accompany Jess to the castle. Once again, the woman was in their company. This time, a fourth person had joined them. It was a young man, not yet a score, taller than average height and with bulging arms of muscle.

What surprised him more was that Jess and the man each carried a bundle. His pulse quickened.

Was she joining the troupe?

Marcus watched Elias direct the pair toward the tents where the mummers slept, while Moss headed in their direction.

The owner met them. "It looks as if everything has been unloaded from the carts."

"Aye," he responded. "All the trunks are accounted for and inside. Agatha is rummaging through everything, organizing them in some fashion."

"Good," Moss said.

"Who are the two people with Elias?" he asked casually.

Moss looked over his shoulder and back. "Two new members of our troupe. Peter Gilpin and his sister, Jess."

Marcus let out a breath he hadn't even known he held. Peter Gilpin was Jess' brother. Not her husband. Not a lover. He didn't know why that brought him relief, but it did.

"Come along, Rand. We should greet our newest members," Marcus urged.

They strode toward where Elias stood with the newcomers. As they approached, Jess looked at them. Her brows shot up as a look of disapproval crossed her face. Marcus wondered what he'd done to earn that.

Then it hit him. Moss had said Gilpin. Not Vernon. He wondered if the hauntingly beautiful Jess had been wed and was now a widow.

"Greetings," Marcus called out. "I hear you will be joining our troupe." He offered a hand to Peter. "I am Marcus de Harte. This is Rand Trammel."

"Peter Gilpin," the younger man said. He indicated his companion. "And this is my sister, Jess."

"We've met," she said succinctly.

"I met Jess Vernon," Marcus said. "Not Jess Gilpin." When her eyes widened, he continued. "Moss told us you are brother and sister."

"We are," Peter said firmly, his tone challenging Marcus' words.

Jess laid a hand on Peter's forearm. "Well, half-siblings," she amended. "After my father passed away, Mother married Peter's father. Then she gave birth to Peter." She gave him a warm smile and squeezed his arm. "Peter has never made a distinction between us. Though my name is Jess Vernon, he always refers to me as Jess Gilpin.

Sometimes, I even refer to myself that way."

Peter wrapped one of his huge arms about Jess and plunked a kiss on the top of her head. "We *are* brother and sister," he insisted. Looking at Marcus, he added, "And the best of friends. I can't imagine anyone coming between me and Jess."

Marcus received the warning that lurked beneath the surface of Peter's words. Loud and clear.

Peter Gilpin chief's responsibility would be to protect his sister.

Especially from the likes of men such as Marcus and Rand.

CHAPTER 5

Jessimond finished the last stitch and tied it off. She set her needle and thread aside and flexed her aching fingers. She had never sewn so much as she had in the past week. Once Elias and Moss introduced her to the mummers, all of them had requests to make. Some needed their own clothing repaired, while others brought her their various costumes and showed what needed to be mended. She'd worked as fast as she could. This monk's robe was the final piece.

Not that she would be through with sewing anytime soon. Ralph, the lead actor of the troupe, already had met with her to discuss his ideas for new costumes for the plays the mummers currently performed. The group tried to rotate and do different plays for each day they were at a stop. Ralph also wanted to add a few more plays to the group's repertoire—which meant a vast assortment of different costumes. Jessimond would have plenty of work over the next few weeks if the Vawdrys approved of any of Ralph's plans.

She looked up to the cloudless sky. Most of her sewing had been done under the tree where she now sat. The light was much better outside than if she'd stayed inside the small tent she shared with Agatha. Jessimond had spent her week with the mummers in the area where the group ate and slept, not wanting to interact with the crowds at the faire. She hadn't wanted to run into anyone from Kinwick lands or the nearby village—and she hadn't—being removed from the wares sold and the troupe's performances. Once they were on the road and settled at the next stop on the tour, she planned to visit the stalls and attend some of the plays.

And mayhap the joust.

She felt her cheeks grow warm thinking about the joust—or rather, the men involved in it. While she'd met everyone in the company and knew all of them by name, Jessimond had avoided speaking directly to either Marcus or Rand, the two men she suspected were knights-errant. Watching the way each man moved was enough to give away their identities. Both were graceful and comfortable in their bodies. They carried themselves with a confidence that only a knight possessed. They might pretend and pass themselves off as mummers to others, but they did not fool her.

Each night, the entire troupe gathered for a meal after the last play had been performed and the stalls closed. Jessimond enjoyed hearing all of the stories told, some from that day and others from previous times on the road. She sensed Marcus and Rand watching her but never met their eyes, preferring to listen to the tales recounted or talking with Agatha or Jopp. The young boy had stolen a piece of Jessimond's heart with his eagerness to please and smile that never ceased. Jopp had taken to following Peter about and the mummers teased Peter about his newfound shadow.

"You've been busy."

She looked up and saw Peter hovering above her. He smiled and sat next to her.

"I just finished the last piece. For now."

"You haven't really left this area, Jess." He glanced around to make sure they were alone. "I'm concerned about you. Are you avoiding others?"

"Aye. Until we leave Kinwick. Then I will mingle more. Explore the faire. And I am getting to know the other mummers." She paused. "Agatha's quite nice."

As she suspected, Peter's blush told her all she needed to know.

Then he grimaced. "Agatha's a sweet lass but her cooking?" He shuddered. "You've got to do something, Jess. I would have starved by now if there hadn't been food to sample and purchase at the faire each day."

"I've appreciated the savory meat pies you've brought to me, Peter. But I wasn't hired to cook. I won't take that away from Agatha. 'Tis her job."

"Then she needs another one."

"I agree," a deep voice said.

Jessimond looked up and saw Marcus de Harte standing there. She hadn't heard him approach and was thankful they hadn't been talking of things he shouldn't hear. He squatted and then sat cross-legged on the ground in front of them.

"Rand and I spend all the coin the Vawdrys pay us purchasing food," he admitted. "If you have any knowledge of cooking, Jess, we would appreciate you making our evening meal."

"Agatha does most things right. All it would take is a few spices added to the pot," she shared.

"I doubt Agatha has ever seen a spice," Marcus said. "Much less how to use it to flavor stew."

Jopp came running up, his face flushed. "Peter! Can you come help? Moss needs you."

"Of course, little man." Peter rose, his eyes meeting hers. Jessimond nodded, answering his unspoken question and letting him know she would be fine. He left with Jopp, the boy scurrying to keep up with the blacksmith's long strides.

"Your brother has been quite useful," Marcus remarked.

"Peter is capable of doing anything he sets his mind to."

"You seem close," he noted.

Jessimond nodded. "I can honestly say that we've been good friends all of our lives."

"Not all siblings can say that. Sometimes, there's rivalry between them."

"Not between us." Curiosity made her ask, "But what about you, Marcus? Do you fight with your brothers?"

An odd look crossed his face. "Nay. I have no brothers. Merely sisters."

"*Merely* sisters?" She sniffed. "I see women hold no importance to you."

Without warning, he took her hand and held it, his thumb caressing her palm. "Some women are important to me."

Jessimond jerked her hand from his. "I don't plan to be one of them."

He gave her a lazy smile, causing her heart to skip a beat. She held her ground, though, not blinking. But the longer she gazed into his piercing, blue eyes, the harder it became to breathe.

His fingers captured her chin, the gentle pressure holding her in place. "I mean it, Jess. I'm not Rand. He's my closest friend and I would die for him, but Rand's a charmer when it comes to women. You should stay away from him, for he would only break your heart."

"And you wouldn't?" she asked softly.

Jessimond wrapped her fingers around his wrist, in order to pull his hand from her face. Already, his touch singed her skin, as if her face had caught fire.

"I don't know," Marcus replied, his thumb stroking her bottom lip. "I fear you might break mine."

She swallowed, her hand falling from his wrist. He released her chin and stood, offering her a hand.

"The faire will be closing soon. Come around to a few of the stalls with me. Let's see if we can purchase a few spices to liven up our evening meals."

Jessimond hesitated a moment before placing her hand in his. His large one engulfed her much smaller one as he easily pulled her to her feet. She stumbled, falling against his chest. His free hand clasped her arm to steady her. They stood speechless for a moment and then she pulled away, bending to retrieve the robe she'd worked on and her sewing kit.

"Let me put these in my tent," she said and hurried away.

She lifted the flap of the tent she shared with Agatha and rested her things on top of her pallet. Closing her eyes, Jessimond balled her hands into fists and took a few calming breaths, trying to steady herself.

No man had ever stirred these kinds of feelings within her. She would need to be careful around Marcus de Harte. It would be dangerous if he knew how much he affected her.

Returning to him, she held her chin high and gave him a confident, de Montfort smile. If she'd been a lady, he would have taken her arm and tucked it into the crook of his elbow in order to escort her. Jess Gilpin wasn't, though, so she walked briskly past him and said, "Come along," her skirts swishing.

He caught up to her. "I haven't seen you at any of the stalls."

"I wanted to finish everything I had been given to do. I think almost every mummer made a request. And Ralph is already full of ideas for new plays, which means fresh costumes. Now that I've completed what I was given, I hope to spend more time seeing the faire while I work on different items for the troupe."

"Have you watched one of the plays before?" Marcus asked.

"Aye. The mummers have been coming to Kinwick for a few years. The earl and countess allow their servants time to visit the stalls and see the plays."

"So you worked as one of their servants in the keep?"

"I did. I was ready for a change, though. I thought coming along with the mummers would be interesting. I could see a bit of the world. Meet new people."

"What will you do when the season ends?"

Jessimond had been prepared to be asked that question. "Lady Merryn was kind enough to tell me that I will always have a place at Kinwick if I care to return. One season with the mummers may be enough to satisfy my wanderlust." She glanced up at him. "What about you, Marcus? Do you plan to stay with the troupe?"

"I am at a crossroads," he confessed. "Joining the mummers was a distraction I sorely needed and Rand was good enough to humor me and come along. I will stay through this season, but beyond that?" He shrugged.

Jessimond wanted to ask him more about the dilemma he faced but they had arrived at the row of booths. Since it was the last day before their departure, most of those at Kinwick and in the neighboring village had already completed buying their wares. She could hear laughter coming from the west and knew most visitors to the faire now attended the last play, which should be over soon.

Marcus took her elbow. "Come over here, Jess. Have a look at these herbs and spices."

Once again, a sensation of being scorched occurred when he touched her. Her belly felt full of butterflies spreading their wings and flapping them rapidly, yet having nowhere to fly. Her mouth grew dry. She let him lead her to a stall where a rotund woman with a few missing teeth gave her a grin.

"Come to look, dearie?"

"Aye," Jessimond said and reached for a jar, breaking the contact between her and Marcus. Part of her was grateful as her pounding heart began to slow. The rest of her longed for him to touch her again and bring that giddy feeling to her insides once more.

"That's cinnamon you hold," the woman told her.

Jessimond smiled. "Cinnamon has always been one of my favorites."

"We'll buy it," Marcus proclaimed.

"Oh, no," Jessimond swiftly replied. "We are merely looking now."

She asked the booth's vendor about other jars and opened a few to inhale the pungent aromas. She asked the cost of a few of the spices and then put each jar back on the wooden board that served as a shelf to display the merchandise. Though Jessimond never looked at him, she sensed impatience humming about Marcus.

"Thank you," she told the woman. "We may be back."

Strolling away, she moved to another booth and repeated the process with a man who reminded her of Michael Devereux, husband to her cousin, Elysande. He had Michael's coloring and vivid blue eyes but was a good foot short of the earl's height.

As Jessimond went to a third booth, Marcus cupped her elbow and pulled her away.

"What are you doing?" he hissed into her ear. His lips brushed the lobe, causing a frisson of pleasure to simmer through her.

She pulled away and frowned at him. "Have you never purchased goods before?"

"Of course, I have," he snapped.

"How do you do it?"

"Do it? Do what?"

"Buy something," she said soothingly, trying to calm him.

Marcus frowned. "I pick it up. If 'tis what I want, I ask the price and hand over the coin."

"Ah." She shook her head in understanding. "You are a typical man."

His crooked smile warmed her heart. "My gut tells me there's something more to this game."

"That's exactly right. It is a game and you must learn to play along, lest you disappoint the seller."

"Show me," he urged, his cool, blue eyes warming as he studied her.

"We will need to go to a few more stalls."

Marcus shrugged. "You are in charge."

"You do have the coin?" she asked, knowing she didn't.

"Aye. You'll be able to purchase what you wish."

With that knowledge, Jessimond went into action. She visited five booths in all and then began going from one to another, bickering in a friendly but firm manner with each of the owners. Soon, all five of the vendors knew they were in the game and played accordingly, trying to outbid one another. Some cut their price. Others offered her two spices for the price of one. Another agreed to give her three for what she would pay for two.

"I really had my heart set on some saffron," she mused.

"I don't think any of these people have made you a good price, Jess," Marcus said, finally joining in. "Mayhap when we leave tomorrow, you can stop in the village we pass to see their prices."

"Nay, Jess," called out the toothless woman, ready to make her final pitch. "Come here. You, too, Marcus."

Soon, the seller had made them a good deal on the saffron. Jess wound up buying something from each of the five stall owners. She hiked her tunic as she had seen others do in order to cradle some of the jars, while Marcus held on to the others.

They made their way back to the company's tents, applause erupting from the area near the stage.

"It sounds as if the play has concluded," she said.

"You drive a hard bargain," he told her, admiration in his tone. Grinning, he added, "I never knew purchasing goods could be so entertaining."

"Believe me, they enjoyed it even more than you did. Next time you go to buy a belt or trinket, be sure you barter for it. Negotiating a price is what makes the process so much fun."

They arrived at the tents and Jessimond saw Agatha standing over a huge pot resting over a fire.

"We've brought some herbs and spices for you to cook with," Jessimond said.

Panic flooded Agatha's pretty face. "I barely know how to cook, Jess." She glanced at the jars they held. "What am I to do with these?" she wailed.

"Don't worry, Agatha. I am well versed in herbs and spices. I can show you what to add in order to make food more flavorful."

Agatha made a face. "I hate cooking. I wish you would take over the task, Jess. I only do it because no one else bothers to."

"An excellent idea," seconded Marcus. "You don't mind, do you, Jess?"

"Nay. I enjoy cooking. I will need help, though. The troupe has many members."

"Oh, I don't mind helping you, Jess. Just tell me what to do." Relief settled over the young woman, as if a heavy burden had been lifted away.

"Take the jars Marcus bears. We'll bring them to our tent and decide what to use tonight. I think some of the saffron and long pepper will do for a start."

"I'll carry them," Marcus offered.

He accompanied them to their tent and handed the containers over since Jessimond didn't think he would fit inside the small space.

"I'll line everything up," Agatha said enthusiastically. "I'll let you know when you can see." She closed the tent's flap, leaving Jessimond alone with Marcus.

"She's happiest when she's allowed to organize something," Jessimond said.

Marcus took her hands in his. This time, she didn't yank away.

"Thank you for spending some time with me today," he said. "I enjoyed being in your company."

"I enjoyed it, as well."

They stood gazing at one another. Jessimond suddenly had a fierce urge to kiss him. Such a thought had never crossed her mind before.

As if he knew what went on inside her head, Marcus asked, "Have you ever been kissed, Jess?"

"Nay," she whispered, her heart beating rapidly.

He bent and brushed warm lips against her cheek. Her fingers tightened against his as light filled her. His breath fanned hot against her face. She turned her head slightly so her mouth could meet his. Before it did, Agatha called out.

"Ready, Jess!"

Marcus released her hands and stepped away. Disappointment flooded Jessimond.

"Coming!" she called over her shoulder.

As she turned, Marcus caught her elbow and turned her so that they faced one another.

"A first kiss is something special, Jess," he said softly. "It takes time—and requires privacy. I promise you this—we'll find both.

"Soon."

CHAPTER 6

MARCUS GNAWED ON a hard crust of bread and washed it down with some ale. He and Rand rose earlier than usual, since today they would need to break down the tents and load the wagons in order for the troupe to head to their next venue. Elias had said it would be the estate of Lord Guy Tibbett and his wife, Lady Jeanette. Once the carts were ready, they would travel all of today and part of tomorrow, arriving at Fullminster mid-afternoon.

By now, he and Rand had done this several times and had a pattern down. They made sure everything had been cleared from the tents and all of the trunks loaded before they tackled striking the tents. Though the actors all pitched in, the two knights did the bulk of the work. Marcus wondered what the Vawdrys had done before he and Rand had come along.

After feeding Storm, his horse, he was soon hard at work—but Marcus still had time to think about Jess Gilpin.

He'd watched the blond beauty for the past week before he approached her yesterday. He noted how diligently she worked but how easily her laugh came as the mummers shared a meal and conversation every evening. Marcus hadn't tired of looking at her and enjoyed when she spoke, which wasn't often. Her low, musical voice sounded as smooth as velvet. While he noted her sweet, kind nature, it surprised him that she could be outspoken and opinionated when pressed—and that those opinions were thoughtful and had substance.

In many ways, Jess reminded him of his mother. Margaret de Harte was not only a noted beauty; she proved practical and intelligent. She'd ruled Harte Castle with a firm but gentle hand, assisting everyone so that they worked together to make Hartefield run smoothly. She was well versed in not only domestic issues but knew about livestock and crops and how best to manage an estate, things that had never held his father's interest.

His mother would have approved of Jess.

When the seed had been planted, Marcus didn't know. It formed gradually within him but the more he was around Jess, the more certain he became.

Jess Gilpin would make him an excellent wife.

True, she was of peasant stock but she carried herself with both grace and dignity. Since she'd been a servant inside the castle walls of Kinwick and seemed most observant, Marcus had no doubt she would be able to run a household if given the task. Next to his mother, Jess was the most capable woman he'd met. Already, she had the mummers eating from the palm of her hand. He saw how she truly listened to each one and treated them as individuals, always showing respect. She was friendly without being overfamiliar. Intelligent without rubbing others' noses in it.

And enough of a challenge that Marcus knew he would have to work at winning her affection.

The fact that she'd never been kissed appealed to him immensely. To know no man had come before him, sampling those sweet lips and touching her curves, gave him satisfaction.

Marcus could only imagine what Rand would think if he shared these notions with his friend—which is why he'd kept silent. Rand would howl with laughter when Marcus told him he'd decided to wed, much less that it would be Jess. Rand would remind him of how many women he'd coupled with in the last few months and how Marcus had enjoyed it.

He had—to a point. But somewhere along the line, all the women had become nameless and faceless as he searched for something deeper. Something more meaningful.

Something he thought he had a chance to capture with Jess Gilpin.

That's why he'd bided his time. Approached her slowly. Now, he would woo her carefully as summer unfolded and eventually fled, turning to autumn. The Vawdrys had told him they usually brought their tour to an end by the beginning of October, even mentioning they would finish the season at Glenmore, in Suffolk. Ironically enough, Glenmore, home of Lord Simeon de Grey, was the estate situated to the west of Hartefield. The mummers' travels would be complete and Marcus would finally be home, where he knew duties awaited him.

He planned to return to Harte Castle with Rand—and Jess.

All it would take now would be convincing her. Marcus sensed she understood the simmering attraction between them. He had felt it from the moment they met. He would court her carefully over these next weeks so that by the time they arrived at Glenmore and the troupe dissolved, she would be more than willing to become his bride. Marcus didn't care what his father thought of Jess' low birth. She offered much more than any noblewoman he'd met. He looked forward to their spirited discussions, both in and out of bed.

And teaching her everything she needed to know about love play.

His cock began to respond at that thought and, immediately, Marcus began to conjugate Latin verbs in his head. Nothing dulled him more quickly than repeating the Latin that his tutor had ground into him before he left to foster. The exercise had helped put him to sleep many a night when the sounds and smells of battle refused to leave him in peace.

As he heaved a trunk from the ground and rested it atop his shoulder, Gylbart joined him, carrying a smaller one. The actor was lean and lithe, and Marcus had taught him a few moves with a sword since he and Rand had joined the troupe. Oftentimes, the plays included sword fighting. All the actors tried their hand at it, but Gylbart wanted to be known as the best in their little group. Marcus suspected 'twas because Gylbart had plans to knock King Ralph off his throne. All the actors referred to the lead actor in that manner since Ralph tried to control every aspect of each play and, without fail, always won the lead role in the plays performed. If the Vawdrys didn't start sharing the wealth more and passing around the choice roles so that others might have a chance, they might have open rebellion on their hands.

Or find themselves short a mummer or two.

"King Ralph is interested in performing some new plays," Gylbart confided. "He's already met with Jess and told her what kinds of costumes he'll need her to produce."

"Has he mentioned this to Elias or Moss?" Marcus countered, thinking Ralph bold to have already cornered Jess, demanding more costumes be made.

"I suppose so," the mummer said sullenly. "I still don't see why he wins the lead in all the plays we do. He's not nearly as talented as he thinks he is."

They reached a wagon and both men hefted their loads in its bed. "But Ralph is a quick study," Marcus pointed out. "He knows his lines and everyone else's."

"True. But I'm starting to be better with a sword now, thanks to you, Marcus. I hope you'll give me more lessons soon."

"I can do that," he promised, knowing it would take quite a bit of work to make Gylbart more believable in a staged sword fight.

The two men went back to the tents and joined the others, pulling up stakes now that the last of the trunks had been loaded.

"The stew last night was most delicious," Gylbart said. "I'm glad Jess will take over the cooking from Agatha. Reba did it the last few years."

"Who is Reba?" Marcus inquired.

"Agatha's older sister. Their mother used to sew all our costumes and cook for us. She died several years ago and the two girls remained with the troupe. Reba took over the cooking and sewing until last season. She found a man she couldn't live without and left the mummers to wed him."

"So she left Agatha behind?"

"Aye. The poor girl had nowhere else to go. Reba was so wrapped up in her new lover that I doubt she gave her a sister a thought."

"How old is Agatha?"

Gylbart pondered a moment. "I think ten and five now."

"And where does she go when the mummers retire from the road each year?"

The actor shrugged. "I haven't a clue."

As the tents slowly came down, Marcus decided when he returned to Harte Castle that he would offer Agatha the choice to come with him and work in the keep. He thought he might have to do the same with Peter Gilpin. Jess and her brother were especially close. Marcus didn't think they would care to be split up. The castle was large and had plenty of room and in a week, Peter had proven to be an excellent worker, both bright and industrious. Marcus would be able to find something for the young man to do at Harte Castle.

He finally caught sight of Jess coming toward him. She had several cups in her hand, giving them to the actors as she passed by.

Reaching him with the final one, she said, "May I offer you something to drink? You look parched with all the loading you are doing."

Marcus rose and grasped the cup, allowing his fingers to graze hers as he took it. Her cheeks pinkened slightly. He longed for the day when he did things to her body that would cause not only a blush to rise, but a fever to take hold of her.

The fever of desire.

His desire for her had grown over this past week. Marcus knew it would continue to rise as they remained in close quarters. He would need to keep it in check and not frighten her away.

But, as he'd promised her last night, he would find a time and place to kiss her. To thoroughly explore those berry-colored lips. Nip and lick them as he listened to her moan. It would be difficult. Not only would he need to be free of any mummers stumbling across them but far enough away from any crowds that also attended the faire.

As much as he wanted this, Marcus was determined to find that occasion. Multiple times. Already, he fantasized about Jess as he lay awake at night. He'd done the same today as they prepared to leave Kinwick. For his own sake, he needed to kiss her.

Soon.

Downing the liquid in one swallow, he returned the cup to her. "Thank you, Jess. I certainly needed some refreshment."

She glanced around. "Will we leave before long?"

"Aye. When this last tent comes down."

He paused. Though he'd ridden Storm each time they'd left for a new place, Marcus decided Jess would never accompany him that way. At least, not yet. Mayhap in time, she would agree to ride nestled against him. For now, he had a different idea.

"If you haven't a place set to ride yet, I would enjoy your company as I drive one of the wagons."

Those amethyst eyes seemed to see right through him as she studied him a moment. "All right," she agreed, twirling the cup. "I will see you shortly."

JESSIMOND TUCKED HER possessions into the wagon, carefully sliding in her lute and cushioning the instrument with her spare clothes on either side. Her case of medicinal herbs went after it. She looked in the distance and could see Kinwick rising majestically. A lump formed in her throat. She hadn't seen her parents in the week she'd lived among the mummers, nor Hal or Elinor and their children. Now, she would ride off without saying goodbye.

Blinking back tears, she avoided the large horse tied to the back of the vehicle and came around to the front of the cart. Marcus already sat on the bench. He gave her a ready smile and leaned down, his fingers capturing her waist and lifting her to him. Jessimond sat and found Marcus took up most of the bench, his thighs as large as tree trunks. She had nowhere else to go and wiggled her behind, trying to lodge into place. Still, her leg rested snuggly against his, as did her shoulder. She barely had space to claim as her own.

She rather liked it.

"Are you sad?" he asked.

"A little," she admitted. "Kinwick has always been home." Though she had spent large amounts of time away from the estate, it had always been to visit her siblings and other relatives. This time, Jessimond would be on her own.

"You'll enjoy the road," Marcus predicted. "If you are adventurous enough to leave the employ of a kind noblewoman, you are ready for anything."

With a flick of his wrists, the horses surged forward.

They didn't talk for the longest while but Jessimond didn't mind. She enjoyed sitting next to Marcus and watching the passing countryside. England in spring was always beautiful as nature came to life again, but she'd found she enjoyed the full bloom of summer even more and then the wild colors of autumn that followed.

After they'd left Kinwick lands far behind, Marcus began humming one of the songs Bartholomew sang when he entertained the crowds before a play began. Jessimond joined in, humming softly, and finally began to sing. Gradually, he ceased and allowed her to finish the song.

"You should be the one singing, not Bartholomew," he told her. "Have you always sung? I noticed you brought a lute with you."

"I received it as a gift many years ago. 'Tis my most treasured possession." Actually, her amethyst brooch was what she cherished most, a link with who she had been before she became a de Montfort, but she couldn't reveal that. "When I strum its strings," she continued, "it seems to become a part of me. I enjoy singing and do so whenever I can."

"Mayhap you can entertain us as you cook each night. I can't thank you enough for easing into that task."

"Several people complimented me after last night's meal. I enjoyed preparing it. And Agatha was most helpful. Did you know her parents used to be a part of the troupe until they passed away?"

"I'd heard her mother once cooked and sewed for the group, and that she had a sister who also worked for the Vawdrys until last season when she left to wed."

Jessimond frowned. "She didn't take Agatha with her?" She didn't anger often but the thought of Agatha being abandoned by her only relative caused Jessimond pain. She determined when the season ended and the troupe disbanded for winter that she would bring Agatha with her to Bexley and on to Kinwick. Merryn would mother the orphan and find work for Agatha. She might even enjoy helping Elinor manage her growing brood.

They drove for many hours and finally stopped as the sun began to descend upon the horizon. No tents would be raised tonight. Instead, the mummers and vendors who traveled along with them would either sleep in their wagons or place their pallets on the ground under the night sky. Jessimond saw that they ate a hearty, flavorful soup and served some of the bread Moss had purchased today as they traveled. The remainder of it would be for breaking their fast in the morning.

As they sat in a circle, Jopp spoke up. "I heard you singing today, Jess. It was pretty."

"You sing?" A sleepy Bartholomew sat up, now interested in the conversation.

"Some."

"Jess is being modest," Marcus interjected. "Her voice is quite good."

"We should sing together." The troubadour retrieved his lute. "Come, Jess. Sit next to me."

She set aside her tin plate and moved to the log Bartholomew rested his back against.

"What songs do you know?"

Jess chuckled. "Every one you sing and many more."

"Join in when I tell you."

Bartholomew began strumming the strings and started to sing a ballad. When he reached the chorus, he gave Jess a nod. She joined in, harmonizing beautifully, and then sang the next verse by herself.

Marcus enjoyed not only her rich voice but her celestial looks. He almost believed God had placed an earthly angel among them.

One that he was determined to make his.

The song ended and enthusiastic applause for the duo broke out. They acknowledged the compliments tossed their way.

Elias said, "We've wasted you on sewing, Jess. You need to be singing in front of the crowds."

"Nay, that is Bartholomew's task. Not mine. Besides, I have plenty to keep me busy."

The troubadour draped an arm around her. "I insist you sing with me, Jess." He gave her a charming smile.

Marcus noticed the man's fingers squeeze her playfully. A sudden rage filled him. He wanted to smash his fist into the musician's handsome face.

Rand leaned close and whispered, "Don't do it."

He whipped his head around and glared at his friend.

"You'll frighten your little songbird if you resort to violence. She might fly away for good," Rand told him, a knowing look on his face. "Besides, she's not yours. Yet." He chuckled quietly.

Marcus glanced back at Jess' flushed, happy face as she and Bartholomew began another tune. It struck him like a lightning bolt flashing in the sky.

He was jealous.

CHAPTER 7

MARCUS FINISHED SECURING Storm to the back of the wagon, eager to be on the road to Fullminster, their next stop.

Or eager for Jess to ride with him again. He'd enjoyed the time they'd spent together alone on the road as they traveled to Lord Guy's estate and hoped the blond beauty would agree to accompany him today. They wouldn't reach Fullminster until afternoon, giving him several hours to spend in conversation with her.

He turned and saw Jess approaching and gave her a smile. "Ready for another day of travel?" he asked pleasantly. "I've room in my wagon if you wish to travel with me. As the first wagon in our caravan, it will be easier to view the passing sights."

"I am excited to be moving to a new estate," she began, "but I'll be riding with Elias. We have business to discuss about costumes for the new plays Ralph wishes to perform."

The soldier in Marcus contained his disappointment, not wanting to reveal his frustration with her decision.

"Then I will see you when we arrive at Fullminster." He climbed into the vehicle. Lifting the reins, he clicked his tongue and started off as the lead wagon.

Something so small as where Jess Gilpin rode during their journey shouldn't have bothered him so much—but it did. A growing need for her had come to the forefront and wouldn't be banished easily. It wasn't just a physical need, though his desire for her deepened each day. Marcus found her joyful to be around. Her happiness was contagious, making everyone wish for more time with Jess, not just him.

She also seemed somewhat of a mystery to him since the first day he'd laid eyes on her. Jess had claimed she and her brother were servants at Kinwick Castle. That it was the only place she'd ever known. Though her clothes were definitely ones that reflected her station, her speech and manner were of one much higher born. As a knight of the noble class, he had been around enough noblewomen both at Hartefield and while fostering to know how they conducted themselves. How they gave orders. How they comfortably managed people. Jess had a deft hand in directing others and handled situations with ease. He suspected there had to be more to her story than what she'd revealed thus far.

Marcus supposed part of it had to do with her keen intelligence. Her opinions had substance, as if she listened carefully to what others said and then used the evidence to support her own conclusions. She articulated well. That could also be due to her cleverness. If Jess had grown up serving the earl and countess, she would have been exposed to them and their guests for years. She might very well be imitating what she had seen and heard her entire life and not even realize it.

A thought occurred to him. Jess might be a bastard child of the Earl of Kinwick. Though it wouldn't have pleased the countess, Geoffrey de Montfort might have installed Jess within the castle as an upper servant in order to keep his eye on her and watch her grow up, especially if the earl had a fondness for Jess' mother. De Montfort could even have encouraged Jess to mimic the ways of him and his family. If that were the case, then Jess was only part peasant and noble blood flowed through her. That argument made the most sense to him, watching how gracefully she moved and spoke.

Marcus would continue to observe her and see if he could solve the riddle of Jess Gilpin.

JESSIMOND WATCHED AS other carts began falling in behind Marcus. She'd had trouble speaking to him because she couldn't help but admire his height and strong build. She'd never paid any attention to how a man was put together.

Until now.

She hurried to the rear, where Elias was already seated behind the horses, waiting for her. He gave her his hand and hoisted her up.

Once their turn arrived, he started the horses.

"Marcus said we would arrive sometime this afternoon at Fullminster."

"Aye. 'Tis a good place for us to stop. Lord Guy and Lady Jeanette are always welcoming and the crowds are large and lively."

"How long will we stay there?"

"Two weeks."

Jessimond looked ahead, counting the number of wagons as the procession began to round a curve in the road.

"It looks as if we are missing some people."

"Not everyone travels with us to each site," Elias shared. "Of course, my mummers are along for the entire journey. Many of the vendors who have wares continue with us, especially those with cooking utensils, cloth, or leather belts and shoes. Others who sell rounds of cheese or soap often are local people. I allow them to join the faire for a price. They either return to their village when the faire moves on or follow us on the road a day and then veer off to make for home."

"How long have you owned the troupe, Elias?"

His brow wrinkled in thought. "Mayhap ten and eight years. Or nine? Ask Moss. He's better at remembering things than I am, especially where numbers are concerned."

"Have you always done this together?"

Elias laughed. "Moss and I are inseparable. We do everything together." He gave her a furtive look and said, "We aren't truly brothers, you know."

Jessimond nodded. "Though you claim to be, you look so very different. Your great height and flaming red hair and beard are such a contrast to Moss."

"Aye, Moss is short and round and brown," Elias agreed. "But we met on the streets of London when we were boys. Both orphans. Scrounging to survive a day at a time. It's hard to be alone, on your own, in a city so great. Together, Moss and I had each other's backs. There's safety in numbers and we two formed a bond greater than blood brothers. Moss will always be family to me. I'm sure we'll be buried in adjoining graves when the time comes."

Curious, she asked, "What do you and Moss do when the troupe disbands for winter?"

"We return to London and put the costumes and props into storage. Keep some of the horses and wagons and sell the rest. We live near the river and deliver goods coming off the boats." He shrugged. "Eventually, I suppose we'll do that instead of hitting the road each spring."

"Where do others in the troupe go?"

He explained how Gylbart stayed in London and worked at the tavern his sister and her husband owned. Oddo left for Sussex, where he worked in his family's inn and tavern. Hamlyn went north, where he had a wife and children, but never revealed what he did once he arrived there.

"And King Ralph, believe it or not, gets his hands dirty as a carpenter. Jopp is also learning the trade. Ralph's brother has five daughters and no sons so he welcomes Ralph and Jopp back each autumn. They build mostly furniture."

"Speaking of Ralph, we need to discuss the new plays and costumes he's interested in me making," Jessimond said. "His list was a long one. I didn't want to start anything until we had spoken."

Elias chuckled. "Ralph is always full of ideas. Frankly, most every play is the same story. There's a struggle between good and evil. Some type of devil who makes an appearance, tempting the hero. A sword fight or two. Death. Then someone rising miraculously from the dead and ridding the world of all that is bad."

She chuckled. "You're telling me we don't need any new costumes."

"Not really. Oh, once we arrive at Fullminster, I'll give you coin to purchase some new cloth. You can make up a few new things to please Ralph. He is an excellent actor. I would hate to lose him over something like this."

"Do you think he would leave the troupe?"

"Ralph's temper can be fierce, especially when he's not getting his way. He threatens to leave at least seven times a season. He's never made good on it, though, and I doubt he ever will. Still, if I can please him in this small way, I will. If merely to keep peace within the group."

Jessimond hesitated and then said, "Do you realize some of the other mummers are tired of Ralph playing the lead role every time?"

Elias snorted. "I'm sure you're meaning Gylbart. He's never satisfied with anything. As for any others?" He shrugged. "They can stay or leave. 'Tis actually easy to find people to replace them. You'd be surprised how many seem to have the urge to roam the countryside and pretend to be someone they're not."

Jessimond thought that description sounded like her but remained silent, nursing hurt feelings.

Finally, she asked, "What of Agatha? Where does she go when the troupe scatters?"

He frowned. "I never really thought of it. When her parents were alive, they went to Kent. She and Reba did the same after their mother passed."

"I heard Reba left the troupe last year and wed. Would Agatha have gone with her sister?"

"Nay. Reba was always full of herself. Would argue with a log if given the chance. She could be something spiteful to Agatha. Even cruel at times. Reba would not have wanted the girl to visit for any length of time, especially with a new husband." Elias paused. "I'm afraid I have no idea what Agatha did. She merely showed up again when it was time to leave London."

Jessimond bit back the sharp retort on her tongue. No one in the company seemed to care about the girl. It reinforced her decision to take Agatha with her at the end of the season. Someone had to care for her.

That someone might be Peter. Jessimond knew he had eyes for the young woman. Bringing Agatha back to Kinwick would not only secure her future but might also lead to marriage with Peter. She would try to see how Agatha felt about life on the road with the mummers and if she ever had any interest in settling down in one place.

They rode several more hours. Elias answered all of Jessimond's questions about where the mummers would travel the rest of the season and about various members of the group. By the time they arrived at Fullminster, she knew much more than she had about the troupe.

"Remember to look at the various stalls offering cloth for the new costumes once the vendors have set up their wares," Elias reminded her.

"I will spend your coin wisely, Elias. I drive a hard bargain."

As they had at Kinwick, the mummers pulled the carts close together and began unloading their goods in a large field. She noted how Peter blended seamlessly with the others and did his share of the work. Soon, the wagons had been unloaded and the men began erecting the tents. She would need to think about a hearty meal because everyone would be hungry after such physical labor.

Jessimond saw a couple heading toward them. By their dress, she assumed the pair to be Lord Guy and Lady Jeanette.

The nobleman gathered the troupe members and said, "We are, indeed, happy to have you back at Fullminster this year. My wife and I look forward to hearing your songs and seeing your stories acted out. As a thanks, a stag has been butchered and prepared for you so that you can feast upon it tonight."

The group cheered loudly and Elias and Moss thanked their host and hostess. The couple left and a cart appeared soon after with the promised meal in large pots. By then, the tents had been set up and the men had gone to the nearby stream to wash. Jessimond and Agatha helped distribute the food, ladling the thick stew into bowls. Besides the stag, Lady Jeanette had sent stewed apples and several rounds of cheese. The troupe ate in silence, exhausted after their long day.

After the meal, Elias and Moss approached her.

"We think it would be a good idea for you to sing some with Bartholomew," Moss began. "Your voices blend well together. We've never seen a man and woman perform with one another as troubadours. It would draw greater crowds."

"Bartholomew is the troubadour," Jessimond countered. "I merely sing for fun. Besides, I wouldn't want him to resent me."

"He wouldn't," promised Elias. When she hesitated, he said, "Think about it, Jess. You don't have to sing tomorrow. In fact, come see the plays. Listen to Bartholomew perform. Get a feel for what goes on in the entertainment area. Then you can make a decision."

Jessimond thought that a good compromise. "I'll do that. After I shop for new material."

She turned and found Marcus at her elbow.

"You'll be making new costumes?"

"Aye. Not as many as Ralph would prefer but enough to please him."

"The stalls will be set up in the morning. May I accompany you as you look for what you need? I can hold whatever you buy."

"Don't you have better things to do than carry my goods?" she teased.

His warm gaze caused her belly to turn over. "I have plenty of time to help you, Jess, before I am needed elsewhere. Besides, I need more practice at buying goods under your watchful eye."

"All right," she agreed, looking forward to spending more time with him.

The troupe bedded down for the night. Jessimond returned to the tent she and Agatha shared.

It took her a long time to fall asleep.

JESSIMOND AWOKE EARLY after a night of tossing and turning. She hoped she hadn't disturbed Agatha's sleep. She emerged from the tent as the camp began to stir and made sure those already up had bread and ale to break their fast.

Marcus appeared, his dark locks tousled. He raked his fingers through his thick hair, which only made her wish she were the one taming it. The thought troubled her. She barely knew this man yet already her body quickened and came alive when he drew near.

"Are you ready to walk the stalls in search of bargains?" he asked.

"Do you think they will be open this early?"

He shrugged. "Most should be. Once they see a paying customer is at hand, they will make themselves available."

They strolled side-by-side to the area where the booths stood. A few were empty but most already had someone stationed with the displayed goods, ready to negotiate with buyers.

Marcus pointed out various stalls for her to visit, noting which might give her a better price.

"You seem very familiar with the sellers and their wares," Jessimond noted, wondering how many of the women he'd made friends with since he'd called everyone by name as he described their booths and what they sold.

"I have a lot of time on my hands. After Rand and I exhibit our sword skills or perform our joust, I am free to come and go as I please. Sometimes, I go to the plays and have even acted in a few in a minor role. It's allowed me to wander around and get to know the others traveling with us, beyond the mummers."

"Where should I start?"

He told her the three stalls to visit that would have the best quality of cloth. Knowing she spent another's coin, Jessimond wanted to get the most for the money Elias had given her last night. Both she and Marcus bid for material in wool and linen for the next half-hour, and she came away with exactly what she would need to complete the costumes Ralph had urged her to make.

Marcus accompanied her back to her tent. They saw Agatha rolling a wheelbarrow, taking the last of the props to the stage area.

"I'll be behind the stage if you want to come watch from there," Agatha said. "You can even help me hand out some of the props if you wish."

"I'll see you soon," Jessimond promised.

She held the flap of their tent open. Marcus ducked inside so he could lay their purchases on her pallet. His large frame filled so much of the space that her movements were restricted. Jessimond knelt so she could separate the cloth into different piles and think about what she would start first. She would begin sewing after she'd spent time observing Bartholomew sing and the mummers' first performance of the day.

As she moved the cloth, she discovered a rich, red wool that resembled rubies in the depth of its color. She rose, the material in her hands.

"I'm afraid one of the merchants accidentally included something we didn't buy," she told Marcus.

His eyes only gleamed at her. "'Twas no mistake."

Confusion filled her. "I did not pay for this, Marcus. I need to return it."

Jessimond started around him but he caught her arm.

"I did pay for it, Jess," he said softly.

"You . . . do you wish for me to make a new tunic for you or Rand?" His fingers scorched her arm. She was aware how close their bodies were to one another.

"Nay." His eyes glowed at her. "I bought it . . . for you."

"For me?" She hated how her voice squeaked. Swallowing, she asked, "Why?"

Marcus lifted the material from her hands and placed it on the pallet again. "I thought the color would suit you. I want you to sew something for yourself. You've taken care of the mummers this past week. Now, do for you."

Her knees grew shaky. "Marcus, I cannot accept a gift like that. The wool is very fine. I'm sure it was terribly expensive."

He placed his hands on her shoulders. "You're worth it, Jess."

At that moment, Jessimond knew Marcus was going to kiss her.

CHAPTER 8

Marcus saw in Jess' eyes that she knew what was coming. A moment later, his lips brushed against hers. He didn't know the last time he'd kissed a woman who'd never been kissed. Mayhap never.

Marcus planned to take his time. The mummers were all at the play, including Agatha, getting ready for their first performance of the day. No one would miss them.

And no one would interrupt.

His fingers lightly held her in place as he continued to softly move his lips against hers, setting a languid pace that would be hard to keep. Already, her scent drove him wild. She smelled of vanilla and warm sunshine, a delicious combination.

Jess hadn't moved beneath his fingers. For a moment, the look of panic in her eyes had made him believe she might flee. She'd stayed, though.

Now, he wanted to show her why that decision was wise.

Slowly, he took small nips at her full, bottom lip, the one which had tempted him beyond measure. Marcus heard each quick intake of breath every time he did so, followed by a tiny whimper. He ran his tongue along that sweet, lower lip, gaining a small taste of the woman who had haunted his dreams.

But when it came to Jess, he was a greedy man.

His tongue found the seam of her mouth and teased her lips apart. He dipped inside, still holding her steady, and tasted the honey of her mouth. An unexpected ripple of pleasure ran through him.

It made him want more. Much more.

Marcus drew her to him now, needing the feel of her body next to his. Her full breasts pressed against his chest. His hands slid down her slender back. He spread his fingers wide, keeping her against him even as he sampled her again and again.

He became aware of two things at once. One, Jess' arms had wrapped around him, letting him know she wasn't going anywhere. The outline of her hands branded his back. The second surprised him, though it shouldn't have.

She began kissing him back.

At first, she was tentative as she felt her way, her inexperience showing. But Jess Gilpin was a clever woman. Within minutes of being kissed for the first time, she imitated—and then improved—on what he did. As her hands roamed his back, she kissed him eagerly, with passion, stroking his tongue with hers until he groaned into her mouth.

A war now ensued between them, one for domination and control. His hands moved past her waist and cupped her rounded buttocks, kneading the tender flesh. She clutched him more tightly, her breasts swelling against him.

Marcus longed for more but knew they must stop. Gradually, he went from deepening each kiss to slowly withdrawing, until finally he forced himself to totally break the kiss.

Still, he held her close, reluctant to part from her, his lips traveling up her delicate nose and landing on her brow. He pressed one last, tender kiss there and then studied her face.

Jess' lips were bruised from their love play. Her eyes appeared dazed. Clouded. Finally, they cleared and focused on him. Slowly, the corners of her mouth turned up.

"I rather like kissing," she informed him, her smile growing.

Jess brought her hands from his back and moved them along Marcus' chest, hard as a stone wall. They rose higher until her fingers locked behind his neck and pulled him toward her. Marcus might think they were finished but Jess was only starting. She yanked down hard and his mouth crashed against hers, his fingers tightening on her bottom, digging into her flesh.

She teased him as he had teased her, nipping and licking her way until she slipped her tongue inside his mouth.

Oh, praise the Virgin Mary! This. Was. Heaven.

Jessimond remembered every little trick Marcus had taught her and then added a few of her own. She knew they worked their magic. Not only did the fever within her grow, but she felt the pounding of his heart against her breast increase until it drummed out of control. His hold on her tightened. His mouth took command once more and, this time, she let him, giving in to the soaring feelings within her.

They kissed until she thought their lips might fall away, scorched until the fire ignited between them had consumed them whole, the flames burning high into the sky.

Then suddenly, Marcus released her, pushing her away, confusing her. Jessimond's entire body trembled. She found it hard to stand on her own. Tears threatened to fall when she realized she had disappointed him.

"What . . . did I . . . am I doing something wrong?" she asked.

Marcus stood panting, raw need written across his face.

"I'm sorry," she said. "I can do better."

He jerked her toward him, enfolding her in his massive arms, his lips brushing her hair. "Nay, sweetheart, you did nothing wrong. In fact, you did everything right. Too right, I'm afraid."

Jessimond wriggled in his arms and then discovered something stiff and uncompromising between them. She realized his member had grown as hard as a rock. Glancing up, his brilliant blue eyes had darkened in passion and desire.

"We must stop, Jess," Marcus said softly. Giving her a wry smile, he added, "You can feel why."

"You want me?" she asked breathlessly, secretly delighted at the notion.

His hand cupped her cheek. "Aye. More than I have ever wanted another woman."

"I doubt that," she said, unable to believe she could have that great an effect upon him. "You are a very physical man, Marcus. I'm sure you've coupled with dozens of women. Ones far more experienced than I. Ones who have brought you pleasure."

He smoothed her eyebrows and then traced his finger down the slope of her nose until he placed it against her lips.

"I'm no saint, Jess. I don't claim to be. But your kiss has kindled something within me that I've never felt."

She started to speak but he pressed his finger against her lips to silence her.

"I want to kiss you again, Jess Gilpin. I want to do more than that. I want to bury my face in that glorious mane of golden hair. Press it between your breasts. I want to feel those breasts. Lick them. Suck them. My cock wants to bury itself deep inside you and never leave."

Jessimond shivered at not only the words but the passion behind them.

"Those are things for you to do with a husband, sweetheart. Not me."

He gave her a hard, swift kiss and released her. Jessimond felt woozy, as if she'd had too much wine to drink.

"Stay in your tent for a while," he warned. "Your lips are swollen and your face is flushed."

Marcus stepped to the tent's flap, his eyes still burning. "I will see you later."

With that, he was gone.

Jessimond sank to her knees, knowing her feet could no longer hold her up.

She had wanted to leave Kinwick to find adventure and experience love.

Was this the start?

She touched the tips of her fingers to her lips in wonder. Marcus' mouth had been there just moments ago. Already, she craved his kiss again. His touch. Never had she felt safer and yet more exhilarated than in the circle of his arms.

Gradually, her breathing came under her control and she once more was the master of her body. She looked at the various materials they'd bought and fingered the ruby wool that he had purchased for her. With a knowing smile, she decided she would keep it and sew something spectacular for her to wear.

Jessimond pushed herself to her feet and decided it was time to attend the mummers' show. Stepping outside, she immediately became aware of a buzz vibrating in the air. She rounded the corner, the tents no longer blocking her view.

People were everywhere.

The stalls she had visited early this morning now held throngs of buyers in front of them. Voices called out as prices were negotiated. Jessimond cut through one of the long rows where booths faced one another, weaving her way in and out of the crowds. She waved to a few vendors that she had come to know, caught up in the excitement that filled the air.

Leaving the merchants' area, she heard the strains of music over the din and hurried toward it. Bartholomew had already begun, his voice soaring as he sang. As she drew closer, she noticed the mass of people gathered around the stage that had been set up the day before after the mummers' arrival. Jessimond moved as near as she could and then got no further, so she stayed in place and listened.

Bartholomew finished his song and sang three more. Sometimes, he closed his eyes, lost in the music. At other times, his eyes roamed the crowd and settled upon a person to sing to. Knowing the troubadour, his gaze always settled upon a woman—and a pretty one at that. He had a roving eye and several of the mummers had warned Jessimond to be wary around the musician.

He finished his last song and bowed, the crowd clapping loudly in appreciation of his talent. Bartholomew exited the stage and a hush fell over the assembled group. Hamlyn stepped out from the left of the curtain and began painting a picture for the audience, taking them back to a time long ago and very far away. His melodious tone set a perfect stage for the action that followed.

The play incorporated most of the members of the troupe. As Elias had noted, it was about the age-old struggle between good and evil. Hamlyn kept the narrative going between the scenes. Jessimond thought some of the mummers excellent in their roles, though a few could have said their lines with more feeling.

Then a final scene occurred with a long fight between the personified Good and Evil. Ralph, naturally, was cast as Good. Gylbart played the role of Evil, as a devil who'd tried to tempt Good away from what he knew to be right and true. Jessimond assumed the moves of their swordplay had been planned in advance, just as their lines had been learned and rehearsed. Gylbart wasn't the most talented swordsman, but he did an adequate job. She would have found the ending more believable if Ralph had been forced to work for his triumph a bit harder. Knowing swordplay as she did, thanks to Raynor's tradition of gifting each de Montfort child with a sword and then Nan working with her until she was more than competent, Jessimond thought to offer some help to Gylbart.

Gylbart fell as Ralph struck the deathblow, then hovered over him, waving his sword high.

"This is what it means to defeat your foes," Ralph extoled in a deep voice. "For Evil—for Death—to lie at your doorstep. I have vanquished my enemy. He will haunt me no longer. I will go forth now, seeking truth and justice for all."

With that, Ralph threw his arms to the sky in victory.

The crowd erupted with cheers and applause. Ralph bowed several times and then Gylbart leapt to his feet and did the same. The other mummers came out as a group and bowed together and then individually. Ralph, as the lead, once more stepped front and center and bowed graciously as the audience chanted his name. He must be familiar to them after the Vawdrys coming to Fullminster several years.

Finally, the actors left the stage and the audience began to disperse. Jessimond fought against the flow in order to make her way to the stage and beyond. She finally climbed onto the raised platform and then exited from the back, seeing Agatha and waving at her.

"I thought you were going to watch the play with me," the young woman said, disappointment evident in her tone.

To assuage her, Jessimond said, "I thought I would first view it from the front, as an audience member would, in order to see how it went. For the next performance, I plan to stay with you and see how things unfold backstage. I'm sure there'll be a great contrast in what goes on."

Agatha seemed placated by her explanation. "Here. You can help me put these props away."

As Jessimond helped sort and put away the props, the actors stepped out of their costumes, dressing quickly in their own clothes, which Agatha had laid out atop wooden crates. Some had on clothes beneath their costumes but a few were as bare as a newborn babe once they shed their costume. Jessimond tried not to look—and tried not to think of what Marcus de Harte would look like with nothing on. She'd already seen him stripped to the waist that first day at Kinwick. Now that her body had been next to his, she wondered what it would be like to run her hands along his skin, feeling the ridges of muscles.

"Jess?"

She turned and saw Agatha looking oddly at her. "What?"

"Did you not hear me?"

"Nay. I was thinking about the play." *Or rather playing with a bare-chested Marcus.* "What do you need, Agatha?"

"Never mind."

She finished setting the props aside, knowing Agatha would merely reorganize them again, based upon the next play the mummers would perform and which ones would be in use. Jessimond folded the garments worn during the play, checking to see if any new holes were present or if a hem needed to be re-stitched. Satisfied that no repairs needed to be done, she decided to seek out Gylbart.

Jessimond found the mummer at a stall selling soap, flirting with a woman old enough to be his mother—and then some.

"Come with me," she told him, linking her arm through his and pulling him away.

"Jess, I was making progress with her," Gylbart complained good-naturedly.

She gave him a stern look. "We'll be here two weeks. If you feel the need to couple with someone who looks like she could be your mother, you'll have plenty of opportunities to do so."

"You think I can do better?" he asked earnestly.

She stopped. "Don't fish for compliments, Gylbart. You are a fine-looking man."

He shrugged. "I don't seem to have much luck with the ladies."

Jessimond clucked her tongue. "Instead of immediately trying to get under their skirts, you might wish to talk with them first."

"Talk? What good is talk when there's pleasure to be had?"

She narrowed her eyes. In a stern voice, she said, "Most women would rather talk with a man first, especially if he's a stranger. If bedding a female is your goal, Gylbart, I would suggest getting to know her first. Woo her a little. Treat her with some respect. Then you can see if the both of you are interested in . . . mutual pleasure."

The mummer shook his head. "You have some peculiar ideas, Jess."

"I have an even better one. Come along."

She led him back to the stage area, where Agatha bustled about moving items. Jessimond had seen where several swords lay, so she plucked two from the group of weapons and brought them to where she'd left Gylbart.

"We're going to practice," she told him as she breezed by.

As she expected, he followed her, catching up and full of questions.

"You have swords, Jess. Why do you have swords? What do you mean, practice? Be careful there. Those can be dangerous. Oh, I know the tips have been blunted but you could injure yourself all the same. Women don't hold swords. Slow down, Jess. Why are you in such a hurry? Why do we need swords? And what do you mean to practice?"

She weaved through the crowds again situated at the vendors' booths and continued, not answering his questions until they arrived back at the tents.

"I'm going to help you learn true swordplay," she said, continuing past the tents and going further away until they were alone, not an easy thing with so many people roaming Fullminster lands.

Finally, she came to a halt and handed Gylbart a sword.

"I have a few things I can teach you that will make you markedly better," she promised. "Ralph's defeat of you in the play seemed much too easy."

"He's very skilled with a sword," whined Gylbart.

"You say you want better roles? That you could replace Ralph?" Jessimond paused. "Then you need to learn to be better than Ralph. In every way. Prove to the Vawdrys that you are an actor to be reckoned with.

"Starting now."

CHAPTER 9

MARCUS LEFT JESS, shaken to the core. He blindly walked through the booth area, where vendors bargained with buyers, not hearing any of their conversations. Eventually, he found himself near the stage and decided to attend the first play of the day. Soon, a crowd swelled about him and he became lost in his thoughts.

It was obvious to him that he should stay away from Jess Gilpin. Though Marcus was determined to settle down at Hartefield once the mummers' season ended, he'd believed he would bring Jess with him, ready to make her his wife. Now, that idea frightened him beyond words.

Never had a woman moved him so much—and they had merely shared a kiss. Actually, dozens. Or hundreds. One kiss had blended into the next until Marcus understood that the two of them had become one. It was as if Jess had a window into his soul and had opened and then climbed through it, totally inhabiting him inside and out. That wasn't what he desired in a marriage. He wanted a wife who would help him run Hartefield once his father had passed on, a woman who could manage all of the keep's domestic matters. One who would birth his children and keep his people happy. One he could say goodbye to each morning as he headed to the training yard to work with his soldiers and not give her another thought until he returned at night.

Jess was definitely not that woman.

Instead, she was one already under his skin, a woman who dominated his waking thoughts. One he would need by his side each minute of every day. If she were out of his sight for long, he wouldn't be able to go about his duties. Marcus had heard of women who bewitched men in such a manner, so that they became weak and unreliable, thinking only of their woman and how to please her. He didn't have the desire to bend until he broke, caring for a single woman above all else. By the Christ, he was a knight. The future Baron of Harteley. He must only rely on himself and not have his attention dominated by a beautiful wife. True, he would need to marry and provide an heir of his own, but any woman would do. He would lead his life and she would do the same. They would couple when needed and come together to strengthen their common interests, making Hartefield a productive place.

And every moment of that life would be empty without Jess in it.

Marcus cursed under his breath. He felt as if he had no choice. Wed the wench and face being besotted the remainder of his life—or push her aside and never see her again—and still be miserable for decades.

How had it come to this?

He'd only known her a short time. Hellfire and damnation, they'd only kissed today. *Kissed!* Nothing more. Why did Jess seem like a part of the fabric of his life, already woven into his story, a part that couldn't be ripped out or patched over?

Marcus had never been more confused or unsure of himself. He was a responsible man, at least until he'd stormed from Harte Castle two months ago. Even now, he knew he would soon return and dedicate himself to Hartefield and its people. Confidence had never been an issue. He rode well. Was an excellent swordsman and archer. He was loyal and trustworthy and above average in intelligence.

How had Jess, a simple servant and mere woman, made him question everything about himself—including the man he was—and the one he might become if she were by his side?

Marcus suddenly became aware of the tension surrounding him. He cleared his mind and saw the morality play had almost come to an end. The great battle between Good and Evil was about to commence and the audience watching held their breaths in anticipation of its outcome.

Fighting to stay in the moment, he banished all his dark thoughts in favor of watching Gylbart, who played Evil. After first seeing the mummer with a sword, Marcus had pulled him aside and given him a few lessons in swordplay. As he now watched the very fight scene he and Gylbart had perfected, it seemed every move they'd practiced had been forgotten by the mummer. Marcus winced at how wooden Gylbart appeared. The actor proved adequate enough for the audience he performed before, but Marcus believed the friction between the pair could be escalated, and the crowd more entertained, if Gylbart appeared to be more of a threat to Good. Ralph's talents included wielding a sword in a credible manner, so there was never any doubt about the outcome once the battle began.

Finally, Good vanquished Evil and Ralph started into his last soliloquy. Having heard it several times before, Marcus turned and moved through the enthralled crowd.

Then he spied Jess as she watched the play. Never had he seen a lovelier sight. The sun struck her long, golden braid, warming it. Her eyes glowed with interest. Her parted lips, still slightly swollen, tempted him beyond compare. Marcus wanted nothing more than to sweep her into his arms and march away, her hands clinging to him, eyes wide yet knowing what was to come. He wanted to kiss her until she grew so weak that she couldn't stand. He craved her touch, those small, callused fingers of hers cradling his face.

Oh, then he would whisper all the wicked things he planned to do to her in her ear—and act upon them. By the time Marcus finished, he would have explored every inch of Jess Gilpin. Multiple times.

Her face lit up as Ralph's lines ended and she began clapping enthusiastically. To see her joy almost caused him physical pain. Marcus pushed through the crowd and departed the stage area. He made his way over to the faire's stalls and lost himself among the crowds, swelling to a greater size now that the play's audience mingled in. He wandered restlessly up and down the various rows, glancing at the displayed wares but not really seeing them. Several people called out to him but he dismissed them with a wave and kept moving.

Finally, he decided to return to his tent. No one should be nearby since another play would be enacted in another hour or so. After that performance concluded, he and Rand would put on their own demonstration of swordplay. Marcus looked forward to some quiet time to reflect on what he needed to do about Jess. How he should behave when he next saw her.

Would he commit to bringing her to Hartefield once the season ended? If so, he should make it clear that he had no interest in pursuing her—or rather pretend to claim no interest in her. His gut told him if he didn't stay away from Jess, he wouldn't be able to control his desire. She was a true innocent. The least he could do was respect that innocence and keep from sullying her until after they made their vows. Yet, if he did pull away, how could he subtly woo her? When it came time for the troupe to disperse, he needed Jess to care enough about him to trust him so he could bring her to Hartefield.

Marcus' head ached from confusion. As he moved further from the crowds, the noise lessened until it was barely audible by the time he arrived at the circle of tents. Then he stopped.

What was that?

He thought it might be the clang of steel but knew that couldn't be the case. Then it sounded again. Had Rand decided to practice with one of the mummers? That would only lead to trouble. Unlike the mummers, who used swords with blunted tips and dulled sides, he and Rand fought with their own weapons. Though Rand was very skilled with a sword, he might go too far and hurt one of the actors.

Marcus raced across the open area and crested a hill. Immediately, he saw two men engaged, their swords clashing against one another, the sound echoing in the still air. They stopped abruptly and one stepped next to the other, demonstrating a move. He realized the one on the left was Gylbart from his stance. The mummer imitated the other man and nodded, then tried the move again, this time with more confidence.

Then Marcus sucked in a quick breath. The slender fellow wasn't a man at all.

It was Jess.

She turned quickly and he saw her braid fly in the air, swinging behind her. Lifting her sword, the two commenced again for a few moments before Jess stopped the action.

He sank to the ground, fascinated at what he saw.

Jess knew exactly what she was doing, better than some soldiers he had trained. Her movements were both fluid and fearless. She was also patient, showing Gylbart over and over certain moves, from footwork to how to arc the sword gracefully and with power. Marcus admired her skill—and then some.

What now caught his attention was what she wore. At first, he'd thought her a man. The more he studied her, though, he realized how foolish that notion was. Though dressed as a man, Jess filled out the clothing in wicked ways. The dark pants fit her snuggly, emphasizing her rounded bottom and slender legs. The tunic's sleeves fit tightly around her arms, allowing her better movement. But it was the front of the tunic that drew his eye. Jess had an ample bosom and the simple, tan tunic emphasized every curve.

Marcus' mouth watered simply gazing upon her. The desire he'd wanted to rid himself of magnified a thousandfold, seeing her garbed in such a manner and witnessing how accomplished she proved with a sword. This woman caught his imagination. Hunger for her increased the longer he observed her.

But who was Jess Gilpin? No servant would have access to weapons, much less grow so talented in the use of one. The skill Jess showed had been achieved over time. It would take years of practice to develop that level of adroitness.

Marcus determined to find out exactly who this woman was.

JESSIMOND CALLED A halt, her breathing rapid and her mouth dry. She was glad she'd taken time to change her clothing. Movement using swords was much easier when she wore a man's garb.

"You showed tremendous improvement, Gylbart," she praised.

His eyes lit with enthusiasm. "I cannot wait to practice again with Ralph with what I know now. The audience will cheer like madmen when they see us attack one another." He frowned. "I did not do nearly as well as when Marcus worked with me."

"He did?"

"Aye. When he and Rand joined the troupe, Marcus told me my sword skills were lacking. He tutored me." A sheepish smile crossed his face. "He didn't show nearly the patience you did, Jess. He's so tall and commanding. I'm a little afraid of him. I just hope I can remember everything you've shown me."

"If you don't, we can always go again. It would help if I could witness you and Ralph at practice and make a few suggestions."

Gylbart shook his head. "Nay. Ralph would never listen to advice given by a woman."

"We'll see about that," she said, determined that King Ralph would work with Gylbart and allow her to watch—especially if he wanted those new costumes made up.

"I need to return to the stage," Gylbart said, panic in his voice. "I've lost track of the time. Thank you, Jess." He gave her a quick kiss on the cheek and hurried away.

She watched him running up the rise and noticed Marcus sitting at the top of the small hill. Jessimond wondered how long he'd been there. Gylbart greeted Marcus and disappeared. Marcus rose and came down the hill. Jessimond's heart began beating rapidly.

"I see you took Gylbart under your wing."

"I heard you did the same," she countered.

He chuckled. "You seemed to have had better success tutoring him than I did."

"Gylbart's a bit afraid of you," Jessimond said. "I think both your size and skill with a sword intimidated him. And mayhap, you were a bit gruff during your lessons. I am much calmer and more suited to teaching someone."

He eyed her a long moment. "I'm surprised Gylbart listened to a thing you said."

"Why?" she asked. "Because I am a woman—and only a man can teach sword skills?"

A slow smile lit his face. "Because if you'd been showing me how to swing a sword, I wouldn't have heard a word you uttered. I would be mesmerized with how beautiful you are."

Jessimond felt her face go hot, both at his compliment and how he stared at her. She looked at the sensual lips that had been next to hers only a short while ago and a yearning for them, as wide as an ocean, enveloped her.

Marcus took a step toward her. Jessimond hoped he would kiss her again. They were alone and that was not a frequent occurrence when part of a large troupe.

He reached out and captured her braid, which had fallen over her shoulder. Lifting it to his face, he brushed the tail against his cheek. He lowered it—but didn't release it. Instead, he wound it around his fist, ensuring she wouldn't go anywhere. They stood so close that her breasts almost touched his chest.

Jessimond knew what was coming and prepared herself. She only hoped she would be as believable as one of the mummers speaking his lines.

"Where did you learn how to fight like that?" Marcus asked, his gaze unwavering.

"At Kinwick."

She didn't know him well enough to trust him with the entire truth. Even if she did, he might accidentally let it slip and then the others would learn of her true identity. Already, she had enjoyed being a part of the company and living a different kind of life. She wasn't anywhere near ready to give that up.

Not even for a man who kissed like Marcus de Harte.

"Kinwick. Where you were a servant." Doubt lingered in the air.

"Aye. I helped care for some of Lord Geoffrey and Lady Merryn's grandchildren. Their son, Sir Hal, is Kinwick's captain of the guard. He and Lady Elinor have three children. As a knight, Sir Hal believes it important for his children to learn sword skills from a young age. In fact, 'tis a family tradition that Lord Geoffrey's cousin, Lord Raynor Le Roux, carve and gift a wooden sword to each de Montfort child. He has continued this practice with every grandchild who has arrived."

Jessimond took a breath and laughed. "Poor Lord Raynor is kept quite busy since there are six de Montfort children. It seems one of the wives is always birthing another babe."

Marcus took in what she said and then asked, "But what does that have to do with you?"

She was now ready to make the connection for him.

"Since I watch over the children, I do more than feed and bathe them. I sing to them. Tell them stories. Play with them. I also take them all around the estate. After they were given their swords, sometimes they needed someone to spar with them. The soldiers in the training yard didn't have time to do that. The children grew to learn one another's strengths and weaknesses and tired of fighting each other."

"That's where you came in?"

"Aye. I had been present at all of their lessons and assimilated the knowledge. It took several tries once I put a sword in my hand to physically understand what my mind already knew. Once I did, I truly enjoyed sparring with all of the children. I've done it for several years now."

He tugged on her braid. "You are exceptionally good at it. Better than some men I've known."

Jessimond smiled. "I will take that as a compliment, coming from a knight." She paused. "You are a knight, Marcus, aren't you?"

She asked not only to draw attention away from her, but to learn something more about him.

When he remained silent, she said, "I figured you and Rand to be knights-errant, not associated with any liege lord, and that is why you were able to join the Vawdrys' troupe."

"I do give allegiance to a lord," he finally said. "Rand, as well. We are on an interesting mission. Taking the long way home."

His words puzzled her. "Your lord does not mind you doing so?"

Marcus shrugged.

Jessimond wasn't satisfied with his silence. Before she could call him out, though, Jopp interrupted them.

"Jess!" the boy cried.

She looked up and saw him running down the hill.

"What's wrong, Jopp?"

"Hamlyn stumbled and fell against the stage. His forehead is split open and he's not making much sense. Moss said you are a healer. Can you come help?"

"Of course," she assured the boy. "Let me get my case of herbs. Run back and let Moss know I'm coming."

Jopp took off again like a bolt of lightning and disappeared over the rise.

Marcus released his hold on her braid and took her elbow, helping her up the hill. Jessimond retrieved her case and exited the tent.

"You're going . . . like that?" he asked, waving his hand up and down her. "'Tis not decent for you to be seen in such a way, Jess."

"I'm not going to take the time to change my attire when a man needs my help," Jessimond said curtly and strode off.

CHAPTER 10

JESSIMOND IGNORED MARCUS when he caught up to her. She'd done her best to explain how she came to have such unusual skills for a servant, much less a woman. Either he would believe her or not. She didn't want to waste any more time trying to convince him.

As they arrived at the booths, she asked, "Do you still have coin?"

"What do you require?"

"A cup of strong wine to bathe Hamlyn's wound."

"Wait here."

Marcus ventured to a nearby stall and soon returned with a cup he'd promised to bring back. They continued on their way until they reached the stage. Several mummers either stood or knelt in a circle. Hamlyn lay in the center of them, a large gash across his forehead. Blood streamed down his face and covered the front of his tunic.

Jessimond sat next to him, opening her case. "I heard you took a nasty fall."

"Bloody knee gave out on me," the mummer complained. "Made me stumble. Fell head first into the corner of the stage."

"Jopp said you were a little confused."

"Nay. Not anymore, Jess," Hamlyn assured her. "You're Jess. I'm Hamlyn." He pointed to and named several of the mummers hovering nearby. "We're at Lord Guy's estate. 'Tis a Tuesday. Truly, I'm right in the head. Saw a few stars when it first happened but I've been awake the entire time. Hurting," he added, looking as if he wanted her sympathy.

"Well, I'm here to fix you up," she promised.

Jessimond had been around others who'd suffered head injuries, a few who remained confused for several days. Hamlyn had his wits about him, which was very good news.

"First, I'm going to cleanse your wound," she explained. "I'll sew it up after that and you already know I'm an excellent seamstress. It will only take a few stitches to close."

She opened her case and took out a bit of ginger. "Chew on this."

Hamlyn eyed it with suspicion. "What for?"

"'Tis ginger. In case your head is aching or you feel a bit of nausea, it will help calm your stomach."

He thought it over a moment and then slipped it between his lips. "That's strong," he declared.

When he didn't spit it out, she thought that was a good sign. Jessimond took small bits of linen from her case and motioned for Marcus to hand her the cup of wine. She dipped a square into the liquid and smoothed it over the gash, repeating the action several times until the area was free of blood. She would use water to wash his face once she got him back to the camp.

"I'm going to sew the slice together now. It will sting some," she warned.

Hamlyn eyed the cup on the ground. "Are you through with the wine? I could drink what's left to help with the pain," he offered.

"An excellent idea," she said, handing him the cup.

He drained it quickly and set it aside.

"Lie still." Jessimond thought a moment. "In fact, it would be good for someone to hold your head."

"I will," Marcus volunteered.

He sank to his knees and placed Hamlyn's head between them, then gripped the mummer's head with both hands. Jessimond knew Hamlyn wouldn't be going anywhere.

Quickly, she threaded a needle from her case and pinched the skin together. Using a combination of a fell and running stitch, she mended the skin in a few minutes and then coated the wound with honey to promote healing. Winding a long strip of linen around Hamlyn's head in order to keep dirt from the wound, she secured the end.

"You'll be good as new but will probably have a small scar as a reminder of your misadventure," she told him. "What you need to do now is rest."

"But we have a play to perform in just a few minutes," Hamlyn complained.

"Not today," Jessimond declared. "You need to sleep. I'll even watch you to see that no fever develops."

"You're treating me as a child, Jess. And who will take my place? Next to Ralph, I have the most lines," he lamented.

Jessimond knew that was the true reason he wanted to remain. These mummers fought for time in the spotlight. She believed Hamlyn would go out, bloody tunic and all, merely for the chance to perform and receive adoration from the audience.

"I can," Gylbart quickly volunteered. "I've always thought the role better suited to me than you."

"You're the narrator this time, Gylbart," Elias interjected. "You can't narrate and act at the same time. 'Twould confuse the crowd."

Marcus rose to his feet. "I'll step in," he offered. "I've done that before."

"True," Elias agreed, "but only for a small role. Both Hamlyn and Gylbart have many lines in this play."

"I can do it," Marcus assured the troupe's owner. He turned to Gylbart. "Which part would you rather take on?"

"Definitely Hamlyn's," Gylbart said, his eyes glowing in satisfaction.

"Then it's settled." Marcus looked down at Hamlyn. "Let me help you back to the tents."

"I can do that," Jessimond said. "I'd like to give Hamlyn some chamomile boiled in water. It will help soothe any headache that occurs and possibly prevent fever."

"We'll do it together," Marcus insisted.

He helped Hamlyn to his feet and they got on either side of the mummer. Jess retrieved the wine cup to return to the merchant and told Jopp to close up her case. The boy handed it to Marcus to carry and they set off.

"Are you sure you have time to do this?" she asked.

"Aye," Marcus said. "Bartholomew will play several songs before the play begins."

"Do you really know all the lines?"

"Most of them," he revealed. "If 'twere Hamlyn's part I took, I do know all of them. I'd need to in order to give Ralph the right cues so he could deliver his next line. But the narrator? That's different. I know most of what Gylbart says. As long as I set each scene up properly, the crowd won't know if I've tweaked a line or two."

They gave the merchant his wine cup back and then took Hamlyn to the tent he shared with several mummers. Placing him on the pallet, Jessimond had Marcus remove Hamlyn's blood-soaked tunic. She would try to get the stains out later. Quickly, she bathed his neck and face with water and he lay back, looking exhausted. He thanked them and promptly fell asleep, his snores filling the tent within seconds.

"I was going to boil the water and chamomile for him but I hate to wake him to drink it. Sleep restores good health. I suppose he can sip it later."

Jessimond started to kneel next to Hamlyn and then found herself rising. Marcus had her elbow and tugged her to her feet.

"What are you doing? I need to stay with Hamlyn."

"Look at him. He'll sleep for several hours. Come back and watch me in the play. You can check on Hamlyn after it finishes. I'm sure you'll find him snoring the day away when you return."

His hand still held her elbow, causing a wild flutter inside her. She swallowed, unsure whether to stay or go, but she definitely wanted to see Marcus as a mummer. That won out.

"All right," she agreed.

"We'll have to hurry," he said. "Come on."

Marcus' fingers slid down her arm and caught her hand. He took off in long strides. Jessimond had to trot to keep up with him. The entire time, she was aware of her hand enfolded in his.

It seemed as if it were made to belong exactly where it rested.

They pushed their way through the crowds as Bartholomew sang a stirring ballad. Marcus pulled her to the very front and moved her between two men. One gave him a challenging look. Marcus glared and the man's eyes dropped to the ground.

"I will see you later," he told her. "Enjoy the play."

The audience applauded at the end of Bartholomew's song. The troubadour caught her eye and motioned to her. Jessimond shook her head violently, knowing what he had in mind.

He ignored her protests and said, "My singing companion has just arrived. I know she would love for us to share a song with you. Jess? Come up."

Reluctantly, she stepped forward. Bartholomew grasped her wrist and pulled her onto the platform next to him.

"We'll do one from the other night. Just follow my lead," he whispered.

"I might die before a note comes out of my mouth," Jessimond said, frightened to her core by the large crowd gathered in front of them.

"Then close your eyes. Let the music lead you," Bartholomew advised.

The troubadour began strumming his lute. Immediately, she recognized the song they would sing but she couldn't recall any of the words. Panic squeezed her chest, making it hard to breathe. Then Jessimond did as Bartholomew recommended and shut her eyes. She listened to the music and then Bartholomew's mellow voice. The crowd receded from her mind, replaced by the song.

When the chorus began, Jessimond joined in, harmonizing as they had around the campfire the other night. Even she could hear how well their voices blended together and she started to relax. The second verse began and the words came to her. She sang them and the chorus again. As it ended, Bartholomew nudged her. Jessimond opened her eyes.

"We'll do the final verse together," he said.

She nodded and decided to bravely leave her eyes open as she continued singing. Her gaze never fell upon one person. It simply skimmed over the crowd. All she saw was a blur of faces in the sea in front of them.

Then the song ended. The audience roared their approval, clapping and stomping. Jessimond knew her face flamed as Bartholomew took her hand and had them bow, acknowledging the applause.

"You were wonderful," he said, his admiration obvious. "We should do a few songs together each performance."

"I'm no troubadour, Bartholomew. I'm a seamstress and healer."

He gave her a knowing look. "We'll see about that."

Jessimond hopped down from the stage and returned to her spot in the front row. This time, the angry man made ample room for her, complimenting her on what a sweet voice she possessed. She nodded her thanks and focused on the stage, knowing Marcus would appear soon.

He came out and the crowd's noise began to die. Marcus caught her eye and winked at her, causing a blush to spill across her cheeks. He had changed from his tunic and pants into one of the Greek togas and a pair of sandals and looked divine. His olive skin contrasted sharply with the snowy white toga. Jessimond became fascinated with his muscular calves and thighs, longing to allow her hand to follow their curves. His bare arms appeared massive, as if he could lift felled logs with no effort. Again, she wished to run her fingers up and down them. He wore some type of crown, composed of gold-looking leaves, though his hair looked as wild and untamed as usual.

In a word, he was perfection.

Never had Jessimond been so physically attracted to a man. This knight looked like a god from old, stepped down from Mount Olympus. She wondered again about his odd story of bearing allegiance to a liege lord and yet here he was, a part of a mummer's troupe. Despite that, she'd found him to be intelligent and caring toward the others in the company, always willing to lend a hand and often taking a leadership role. She wished to unravel the mystery that was Marcus de Harte.

He began to speak, scanning the crowd, his voice carrying in rich tones across the area. His voice was like his tongue, smooth and commanding. Soon, the audience was spellbound.

And so was she.

As Marcus spoke, Jessimond realized that somewhere along the way, this knight had captured her heart. Now, it was up to her. Would she retrieve it from him and hide it away—or allow him to keep it? She feared if she stashed it deep within her that she would be making the gravest mistake of her life. If she let him possess it, though, she was afraid, in the end, all that would remain of it might be shattered pieces.

His gaze met hers and he spoke to her. Only her. The ocean of people receded. Only the two of them existed. He wove a tapestry of color around her as he told her of the fight she would behold, one between Virtue and Vice. Who would be the victor?

With a sweep of his hand, the curtain suddenly rose and Marcus faded into the background. The spell had been broken between them.

Or had it just begun?

Jessimond slipped from her place and circled around until she could reach behind the stage. Agatha handed a mace to Otto and nudged him toward the stage. He stepped onto it and she breathed a sigh of relief.

"Worried about Otto?" Jessimond asked.

The young woman nodded. "He knows his lines until the play begins and then he always seems to forget them. Sometimes, I whisper to him a word or two to get him back on track. He does better with a prop in his hand. Otto grips it tightly and it seems to reassure him." She paused. "How is Hamlyn?"

"Sleeping. I left him snoring."

"Good. We were all worried when he fell and began speaking gibberish but he seemed to have recovered his senses by the time you arrived. You did an excellent job stitching his injury. I doubt he'll have much of a scar. I knew you were an excellent seamstress but I did not know you also were a healer until Moss mentioned it and sent Jopp for you."

"I know a little about both."

"Did you learn about these things at Kinwick?"

"Aye," Jessimond said, and decided to press Agatha some about her past. "Has Hamlyn ever mentioned his family? I heard he goes north each winter."

Agatha nodded. "He rarely speaks of them. I first learned of his wife and children when I overheard him talking about them to my father years ago."

"Your father was a member of the Vawdrys' troupe?"

The young woman beamed with pride. "Father was their lead actor. He possessed more talent in his thumb than King Ralph does in his entire body. I watched every performance he gave."

"You sound very proud of him."

"I am. He was not only a fine actor, but a good father and man. A loyal friend." Her eyes filled with tears. "We lost him when I was nine. Mother and I remained with the mummers. It was the only life we'd known. Then she passed away, too."

"What about your sister, Reba?" Jessimond asked. "I heard she cooked for the company until she left last year."

Agatha's nose wrinkled. "Reba was not truly my sister. She was Father's daughter with his first wife. He married Mother soon after his wife passed and then they had me. Reba was jealous because Father loved Mother and me so much. He tried to explain to her that he had enough love in his heart for all of us but Reba didn't want to hear that. She never forgave him for dying and never accepted Mother or me as her family."

Jessimond asked, "Did you go to live with Reba after the troupe disbanded last year? I know she wed."

"I would never stay with her," Agatha said vehemently and then laughed harshly. "Not that she would have had me. The fellow she married had a roving eye. Nay, Reba would not have wished for me to be a part of their merry little household."

"Where *did* you go, Agatha?"

She crossed her arms protectively in front of her. "I stayed in London. I worked."

Jessimond placed her hand on her shoulder. "What happened, Agatha?"

The girl bit her lip. "It was terrible, Jess. I hated it. I barely survived. I didn't realize how cruel people could be. I left several jobs because men... well, they were disrespectful, that's all I'll say." Agatha sniffed. "When it came time for the troupe to gather in early spring, I was more than ready to return to my family."

"Would you like to go to Kinwick with Peter and me once we complete our tour this autumn?"

Hope sprang to Agatha's eyes. "Do you think I could? 'Tis a lovely spot of England. One of my favorite places to visit each year."

"It is, indeed."

"Will you really be able to go back, Jess?"

"Aye. The countess assured me that Peter and I will have a place there come winter. He'll return to the smithy's shop and I will be back inside the keep." Jessimond simply omitted the fact that she would return as a daughter of the house. She would save that information for a later time.

"It is a grand castle."

"The estate is large and has many workers. If you've a mind to work hard and be happy, the earl and countess would be glad to have you at Kinwick." Jessimond paused. "I think Peter would also be most pleased if you came."

Agatha blushed furiously. "You think so?"

Jessimond was happy her suspicions were true and that Agatha had feelings for Peter. "I do. He is a wonderful man. Who knows? You may find a place to work *and* a place with Peter."

"Oh, Jess! We would be true family then. We'd be sisters-in-law." Agatha smiled through her tears.

Suddenly, a dozen mummers descended upon them.

"The scene is done," Agatha said, wiping her eyes with her sleeves.

"Help me, Jess."

Agatha began grabbing various props. Jessimond took and distributed the items to whatever actor reached for them. The chaos calmed as the actors resumed their places. She could hear Marcus transitioning the crowd with his words and then the mummers once more took to the stage.

Agatha came to her and hugged her tightly. "You don't know what this means to me. Thank you, Jess, for inviting me to accompany you and Peter to Kinwick."

"You're going back to Kinwick? With Agatha?"

Jessimond glanced up and saw Marcus standing beside them.

CHAPTER 11

MARCUS WAITED FOR a response from Jess as she released Agatha. "Not now," she informed him. "I've merely invited Agatha to join Peter and me once the troupe disperses for winter."

He wanted to sag in relief. Instead, he stood tall, keeping his emotions masked. "I see. It's a good thing because we would miss having Agatha around. She's the true heart of the Vawdrys' company. If not for her organization, backstage would be in constant turmoil. I don't see how one play could occur without Agatha managing the mummers, their costumes, and props."

Agatha glowed at his compliment. "Thank you, Marcus," she said shyly and added, "You've done an excellent job stepping in for Gylbart today."

"Thank you. Only one more narration to complete and then I'm off for my exhibition with Rand."

Agatha turned to Jessimond. "Oh, Jess, you must go see Marcus and Rand fight. They simply terrify me. All that clanging of steel causes my knees to go weak. It looks as if they are going to kill one another." She grinned. "But it's ever so much fun to watch."

"I'll do so another day, Agatha," Jess said. "I need to tend to Hamlyn now."

"Wait until I finish my final piece," Marcus said. "I need to go back to the tents to retrieve my sword. I'd like to check on Hamlyn when I do so."

She agreed and they stood in the wings until the scene played out. Marcus went before the audience for a last time. This was the most he'd been in front of crowd, saying lines. He found it came rather easily to him, as if he were born to act. He finished with a flourish and knew that he preened a bit in order to impress Jess.

Gathering his clothes and boots, he set off with her. The crowds had died down at the stalls. Most of the faire goers attended the play now. They headed toward the tents and found the way deserted.

"It's kind of you to take Agatha with you when the season is over," he began, wanting to learn more about her plans when their tour ended.

"She's a lovely young woman. I feel sorry that she was abandoned last year when everyone went his own way. Besides, she and Peter are sweet on one another."

"They are?"

Her words didn't surprise him. Marcus had caught the couple staring at one another repeatedly, turning away in embarrassment and then stealing furtive glances when they thought the other wasn't aware.

"Aye. No one has a sweeter nature than Agatha and Peter is quite protective. I think he would make her a good husband."

"What about you, Jess? Have you thought of taking a husband yourself? You seem older than Peter."

She shrugged. "The opportunity has never presented itself."

"I doubt that. Kinwick is a large estate and must be filled with men."

"It does have its fair share."

"I cannot believe that not one man has offered marriage to you," Marcus pressed.

"I didn't say I had never received any offers," she quickly replied, a faint smile playing about her lips.

The thought of another man wanting to wed Jess had him seeing red.

That's when Marcus knew beyond a doubt that he had to have her. He couldn't bear to think of another man touching her satin skin. He certainly didn't see himself with any other woman. He would have to be careful and guard his heart, but he intended to make Jess Gilpin his.

"Then you've refused these offers?" he asked.

"I intend to marry for love."

Her simple statement drove a nail into his heart. Love was something to be avoided at all costs. Marcus didn't want his world turned upside down by it. His mother had loved his father and look what that had gotten her. A one-sided wound that festered painfully the more he berated her and pushed her away. Already, it was difficult enough that Jess tempted him beyond measure. He would enjoy worshipping her body with his but he refused to offer her love.

Marcus stopped and decided to end this nonsense. He needed to plant the seed in her head that what they had between them would be more than enough for a happy marriage without the notion of love being involved.

"You do realize love is a myth," he began. "It doesn't exist. Oh, I know some couples are fond of each other. Some are ruled by passion. But love isn't real, Jess. I do believe love can exist between a parent and child. I loved my mother tremendously and she returned my affection but love is something ethereal. You might think it lives and then it vanishes without warning."

"You actually believe what you just said." She looked at him in astonishment. "That love—true love between a husband and wife—cannot exist. I feel sad for you, Marcus." Sighing, she walked away.

Marcus watched helplessly as she trod on. How was he to convince her that the passion between them would be more than enough? That he would also add respect for her, guaranteeing them a successful union. Yet, Jess said she wanted love. He'd found her inexperienced. That would help. He would show her that he cared for her. Desired her. Needed her.

If she wanted to call that love, so be it.

He raced to catch up with her and they went to Hamlyn's tent. The mummer's loud snores echoed as they entered. Jess placed her palm against his cheek.

"No fever. 'Tis a good sign."

Marcus exited the tent and she followed.

"Thank you for escorting me back," she said politely. He sensed a vast gulf spreading between them.

"Jess."

He placed all he carried upon the ground and grasped her upper arms. Her eyes widened as he stepped to her. "I may not believe in love but I believe in you—and me—together."

Marcus held back. He wanted to crush her to him. Tangle his fingers in her long tresses. Take her mouth by storm. Instead, he softly pressed his lips to hers. He realized his earlier declaration had frightened her. He didn't want to see her spirit broken. He would lure her in gently, like a feral cat. He would build trust between them over the next few weeks and finally ask her to be his. She wasn't ready to hear that now, having foolish, girlish dreams of love.

But he could make her want him. Fan that flame of desire until she needed it like the very air she breathed.

Gently, he skimmed his hands along her shoulders and up her neck until he cupped her face. He kissed her lightly. Softly. Then pressed his brow to hers.

"I must go."

Releasing her felt like cutting off one of his limbs. She'd already become an essential part of him. Marcus quickly turned away, scooped up his things, and made for his tent. He shed the toga and rid himself of the uncomfortable sandals that were too small for him, replacing them with his gypon, pants, and boots. He didn't need his armor today. He and Rand only wore it when they jousted. They'd learned their audiences liked to see their faces and bodies while they fought with swords and had even discovered the crowd enjoyed them bantering back and forth with one another. Fortunately, they knew each other well enough to coordinate their moves. So far, neither of them had suffered even the slightest nick.

And if they did?

Marcus wouldn't mind the angelic Jess tending to his wounds.

THEY ARRIVED AT Whitmore, the estate of Lord Cedric Wariner, a widower who had engaged the troupe because his wife enjoyed them visiting each year. Once they arrived and received word that the baroness had passed away last Christmas, gloom settled over the group as the men set up the tents and stage.

As Jessimond carved up a few plucked chickens and tossed the pieces into a boiling pot for the evening meal, Bartholomew came to her, his distress obvious.

"My throat hurts," he rasped. "I'm having trouble swallowing. I can barely speak, much less sing tomorrow." He began coughing.

"I can give you lungwort for your cough."

"Those bluish flowers?"

"Aye. I'll crush them and steep them in boiled water. You can drink that thrice a day. I'll also rinse sage and thyme with water and mix them together. That, too, will be boiled in water and steeped. Once it cools, you can gargle with it. The scent is very pleasant."

"How soon could I sing again?" Bartholomew asked.

"It depends. I'd advise you to stop talking and rest your voice. I would think two days would be enough time."

The troubadour frowned. "Elias will not be happy."

"You can't help it if you are ill," Jessimond said. "Keep to your pallet and get plenty of rest. I'll speak with Elias and Moss for you." She hesitated. "I'll even take your place tomorrow and the day after if you'd like."

"Would you, Jess?" Relief caused his body to sag.

"Go to your tent. I'll get the lungwort and other herbs now."

She retrieved her case and had Jopp fetch more water so she could put a smaller pot on to boil. Jessimond could divide that boiled water in half and steep the different herbs separately. As she waited for the water to boil, she cut up some onions and dumped them into the pot with the chicken and stirred in plenty of pepper. Next, she crushed the lungwort in one bowl and ground the sage and thyme, mixing them together in another.

Moss appeared and bent over the pot, inhaling deeply. "I see 'tis chicken tonight."

"It will be ready in an hour. In the meantime, I need to let you know that Bartholomew is unwell and will not be able to sing for a few days."

Jessimond was glad she broke this news to the placid Moss, who seemed to take everything he heard in stride. If it had been Elias, the hot-tempered redhead would have exploded with curses.

"I've told him I would step in and take over his duties until he returns," she added.

Moss gave her an appreciative smile. "Our audiences have taken to the duets you do with Bartholomew. I'm sure they will like whatever you choose to sing for them."

"I can perform any of the songs Bartholomew does since I've heard them several times now. I also have others I know and a few original ones I've written that I'd be happy to sing."

"Whatever you choose is fine with me," Moss assured her. "'Tis good to change the pace with each song, though. And most important, make the last song slow and soft. The crowd will quiet and even strain to hear you. That makes it easier to begin the play as soon as you finish."

"I'll remember that," Jessimond promised.

She took both her concoctions to Bartholomew, making sure he drank the lungwort to calm his cough, and instructing him on how to gargle since he'd never done that before. It took him a few tries and a little sputtering before he understood what to do. Once he did, Jessimond told him to continue resting and that she would make sure he had enough of the steeped herbs at the beginning of each day.

By then, the company gathered to eat, most of them seeking a second helping of the stew, thanks to the appetite they'd built up assembling the tents and stage. Elias had stopped in the village they passed just before arriving at Whitmore and had purchased plenty of bread, which they used to sop up the last of the stew from their wooden bowls. Agatha and Jopp collected the bowls and placed them inside a large container. As had become the habit, Marcus lifted the container and Jessimond accompanied him to the nearby brook. They would cleanse the bowls with sand and then rinse them with water.

She'd come to enjoy that part of the day. Marcus was a witty companion and always had interesting stories to tell her. Everyone seemed to understand that they wanted to be alone and never interrupted them. At first, Peter had accompanied them a night or two, but Jessimond explained that Marcus only desired her company.

Much to her chagrin.

She gave the knight every opportunity to kiss her but he never took it. At least not as she wished. Every so often, he would brush his lips against her cheek or upon her brow briefly. Twice, he had held her hand for a moment. But the passionate kisses from before had ceased.

That made Jessimond hunger for them all the more.

Tonight, they walked in silence to the running water and cleaned the company's dinnerware quickly, stacking the bowls back into the crate. Instead of starting back, however, Marcus plopped down on the bank.

"Come join me," he invited.

She sat beside him. Not too close but near enough to feel his warmth and smell the spice of the soap he used as its scent rose from his skin.

"I hear you'll be singing in Bartholomew's place tomorrow." He casually slipped an arm around her waist.

"Aye," she answered, her mouth growing dry. "He's bothered by a cough and his throat is sore. I'm boiling herbs for him to ingest and gargle with."

"I see." His free hand reached up and brushed a stray strand of hair from her face.

Jessimond stared into those mesmerizing blue eyes, willing him to kiss her. She began worrying her bottom lip and his fingers tightened against her waist. Then his mouth descended ever so slowly until their lips met.

That was all the encouragement she needed.

Her hands cupped his face, the stubble rough against her palms. She parted her lips and he accepted the invitation, his tongue slipping inside and gliding along the roof of her mouth, sending chills through her. Her thumbs stroked his cheeks as he kissed her as he had in the tent that first time. Both his arms now encircled her, making her feel safe inside the steel bands. Jessimond almost purred as a contented cat might.

Marcus broke the kiss. "I could do this all night," he murmured against her lips.

She smiled against his mouth. "Do you have the stamina to go all night?" she teased.

He growled and yanked her toward him. Her breasts pressed against the wall of his chest and she linked her hands behind his neck, rubbing against him. His hand slid from her back and cupped one breast, squeezing it. His fingers found her nipple and rolled it, causing shoots of pleasure. Jessimond pressed closer to him as his other hand imitated the first, kneading her breasts and teasing the nipples. The friction drove her mad.

Marcus pulled her into his lap now, his hands gliding along her curves. She kissed his neck and then had the urge to lick it. His skin tasted slightly salty as the growl deepened in his throat. His lips found hers again and showed her just how skilled he was. Soon, Jessimond found herself breathless, coherent thought impossible.

Then he stopped abruptly. Lifted her from him and rested her back on the ground next to him. She heard his rapid breathing and knew he fought to gain control. Quickly, he pushed himself to his feet and then grabbed both her wrists and brought her to hers. Still holding on to her, he dipped his head and gave her one sweet, final kiss.

"Dream of me tonight, Jess," he implored. "I know I will dream of you."

Jessimond wished it could be more than dreams and stolen kisses between them. She wanted to become a part of him. Her mother had explained love play to her long ago. More than anything, she needed this man inside her. She wanted to scream his name as he pleasured her and feel his bare skin, slick with sweat, against hers. She needed to touch him. Ride him.

Love him.

That thought brought her to her senses. Marcus had been frank with her. He didn't believe in love—something every de Montfort lived for. Jessimond didn't know who held Marcus' loyalty. Where he lived. What his situation was. He'd continued to hold back from her, which made her believe he wasn't in a position to commit to her—or anyone else.

"We need to return to the others," he said softly.

"Aye."

She watched him retrieve the dishes and joined him as they returned to the camp. The fire had burned down to embers. Only a few mummers sat around it. The others had already gone to their tents for the night. Marcus set the crate down and walked with her to her tent.

"Are you married?" Jessimond asked him. "Or do you have a sweetheart? You tease me and then stop as if you are guilty of something and then try to put distance between us."

He startled, his eyes widening. "Nay." Frowning, he lifted her braid, toying with the end. "Do you think so little of me, Jess? Or do you know so little of my character that you think I would kiss you like that if I were committed to another?"

Frustrated, she said, "Sometimes, I believe I know all I need to about you, Marcus. Other times, I realize there's still so much I haven't learned about you. Where you live. The name of your liege lord. The mission you and Rand are on. Why two knights joined the Vawdrys' troupe."

Marcus swished the tail of her braid against the tip of her nose. "All in good time, sweetheart. I promise you—those answers will come—in time."

He dropped her braid and took her hand. Turning it palm up, he pressed a fervent kiss into the center. The heat from his lips caused her blood to stir.

"Goodnight, Jess." Marcus kissed her palm once more and released her hand.

As he walked away, Jessimond wondered if she could ever have a future with this man.

CHAPTER 12

JESSIMOND WENT TO Bartholomew's tent and found the troubadour sitting up on his pallet and in good spirits.

"I brought you fresh bread and more to gargle and drink. Gargle first," she instructed, handing over the bowl containing the fragrant combination of sage and thyme.

He took it and stepped outside the tent. She heard him gurgling the liquid several times before he returned. Handing over the bowl of steeped lungwort, he sipped the warm brew and ate the bread she'd brought.

"Do you feel well enough to return to the stage today?" she asked.

He swallowed and said, "I tested my voice this morning. It's too weak to carry across the crowd. I think another day of rest will be best."

Jessimond nodded, glad that the troubadour had come to this decision on his own. She had not wanted to dictate to him what he should do, especially if he thought she might be trying to replace him. Bartholomew was the troupe's only troubadour.

"The crowds have missed you. No one sings quite like you do."

She saw her comment pleased him.

"When I do return, I'll have several shows to do each day. I was thinking that, mayhap, you would continue to join me. At least until we leave Whitmore," he suggested. "We could sing several songs together and then do one apiece on our own. That way, the Vawdrys and their paying customers would still be happy and I wouldn't overtax my voice."

"I think it's a good idea. I will tell Elias and Moss what is planned."

Bartholomew gave her a warm smile. "Thank you for caring for me, Jess."

"Continue to rest your voice today but go ahead and move about the camp. You want to build your strength back up after lying abed these past two days."

Jessimond left the tent and decided it was time to head to the stage area. She fetched her lute and saw Peter emerge from the tent he shared with several mummers.

He waved and came toward her. "Are you going to the stage? If so, I will walk with you." He took her lute in hand.

"I barely see you," she said. "The Vawdrys keep you busy."

"Aye, and Rand has also been teaching me swordplay. I've gotten quite good at it. He said I should be ready soon to spar with him in front of the crowds."

"Be careful," Jessimond cautioned. "While you may be here to protect me at my father's request, I feel equally responsible for your welfare."

"Are you enjoying this summer with the mummers?"

"I am," she replied. "Sewing new costumes for the two additional plays has kept me busy. In fact, I'm working on one for you now."

Peter's face lit up. "I don't have a large role. Ralph drafted me more for my size than my speaking ability. Still, learning a few lines has been different from swinging my hammer. We practice again this afternoon and will perform the new play tomorrow for the first time."

"Then I will make sure you will be appropriately attired."

"How do you like performing, Jess? I know you sang for us in the great hall at Kinwick some, but this has to be different."

"It is. At home, I could sing and be in the background why others conversed or ate or danced. Here, I am the center of attention. At first, I was quite nervous but I've become more comfortable with it. I figured out the crowds are not present to see me but hear me. So I don't worry about how I look. I concentrate on the words and the melody and hope I take the audience on a journey through the music."

"It seems as if you've made friends," Peter said.

"I think we both have. I like going around to the different booths and seeing some familiar faces and then newer ones at each stop we make. I've always enjoyed sewing, so stitching new costumes and repairing old ones has been a pleasant way to pass the time. It's been nice to share my music around the campfire and hear stories from the mummers about tours from the past. I've also made a good friend in Agatha."

"What about Marcus?"

Jessimond took a deep breath and exhaled slowly. "Marcus has also become a good friend."

They walked on silently for a few minutes and then Peter asked, ""How will you feel when we part ways with the mummers? I hear Marcus and Rand are supposed to return to the estate where they serve."

Her belly flipped over once. "Do you know where it is?"

"Nay. Just that they will not be continuing with the mummers next year. The same as us."

"Have you told others we will not be back?" she asked.

Peter shook his head. "It hasn't come up. If it did, I would not commit one way or the other."

"I promise you this is the only time I'll ever do something so frivolous and carefree, Peter. This time next year, you and I will be home." She paused. "Do you miss Kinwick?"

He shrugged. "A little. But like you, I'm making the most of this time away. We're traveling to places I would never have seen otherwise. In the end, though, I will be glad to be home."

"With Agatha?" she teased.

Peter blushed. "She told me that you've invited her to come back with us to Kinwick. That you said the countess would have a place for her inside the keep. Agatha is weary of the road and wishes to find a permanent home. She's hoping that Kinwick may be the answer. She is very excited about that possibility."

"I hope you are, as well, Peter."

He stopped. "I will be ready to tell her the truth soon, Jess. That I am a blacksmith and you are a lady. I hate being dishonest with Agatha. A lie of omission is still a lie."

Jessimond didn't trust if Agatha knew the truth that she would be able to keep it to herself. "Then wait and tell her the truth once we arrive at Ancel and Margery's estate. I'm to send word to Mother and Father once we complete the mummers' tour and they will join us there and then escort us home. It will give Agatha time to become used to who the two of us really are."

"Good. The sooner, the better." Peter hesitated. "I have strong feelings for Agatha, Jess."

"Do you love her?"

"Aye, I do. I won't tell her now. Not with these secrets between us. Once we get to Bexley, though, she will know all. I hope she won't be angry that I—that we—deceived her."

"Agatha will be fine," Jessimond promised.

They began walking again and arrived at the stage.

"I'm off to work with Rand," Peter said, handing the lute to her.

"I will see you later."

Jessimond weaved through the crowds. Reaching the stage, she rested her lute on it and then climbed up. Elias nodded at her, letting her know that she could begin when she wished since so many people had already arrived. Once the music started, the rest would stream in. She plucked a few of the strings, making sure the instrument was still in tune. It was hard to believe that some of her happiest moments this summer had come while performing in front of others, both here and at night after the mummers' evening meal. Jessimond had always been the quiet de Montfort. All her siblings, save for Edward, were outgoing and carefree, easily drawing and basking in attention from others. Even now, ever since Edward wed Rosalyne, her once serious brother now laughed more often and seemed more open than before.

She, on the other hand, had been the one who nurtured others. One who made sure everyone else remained comfortable and happy. If attention rested upon her, she deflected it onto others, wishing to stay in the background. Jessimond had always been content to do for others over herself.

Although this still remained the essence of her character, this summer had seen her begin to change, as if she emerged from a cocoon. Jessimond didn't know who she would finally be once the process ended—or how she would fit into Kinwick when she returned.

Moss brought a stool out for her to sit upon. At first, she had wanted to perch on the end of the stage but Elias said the majority of the paying customers in attendance wouldn't be able to see her that way. It had taken all the courage she could summon to sit atop the stool in the center of the stage. Jessimond was proud that she had done so because now that stool seemed like a second home to her.

A familiar tingling made its appearance after she seated herself. It let her know that Marcus was somewhere in the audience. He didn't attend her every performance but her body seemed to always know when he did. She glanced around and spotted him on the edge of the crowd, to her left, and acknowledged his presence with a nod.

Strumming the instrument's strings, Jessimond began with two songs which she had learned years ago from Beatrice, and then sang another two that Bartholomew was fond of playing. She glanced to the side and saw Elias hold up two fingers. That meant two more songs until the mummers would be ready.

She decided to sing one of her own compositions, a lively ditty that had a simple chorus. Jessimond waved her hand, encouraging the crowd, and soon they joined in each time the chorus came up. When the song ended, the ensuing laughter and clapping had her beaming.

Then she did as Moss had advised before she began performing solo. She allowed the audience to settle down before she began to pluck the strings again, once more choosing a song she had written herself. Unlike the ditty, the first she'd composed, this song had been created during her time with the mummers.

It was a love song.

Jessimond made a deliberate choice and sang it to Marcus, looking only at him while she played. When it ended, she dropped her eyes to the ground.

As the last note faded, no one stirred. Her throat tightened, not only from the emotion she had poured into the song, but from the lack of acknowledgement by the crowd. She realized that they wouldn't like every song the same and she had gotten them involved in the one before, with its lively, spirited pace. She supposed this last tune simply missed the mark and vowed never to perform it again.

Suddenly, shouts of approval sounded. Those gathered cheered loudly, stomping their feet and applauding with zeal. Jessimond's face lit on fire. She jumped to her feet and gave a quick nod before fleeing the stage.

"Well done," Elias said as she rushed by him.

Several other mummers smiled and patted her on the back as she retreated. Agatha slowed her down, grabbing and hugging her tightly, the lute mashed between them.

"That was lovely," her friend proclaimed. "I've never heard anyone with your talent, Jess."

"Thank you," she managed to say. "I'm off to work on the new costumes. I will see you later."

Jessimond escaped the area. Needing to be by herself, she deliberately skirted the faire and its buyers and sellers, giving the area a wide berth. She reached the tents, breathing hard after her quick jaunt. She moved to the shade of a tree and stood a moment, catching her breath.

"Jess!"

Turning, she saw Marcus hurrying toward her. She couldn't read what was in his face.

"You disappeared." His tone was neutral, neither accusing nor questioning her.

"I have many garments to stitch. Peter told me that Ralph intends to put on the first of the new plays tomorrow afternoon. If that's so, I will be busy the remainder of today in order to complete all the costumes."

Jessimond was glad the lute served as a buffer between them. She clasped it tightly to her chest.

Still, he placed his hands on her shoulders. As always, his touch singed her like fire. "Your voice is remarkable. So are your songs."

"Thank you. The first ones I learned from Beatrice, my cousin's wife. Beatrice sings like a lark." Jessimond smiled. "I hadn't thought about it before but she would have made the best troubadour England has ever seen."

"I meant *your* songs, Jess," Marcus said, his voice rough and low. "You did write them. I know you did."

"The last two?" she asked, her nerves fraying. "Aye. The ditty was the first song I ever came up with. I've added to it over the years. My family loves to sing along with it. That's why I encouraged the crowd to do the same. I thought they would enjoy being a part of it."

His fingers tightened against her skin, not painfully, just holding her firmly in place.

"And the last one. What of it? When was it written?"

She swallowed. "It's been coming to me over the last few weeks," she admitted. "All the pieces finally slipped into place last night. I thought I would give it a try."

"It was a love song," Marcus said.

"Aye, though it was more about unrequited love."

"At the end, you left the door open. Did the woman fling herself from the cliff—or did she turn away and move on with her life?"

"'Tis for whoever hears the song to decide that for himself," she stated. "Was her heart shattered so much by her secret lover that she feared she couldn't go on without him? Or did she resolve to show that she was strong enough to survive on her own?" Jessimond shrugged. "I think it makes the song more intriguing by allowing the audience members to decide for themselves."

His gaze held hers. "Was it about you and me, Jess?"

"I don't know," she said candidly. "Our story hasn't been completed yet."

Marcus' hands slid down her arms slowly. He took the lute from her and rested it on the ground.

"What am I going to do with you, Jess?"

"Whatever you like."

Jessimond saw her bold words inflamed the desire reflected in his eyes. He grabbed her hand and strode toward her tent. She stumbled along behind him, trying to keep her balance. They reached it and he lifted the flap, pulling her inside. The flap fell. Darkness surrounded them.

He jerked her toward him. Jessimond crashed against his chest, clutching his gypon, as his hands found her face. The air crackled between them. Then Marcus was kissing her as if she held the answer to every mystery known to man.

Jessimond smiled against his mouth.

CHAPTER 13

MARCUS HAD WANTED to slowly make Jess want him. Instead, he was the one who couldn't seem to get his fill of her. No matter how many times their lips met and their bodies came in contact, it wasn't enough.

It would never be enough.

She had told him he could do whatever he liked. He knew they couldn't live out most of the fantasies that whirled in his head until they were wed and in bed.

But he could give her a taste of what that would be like—and, mayhap, satisfy himself, as well.

He bent, sliding his hands along the sweet curve of her hips and down to her calves, to where her tunic fell. Today, she wore one of hunter green, a sharp contrast to her deep amethyst eyes. Marcus grabbed the edge and pulled it swiftly up, forcing her arms to rise as he pulled it over her head and tossed it aside. He could hear her breathing, already ragged, anticipating his next move.

Stepping so close that their bodies touched, he felt the spark between them. The first time it occurred, Marcus had been surprised. Now, he understood something magical connected them and he expected it each time they came in contact with one another. His hands glided up her hips, the hemp undertunic rough against his palms. When they wed, he would dress Jess in nothing but smooth silks and the finest of wools. She needed something gentle against her satin skin.

Unless it were his hands on her.

He wrapped an arm about her, securing her to him, as his free hand sought her breast. He kneaded it, wishing he could strip the undertunic from her but not daring to do so. Marcus sensed the tension coiled within her and thought she might flee at any moment.

Small steps, he told himself.

Continuing to play with her breast, he brushed a flat palm across her nipple several times, feeling it spring to life. Jess moaned softly and pressed against his hand. He used his thumb and forefinger to toy with the nipple, teasing it to a peak as she continued to make small sounds in the back of her throat. Pleased, he did the same with the other, knowing she enjoyed it.

Marcus had been inside the tent before and guessed her pallet lay slightly to the right. Backing her up, he eased both of them to their knees. Jess' arms went around his waist as he kissed her deeply, continuing to massage her breasts. He lifted her and set her down, feeling around, discovering they had landed on her pallet. She stretched her legs out underneath him as he hovered over her.

He could take her. Here. Now. He was already harder than a plank of wood. That wasn't his plan, though. He needed her to want him enough so that she would agree to wed him—without any talk of love. Marcus intended to show Jess just how passionate her nature was. Already, she kissed better than any woman he'd known, learning the lessons he taught her and expanding on them until she was now a master of the art of kissing.

His fingers skimmed her silken thighs. They trembled, as did the rest of her. Marcus kissed her again for several minutes, allowing his hands to roam until they reached the apex of her legs. He slid a single finger along the seam of her sex. Jess gasped.

"Already you drip with sweet juices, sweetheart," he said huskily.

"Is that good?" she asked, a hitch in her voice as his finger ran along the length again.

"Very good," he assured her. "It shows me how much you want this."

Marcus parted her folds and eased a finger inside her. She groaned.

He stroked. She moaned. He slid a second finger inside her. Jess tightened around them. He pressed the palm of his hand against her. Her hips rose and she squeezed his fingers harder.

He continued to stroke her, enjoying all the little sounds coming from her. It was as if she were an instrument he played and the music came from her mouth. He'd neglected it for a while, so he brought his lips back to hers, allowing his tongue to mimic the action of his fingers. Jess' nails dug into his back as she returned his kiss with abandon. Her hips continued to rise and fall, driving him wild. He wanted to stop and replace his fingers with his cock, and fought the feeling with every bit of discipline he possessed.

Finally, he teased the nub that he knew would bring her over the top. His mouth moved to her throat, nipping and licking, as she whimpered and twisted beneath him.

"That's right, sweetheart. Keep on. You're almost there."

"Where?" she demanded breathlessly, thrusting her hips toward him again.

"You'll see," he murmured.

Marcus sensed her at the precipice. He circled the nub a last time and pushed his fingers deep inside her.

The quivering began, consuming her. Little cries of pleasure erupted from her and she squeezed his fingers, her muscles contracting over and over as she bucked against him. He'd never seen a woman ride a wave a pleasure as long as Jess did. It satisfied him that he'd pleased her so much.

Finally, she stilled, her breathing ragged and uneven. He slipped his fingers from her and lifted them to his lips, licking her juice. Tasting her.

Marcus grinned. That's what they would do the next time.

JESSIMOND SET ASIDE her sewing. She hadn't accomplished much. Her mind had been filled with thoughts of Marcus de Harte and what he could do with his hands and mouth. He had touched her intimately three weeks ago, as she knew a lover did, and he'd done so again twice more since. Both times he had brought her to a point of madness, her body responding to each caress.

The first time he'd put his mouth on her had startled her, but Jessimond soon learned she hungered for it. She constantly seemed in a state of fever, a burning need for Marcus filling her waking moments. Some nights, as well, for she had awakened from dreams of him touching her, her skin hot, her body aching in need.

She took the robe and her needle and thread and left them on her pallet. Taking up her lute, she realized it was time to return to the stage area and sing with Bartholomew. Jessimond looked forward to the next performance by the mummers since Peter had a larger role than ever before. Gradually, his confidence had grown while on stage. Because of it, Ralph continued to cast him in roles with more lines.

Peter, like most of the mummers, couldn't read. Jessimond wished she could help him learn his lines but she couldn't reveal that she could read and write. Instead, she listened as they sat around the campfire at night, Ralph saying the lines over and over as Peter repeated them until he knew them by heart.

She arrived at the stage and saw Bartholomew was already singing. Making her way around the edge of the crowd, she waited until the song ended and then hoisted herself up to join up.

"I'm sorry I was delayed."

The troubadour grinned. "Elias was fit to be tied. That's all right. I managed nicely without you."

Jessimond settled herself on the empty stool and looked out over the crowd. She saw Lord Margrave and Lady Serafina standing nearby. The couple had opened Wenshaw lands to the mummers for half a score and often attended the many plays. She'd overheard Lord Margrave mention to Moss how much they liked the addition of the joust and sword fighting this season.

Watching the joust made Jessimond nervous each time. Though it was obvious Marcus and Rand knew exactly what they were doing, her heart remained in her throat each time the two men made a pass at one another. While she was all in favor of Peter learning sword skills from Rand, she had forbid him from doing the same regarding the joust.

She and Bartholomew sang two more songs together and then he nodded at her. Jessimond knew that was the signal for her to sing something Lady Serafina had requested. The noblewoman had spoken with them the day they arrived, delighted that Bartholomew and Jessimond would sing both alone and together. Lady Serafina had given them a list of songs and requested that they sing one of them at each performance. Jessimond allowed Bartholomew to peruse the list, not giving away that she could read it better than he.

He whispered to her what song to play and Jessimond launched into it. It was a sweet ballad of two lovers torn apart by their fathers when they were young. They'd been forced to wed others but never forgot one another and finally found each other at court years later. Both had lost their spouses and so they were able to reunite in love and marriage.

As she finished the last strains, Jessimond noted the satisfied look on Lady Serafina's face. Glancing to the side of the stage, she saw Elias was equally pleased with her performance.

Bartholomew launched into their final tune. Once it ended, Jessimond joined Marcus in the audience.

"Today is Peter's big day," he said.

"Aye. He told me he had trouble sleeping last night."

"He'll do well," Marcus assured her. "He learns everything quickly. Rand teases me that Peter spars better than I do."

Peter had taken to fighting in the exhibitions with Rand once a day. Jessimond knew how much her friend enjoyed his time swinging a sword and only hoped he would be able to settle back into a more sedate life when they went back to Kinwick.

The play began and Marcus slipped his hand around hers. Warmth spread through Jessimond. The simple gesture moved her more than she cared to admit. She might worry about Peter returning to Kinwick after this summer of excitement—but what about her?

What would her life be like without Marcus in it?

Ignoring the thought, she relished being near him and enjoyed the play. Marcus only released her hand when it ended and they clapped eagerly, especially when Peter made his bow.

He joined them as the crowd dispersed, his face flushed with excitement.

"How was I?"

"I've never been more proud, Peter. You were flawless," Jessimond told him.

"Not exactly. I almost tripped once when Otto moved a way he shouldn't have but I still delivered my line the right way."

They laughed and Peter excused himself, wanting to help Agatha with the props.

"You've come to see Peter in all his glory," Marcus said. "Do you have time to watch me?"

"Since it's the swords, I will."

"You don't like the joust?"

Jessimond frowned. "Not really."

He gave her a knowing smile. "I think you worry about me overmuch."

She sniffed. "Well, someone has to. You can be all too daring."

"Come along."

She followed him to where Rand stood, swinging a sword in both hands. Seeing Marcus, he tossed one to him. Marcus caught it with ease and began using it to slice through the air, loosening up his muscles. The two had already performed for the crowd once today. She hadn't attended that exhibition but was always eager to see Marcus in action. He'd teased her that he might pull her from the crowd one day when she least expected it and let them go at it together.

Jessimond hoped that he would.

Some of the people who'd attended the play came to watch the dueling. Others drifted over from the stalls. Several children gathered around the edge, their mothers urging them to sit. Jessimond looked wistfully at one little girl, toddling about on chubby legs. She had brown, wavy hair and a smile of an angel. A fierce longing for a child of her own suddenly overtook her. And not any child.

She wanted one sired by Marcus de Harte.

A small boy, no older than two years, roamed the area. Twice, his mother called him back to her but as she engaged in conversation with another woman, the boy wandered off again. Jessimond even called to him at one point, urging him to return. She glared at the mother, wishing the woman would pay better attention to her child.

Finally, the two knights began their display. Each of them twirled their swords about, showing skill and finesse, then they commenced. The sound of steel colliding rang through the air as Marcus and Rand fought one another. Though she knew it wasn't truly real combat, it would be hard for an outsider to discern that, for the men concentrated solely on one another. They jabbed, swung, danced away, and even rolled in a somersault as they escaped from harm and then teased each other on again.

Suddenly, Jessimond saw the young boy with the distracted mother move toward the men. Rand had his back to the child and so he couldn't see him coming. Marcus caught sight of the boy and dove, knocking him out of the way. The child hit the ground and then roared like a lion cub, screaming his displeasure.

Her eyes were drawn to Marcus, though. By thrusting himself in harm's way to prevent Rand's arcing sword from slicing the child in two, he had suffered injury instead. Marcus rolled away, landing on his back.

Immediately, Jessimond ran toward him amidst the screams from the crowd. She fell to her knees next to him. Already, the front of his tan tunic darkened with blood. Ripping the cloth away, she saw the slash that started just above his collarbone, slanting across his chest. It looked deep. Though not fatal, wounds like this brought fever—and infection.

She spied Otto and hollered to him. "Bring a wheelbarrow!" Looking to Rand, she added, "Get these people out of here!"

Otto took off running and Rand began ordering the crowd away. She knew some would be eager to depart, while others would have a macabre fascination and want to stay.

By now, Peter appeared at her elbow. "What can I do?"

"Gather clean linen and wine. Find a crock of honey. Put on a large pot of water to boil. Place a blanket underneath a tree at camp. 'Twill be easier to clean him and stitch the wound if I have strong light. Go!"

Peter took off and Jessimond turned back to Marcus.

"You are like a king leading his troops into battle. Go here. Do that." He gave her a crooked smile. "And everyone obeys your command."

Jessimond ignored him and lifted her tunic. She tore a large chunk of cloth from her undertunic and folded it quickly before pressing it firmly against the wound with both hands. Marcus gasped as she did so.

"I'll be fine," he said, gritting his teeth.

"Of course, you will."

"Because you will care for me," he said tenderly.

She kept her hands against the cloth, leaning into him. "Don't speak."

Worry filled her. She had never dealt with such a severe wound before. Jessimond began sending urgent prayers to the Virgin, begging for Her intercession on Marcus' behalf. Rand came and knelt on the other side of Marcus, putting his hands atop hers to keep the pressure steady.

"I'm back, Jess," called Otto.

Jessimond looked around. "We need to transfer him to the wheelbarrow."

Leaving her hands against the material, she rose to her feet as Rand, Otto, and Hamlyn lifted Marcus. He groaned, rending her heart in two.

They took Marcus to the wheelbarrow and set him in it. Rand stepped behind it.

"I'll need to keep doing what I am," she told the knight.

"Get in, Jess," Rand commanded. "'Twill be easier than you trying to run along beside me. I'm strong and can manage the two of you."

Rand was as good as his word. Jessimond straddled Marcus, who kept his eyes closed as they returned back to their camp. Everyone seemed to have heard about what happened and the way was cleared for them.

Marcus gave her a weak smile as they pulled into the circle where the tents stood. "I've imagined you atop me in this very way. Just under different circumstances."

She bent and kissed his brow in reply.

Peter waved Rand toward the tree. Jessimond saw her case lay open and that a large blanket had been spread across the ground under the shade of a large oak. When the wheelbarrow stopped, she climbed from it. Marcus was lifted and placed onto the blanket.

Peter appeared at her elbow. "The water's about to boil." He lifted a bucket. "I brought plenty of wine."

Jessimond lifted a small bit of wood from her case, about the length of a man's finger. Her mother had Kinwick's carpenter cut these and sand them down.

"This is for you to bite down upon," she told Marcus.

His lips twitched. "So, you're telling me this will hurt?"

"Aye." Her eyes filled with tears. She blinked them away. She had no time to show any weakness. Every moment counted.

"Let me have it."

Jessimond slid it into place and he latched on to it. She pulled her baselard from her boot. His eyes widened a bit upon seeing it. He'd already asked her about wearing such fine boots. She'd explained that they belonged to the Countess of Kinwick's daughter. It wasn't a lie but Marcus had assumed the daughter merely passed them down to Jessimond. Now, he saw she pulled a blade from them. She would have to concoct another story of why a mere servant would carry one.

With that, Jessimond swiftly cut away what remained of his gypon and then lifted her blood-soaked undertunic from the wound. She tossed it away and took a deep breath.

"Bring me some of the boiled water in a large bowl," she instructed Peter.

Taking a deep breath, Jessimond readied herself to save Marcus' life.

CHAPTER 14

JESSIMOND BEGAN BY pouring water over Marcus' chest and wiping away the blood. She could see the damage better now. Dipping linen into what water remained in the bowl, she wet the cloth and swabbed away the most stubborn of the blood until it was gone. Next, she dribbled wine liberally along the long slash. She'd learned from her mother to use boiled water first, followed by wine. The strong brew did a better job of cleansing an injury, especially one inflicted by a sword.

Marcus watched her silently as she threaded her needle. Jessimond thought about the best angle to be at in order to sew up the diagonal gash. An idea occurred to her.

"I'm going to sit behind you," she told him. "I'll place your head in my lap. 'Twill allow me to lean over you better."

He nodded in consent, the small block of wood held fast between his teeth, and she moved from his side. Lifting his head, she slipped beneath him, resting his head against her lap. This would get her closer to the wound and she could brace herself better than remaining on her knees, hunched over, for an extended period of time.

"Make any noise you need to," she said softly so that only he could hear. "It won't bother me, and it might make you endure the pain better."

Jessimond began. She knew better than to wince or hesitate. The important thing was to get the gaping wound stitched neatly and efficiently—but as quickly as possible. Her left fingers pinched his skin together as her right hand dipped in and out, binding the two sides.

She paused only once when the sweat on her brow gathered. Not wanting it to drip on him, she brushed it away with the sleeve of her forearm.

It took longer than she thought but when she reached the end, she was pleased with her work. The stitches were evenly spaced, holding his skin together firmly in place.

Jessimond hadn't looked at Marcus' face once during the procedure. He'd groaned a few times but had remained amazingly still. Finally, their gazes met and he relaxed his jaw, allowing her to take the stick from his mouth. She saw the deep teeth marks in it.

He raised his head to view her handiwork.

"You did well," he praised.

"I still have more to do," she insisted. "Stay patient."

Once more, Jessimond poured wine along the new seam that ran across his chest and then dabbed at it. He grimaced but said nothing.

"I will smear honey across it and then apply a poultice. Depending upon how it looks tonight and over the next few days, I will change the poultice once or twice a day." She glanced at the pile of linen and knew they would need more by tomorrow.

Jessimond eased away from him and stood, her muscles protesting after the strain of the past hour. Glancing around, she saw the entire circle of mummers watching in silence.

Finally, Jopp asked, "Will Marcus live?"

She put an arm around the young boy. "We'll have to be wary of fever and infection but I've done the best I can. Marcus is healthy and strong. He should be back swinging his sword in no time." Jessimond looked at the crowd. "Thank you for being here. I know Marcus appreciates your support. I think it best if you go back to the stage now. It should be time to put on another play for the faire goers at Wenshaw."

When protests arose, she waved them away. "There's nothing you can do for Marcus now. I will sit with him and let everyone know how he fares. I think it would be best if everyone had something productive to do."

Moss spoke up. "Jess is right. Come along, everyone."

He sent the troupe on their way, following them. Only Rand, Peter, and Elias remained behind.

"I want him moved to my tent," she told the three men. "I'll need to stay with him constantly during the next few days. Since only Agatha and I share the tent, it will be quieter and less disruptive."

"How should we move him?" Elias asked, his usual bluster gone, replaced by worry.

"Pick him up using the corners of the blanket. You can set it atop my pallet."

Jessimond hurried to her tent and opened the flap. Going inside, she spied the robe on her pallet that she'd been working on before the play. It seemed like a month ago that she had been mending the wool garment, thinking wicked thoughts of Marcus and all the ways he touched her. She set the robe aside as the men entered.

The space was small, so they had to work to get Marcus inside and ease him to the ground.

"What next?" Peter asked.

"I'll need hot water for the poultice. Not a lot. Just enough to make a paste with a few herbs."

"I'll see to it." Peter left the tent, Elias accompanying him.

Rand looked at her. "I can also stay with Marcus. Tell me what to do. How to make this poultice. I must make things right."

Jessimond frowned. "You did nothing wrong, Rand."

"I sliced my closest friend wide open," he ground out, misery written across his face.

"It was an accident. I was there, Rand. I'd seen how the mother wasn't watching her child closely enough. You couldn't have known the boy would impulsively run out during your match."

Rand stood there, looking dejected despite her words.

Then Marcus spoke. "Rand, I don't blame you for anything. I was the one who chose to move in front of your blade."

The knight looked down at Marcus. "You did so to keep me from killing the boy. I don't know which would be harder to live with—

striking down the child—or you."

Marcus smiled weakly. "But look at all the care and attention I will receive from Jess in the coming days. She will be my constant companion and fulfill my every whim."

Rand snorted. "If you're trying to make me feel better, Marcus, it's not working."

"Then go find some lovely young miss that will take your mind off what occurred."

"He's right, Rand," seconded Jessimond. "I need to prepare the poultice and apply it. You can go to the faire for me and purchase several swaths of linen while you're out and about. I will need it as the week progresses."

"All right," Rand agreed reluctantly. "But I will spell you tonight, Jess. That way we each can get a little sleep." He exited the tent.

Jessimond knelt and placed her palm against Marcus' brow. "No fever yet."

"That's a good sign."

"If it comes, it usually takes a few hours. I'll be prepared if it does."

He took her hand. "Thank you. You have taken good care of me."

Peter appeared. "I have the hot water and your case." He brought them to Jessimond. "Do you need anything else?"

"Nay."

"I will check on you later."

Jessimond began making the poultice. She would wait to see if fever came. If it did, she would use stalks of angelica to combat it. For now, she mixed three herbs together. The saffron would treat any possible infection. Myrrh would act as an antiseptic on his wound. Clove would do the same and also serve as a slight painkiller.

As she worked, she said, "If you feel feverish or your head begins to ache, let me know. I can boil yarrow in water and add some chamomile."

"I will."

She coated the wound with her concoction and covered it with squares of linen then used linen strips to fasten it in place. Once she finished, she realized his pants had blood on them.

"I'm going to slip your pants off."

Marcus' eyes were fluttering. She knew he needed sleep, which would be the best medicine for him.

"I don't think I can stay awake to enjoy this," he slurred. "You'll have to do it again when I am better. Promise me."

"I'll make no such promise," Jessimond teased.

His head dropped to the side and his breathing evened out. She removed his boots and set them aside and then pulled his pants down, trying not to stare at what was below his waist. She would wash the pants in the strongest lye soap she could find. Hopefully, the bloodstains would come out. If not, she would make him another pair.

Covering him to his waist with a blanket, Jessimond sighed. Her neck and back ached from bending over for so long. She rubbed her neck, wishing it were Marcus' strong fingers kneading it instead of her own.

Suddenly, a shadow blocked the sun shining into the tent. Jessimond looked up and saw two figures standing there but their faces were in shadow. Then one stepped inside and she recognized Lady Serafina. Quickly, she rose to her feet and curtseyed.

"I heard what happened to poor Marcus," the noblewoman said, glancing down at the sleeping knight. "I've brought Auriol, my healer, to look at him. I also have a litter and men waiting to carry him to the castle. We will care for him until the troupe moves on."

Disappointment flooded Jessimond. She opened her mouth to protest and realized that if this accident had occurred at Kinwick, her mother would have made the same offer—and not expected anyone to question her.

"Of course, my lady," she said. "May I share with Auriol what I have done? My mother is a healer and though I've chosen a different path, I learned many useful things from her."

"I'll leave the two of you to it then," Lady Serafina said. "The soldiers will be waiting when it's time to transport him."

She left and Auriol came into the tent. She had iron gray hair and light blue eyes. Her lined face told Jessimond she was close to three score.

Kneeling, Auriol asked, "Can you tell me about the accident? What the wound looked like and what you've done?"

Jessimond joined the healer and explained everything in detail, including how she had cleaned the wound and what she'd included in the poultice.

The woman unwound a bit of the linen and lifted one of the squares in order to see for herself. She nodded in satisfaction and replaced it.

"You cleansed the gash well and used the correct herbs. Your mother would be proud of you. What impresses me most are your stitches. They are evenly spaced and tightly knit. I couldn't have completed it better myself."

"I am a seamstress," Jessimond said modestly.

Auriol waved a hand in the air. "Seamstress or not, sewing flesh together is far different from cloth."

She rose and Jessimond did the same. "Is it possible for me to visit him as he heals?"

The old woman studied her. "You have feelings for this man."

"I do," she admitted.

"Then why don't you come stay at the keep, my lady? You can help watch over him as he mends."

She sucked in a quick breath. "Oh, I am no lady, Auriol," Jessimond said. "I—"

Again, the healer waved a hand, silencing her. "I know nobility when I see it, my dear. You may have fooled Lady Serafina. The mummers. Even this handsome knight. But your bearing is regal. So is your speech."

She lifted Jessimond's hands and turned the palms face up. "You have the calluses of one who works. I'll wager your mother, the healer, has the same. That you come from a noble family who feels bound to give back to their people."

Auriol dropped Jessimond's hands. "I won't share your secret. I make no judgment. But, you realize, at some point, you will need to tell this young man not only how you feel about him but share who you truly are."

Jessimond looked into the watery, blue eyes that had seen so much. "Aye."

"Then come with me. You can help to nurse him to good health again."

"Will Lady Serafina—"

"You leave her to me," Auriol said swiftly. "Come."

Jessimond closed her case of herbs and the two women left the tent. Auriol gave instructions to the waiting soldiers. They retrieved the sleeping Marcus and secured him to the litter. Both she and Auriol fell in behind them as they started toward the castle.

She saw Jopp on the way and motioned him over.

"Lady Serafina wishes for her healer to care for Marcus within the castle walls," she told the boy. "I am going with him. Please let Peter and the Vawdrys know where we are."

"I will, Jess. Take care."

They arrived at the castle and went through the gates. Minutes later, they came to the keep. The soldiers brought Marcus up the stairs and inside, climbing another set of stairs and taking him to a small bedchamber. Auriol drew the bedclothes back and the men settled Marcus in the bed, drawing the bedsheets to his waist.

"Stay with him," Auriol ordered once they'd left. "I will return to my storeroom and grind some herbs for him to ingest."

"Steeped in water?" Jessimond asked.

"Aye."

"He might need some hops in case he has trouble sleeping," she added.

The healer gave her an approving smile. "You do know your herbs." She left the room and closed the door behind her.

Jessimond pulled a chair next to the bed and took Marcus' hand. It felt odd to be inside a keep after spending weeks on the road, sleeping in tents. She wondered about adjusting to life back at Kinwick once autumn came and the mummers dispersed until spring. She also knew the time was coming when she needed to do as Auriol suggested—tell Marcus of her feelings for him and reveal that she was not a servant, but the daughter of one of the most powerful houses in England. That news could wait until he recovered, though.

Jessimond only hoped that Marcus might wish to spend the rest of his life with her.

And hoped he might grow to love her.

CHAPTER 15

MARCUS SLOWLY OPENED his eyes. His head felt heavy and his limbs sluggish. He glanced around and saw he was in a small bedchamber. A woman dressed in pale yellow cut with scarlet sat next to the bed, her face in shadow.

Where was he?

He closed his eyes. Images danced through his mind. A small child in harm's way. Diving to save the boy. A sword slicing him. Pain. Then Jess ministering to him. Cleaning him. Stitching the wound. A litter. But where did it take him?

Opening his eyes again, he decided he must be inside Lord Margrave's keep. Why, he didn't know. He raised his head slightly and looked down to his bare chest. Large squares of linen still covered it. He could smell the assortment of herbs rising from the poultice underneath the cloth. He remembered his body raging like an inferno. Hands comforting him. Washing him. Cool water touching his inflamed skin.

It must have been the Wenshaw healer who'd attended to him. Then who was the noblewoman beside him now?

She stirred, her head turning, the candlelight striking her face.

It was Jess dressed in the fine silk cotehardie. Where on earth had she gotten such a garment?

Slowly, her eyes blinked open. She sat forward, touching his forearm and then placing her hand against his brow.

"You're awake."

"Aye."

"The fever's gone, thank the Blessed Virgin." She sat back. "You are lucky. We've seen no sign of infection festering."

"How long did the fever last?" he asked.

"Three days. I'm sure you are hungry and thirsty."

She started to rise but Marcus caught her wrist.

"Stay with me a moment."

Jess chuckled and sat again as he took her hand. "I *have* stayed with you every moment."

His eyes roamed over her. "You look lovely."

A blush tinged her cheeks. "Thank you. When Lady Serafina saw that my tunic was covered in your blood, she offered this as a replacement. It belonged to her daughter, who left it here on her last visit. She was with child and it no longer fit her."

"You were made to wear finery such as this, Jess."

"Aren't you full of compliments today?"

"I would see you dressed this way always. In fact, I need to purchase you something to replace what my blood ruined."

"Nay, Marcus. You already bought that beautiful red wool for me. Even though you are a knight, I know you don't have much coin to spend."

Jess stood and leaned over, giving him a soft kiss. She backed away, releasing his hand.

"See, a kiss is something you can freely give me with no cost involved."

If only she knew the cost to his soul every time they kissed. Marcus felt as if he teetered upon a precipice and might plunge over it any minute.

Tumbling into love. With her.

"I will go to the kitchens and return with bread and broth for you."

"I am far hungrier than that." His belly growled loudly, supporting his words.

"We'll start with something light. I'll also have the servants bring hot water. Now that your fever's broken, you'll need a proper bath."

She moved to another chair and indicated the clothes lying upon it.

"What you wore was ruined. The bloodstains wouldn't come out. I've made you something new to wear in its place while you slept."

A knock sounded on the door and Jess went to answer it. She admitted an older woman who came to his bedside.

"You look much better than you did when you first arrived, Sir Marcus," she stated. "I am Auriol, the healer at Wenshaw."

"Thank you for your care," he said.

Her blue eyes assessed him. "I needed to do very little. Jess seems to know as much as I do about herbs and how to tend to an injured man." She glanced to Jess. "No fever?"

"None. I'm off to the kitchens to bring him some food and request hot water for a bath. I know that will make him feel better. Clean bedclothes, too, will help."

Jess left and Auriol asked if she could check Marcus' injury. She gently removed the linen and studied him carefully. Marcus could see the line of neat stitches trailing from under his left shoulder, cutting diagonally across his chest. The healer dabbed along the seam, first with a clean cloth and then inspecting it with her fingers.

"I think since your fever's gone and no infection has arisen, we can dispense with the poultices. You are young and strong and should heal quickly."

"I will need to thank Lord Margrave and Lady Serafina for sheltering me."

Auriol stepped back. "That girl never left your side. If anyone deserves your gratitude, it should be Jess." The healer narrowed her eyes. "And if you have any sense, you'll make sure she never leaves your side again."

Turning, the woman left the bedchamber.

"You should head to the stage, Jess," Elias said. "Bartholomew will be waiting."

Jessimond returned the sewing to her tent and retrieved her lute. A month had passed since Rand accidentally hurt Marcus. The mummers had all watched out for the knight since he'd returned to the troupe, not allowing him to lift or load anything until two days ago. Marcus had declared he was fit to do everything he had before and resumed his usual duties as they packed up and traveled to Lord Burhampton's estate. Denwell was the next to last stop for the company. After this, they would complete their season at Glenmore. From there, she and Peter would journey to Ancel and Margery's estate.

As she walked to the stage, Jessimond inhaled deeply. Autumn had always been her favorite season. She enjoyed the cool, crisp air and changes in the foliage. She thought about the harvest occurring at Kinwick now and how, within a few weeks, she would be back with her family.

She hadn't spoken to Marcus of her feelings for him, despite Auriol's urging. If he would have indicated he still possessed strong feelings for her, she would have in a heartbeat. Instead, the only kiss they'd shared since the accident had been when he'd awakened after his fever broke. Even then, she'd been the one to kiss him. It was brief and sweet but nothing like what they had previously shared.

Since Marcus didn't seem inclined to touch her anymore, Jessimond assumed he was doing what he thought best. The season would soon end. They would be going their separate ways. It would be wrong of her to press him for some kind of commitment. Marcus and Rand would return to their liege lord's estate and whatever duties awaited them. She would take up her old life.

And be miserable, pining for Marcus every day for a lifetime.

Bartholomew awaited her backstage. He handed over his lute and picked up the two stools they would sit upon. Jessimond still felt guilty sometimes when they performed together. She understood how much Bartholomew enjoyed the crowd's attention and hated that Elias and Moss insisted they continue to sing together. Still, Bartholomew was always pleasant to her and never brought up how she had been forced upon him.

Jessimond joined the troubadour, handing his lute to him, and they sat. By now, they could communicate without words, their voices blending seamlessly. Bartholomew continued to select the songs they sang together, while she chose some of her original compositions for when she sang alone. They always closed together with a sweet ballad.

She'd finally grown accustomed to looking out at the audience during the performance. It was hard to imagine only a couple of months ago how frightened she'd been that first time she joined Bartholomew on stage. Sitting with the troubadour and performing before large groups of people now seemed like second nature.

As her partner began plucking his strings, Jessimond noticed a tall man standing near the back of the crowd. His intense gaze caused an eerie chill to creep up her spine. Even as she joined in the song, she continued to sense the heat of his stare boring into her from across the way.

Jessimond forced herself to remain focused on their songs. She looked across the crowd every now and then but never back to where she knew the man stood, not wanting to be distracted. Finally, they ended with a last song and exited the stage. Hamlyn brushed by them and launched into his narrative as Agatha readied the mummers to take the stage.

She decided to return to the camp and finish the gown she'd begun from the material Marcus had purchased for her. The soft, red wool would be a combination of a tunic that mere Jess Gilpin would wear and a cotehardie that Jessimond de Montfort would slip into. She hoped to wear the creation at least once so that Marcus could see her in it. Once she returned to Kinwick, she doubted she would wear it again. It would be too painful to don because it would bring about too many memories of this time with the mummers and the knight who had claimed her heart.

"May I leave my lute with you, Agatha?"

"I'll take it, Jess." Her friend slipped the lute between two crates. "It will be safe there."

"Thank you."

Jessimond started back to the mummers' tents. She decided to stroll through the faire before she did so. It had been several days since she had and was always something she enjoyed doing, meeting new people and viewing their wares.

Then the hairs on the back of her neck stood on end. She looked over her shoulder and saw the man from before. He was about her father's age and dressed as a knight. Mayhap, it was someone who had visited at Kinwick and recognized her. Jessimond decided she should speak to him before he might question anyone else in the troupe about her.

Motioning to him, she moved away from the stalls. She remained in view, though, in case she needed to summon anyone. After all, this man was a stranger to her.

As he approached, Jessimond asked, "Do we know each other?" She had an odd feeling that somehow they did.

He gave her a wistful smile. "Greetings, my lady. I am Sir Rodric Shelley, in service to the Baron of Netherfield."

She didn't recognize the name or face—yet something told her she knew this man.

"I am no lady, Sir Rodric," she replied. "My name is Jess Gilpin. I am with the mummers' troupe."

"Aye. I heard you sing. You look and sound like an angel."

"Thank you. I have not been singing for long. I am a seamstress for the company." She had no wish to share her true past with this stranger.

"They do not need the other troubadour. You outshine him in every way."

"I am happy to share the stage with Bartholomew," she said testily.

"Will you be singing again?" he asked hopefully.

"Aye. I do a few songs with Bartholomew before each play."

"Then I look forward to hearing you again, Jess. I will also bring the baron with me. He will want to hear you perform."

"You are welcomed to do so, Sir Rodric. We will be at Denwell the rest of this week."

Jessimond turned and left the knight. She longed to look back over her shoulder but didn't want him to think she was curious about him. Returning to camp, she put the encounter from her mind and was able to complete her outfit over the next two hours. Deciding to wear it for the first time, she slipped it on and returned to the stage. Smoothing the fine wool over her undertunic, Jessimond felt pretty and confident.

Agatha came up to her. "This is beautiful, Jess. Where did you get it?"

"Marcus bought the material for me several weeks ago. I finally had time to make it up."

"You are so talented. When we reach Kinwick, will you teach me how to sew? I know the basics but nothing ever comes out right."

She hugged Agatha. "I'd be happy to do so."

Once more, Jessimond joined Bartholomew. She decided not to look for Sir Rodric, doubting he would have returned to the faire so quickly, much less with his liege lord. They completed their set and acknowledged the crowd's enthusiastic applause. Since the play following would be the last of the day, she kept her lute and started back for camp. She wanted to add a few leeks and spices to the evening stew that she'd left simmering.

Jessimond passed the area where Marcus and Rand sparred. She stopped and watched the pair at a distance. This was the first stop they had gone against one another again since the accident because Jessimond had not wanted Marcus to burst his stitches. Instead, Peter had taken Marcus' place and done a wonderful job in replacing the knight. Peter had told her while he enjoyed swordplay, he was more than happy to allow Marcus to return to it because what he really liked was participating in the plays. She had teased him about wanting to become a mummer instead of remaining a blacksmith. Peter told her this was his youthful time of adventure and he would be more than willing to settle into life working next to his father. Jessimond thought part of that was because Agatha would return with them to Kinwick, and Peter would not want to go off and leave her behind.

"Celia! Celia, wait!"

Jessimond heard a voice frantically calling and glanced around. She saw no other woman nearby and wondered who the man might be addressing. Stopping, she saw two men rushing toward her.

One was Sir Rodric. The other was a nobleman with dark blond hair edged with silver. As they drew near, she saw he was just over two score and of medium height. His dark brown eyes widened as he came to a halt in front of her.

"God in His Heavens. I cannot believe it." The nobleman shook his head in disbelief and looked to his companion. "Rodric, you weren't mistaken. She is Celia made over."

Jessimond looked at them in confusion. "Who is this Celia, my lord? I am Jess Gilpin, not whom you seek."

He swallowed, a pained yet hopeful expression on his face. "I am Gregory de Challon, Baron of Netherfield. I think . . . nay, I believe . . . that you are my daughter."

CHAPTER 16

JESSIMOND'S JAW DROPPED. *Could it be? Had this nobleman fathered her?* She found no resemblance between them.

The baron took a step toward her, as if to embrace her. She quickly backed away.

"Don't go," he pleaded. "Let me . . . at least let me speak with you a moment."

Warily, she crossed her arms in front of her and held her ground, her lute acting as a further barrier between them.

Seeing that she wouldn't flee, the baron said, "I am ashamed to tell you that as a young man, I was most selfish. I would not have wanted you to know me then. I never thought of others. I sought pleasure through women and drink, never wondering what tomorrow might bring."

He raked a hand through his thick hair. "And then I met Celia. Your mother."

Those two words made her knees turn to water. Jessimond locked them to keep from collapsing.

"Celia was the loveliest woman I'd ever seen when she arrived at the royal court. Nay, she was still a girl. Only six and ten. So beautiful and full of light and sweetness. I wanted her like no one before."

"You seduced her," Jessimond said flatly.

Lord Gregory winced. "Aye. I thought I merely would charm her. Steal a few tender kisses. I never set out to deflower her." He closed his eyes and drew a deep breath before opening them. "Celia stole my heart, though. One kiss wasn't enough. Suddenly, I thought of nothing else, night and day. Every waking moment seemed consumed with thoughts of her."

She could understand what the nobleman said, having been taken with Marcus in the same way.

"Kisses turned into more passionate actions. Before I knew it, Celia was with child."

Something told Jessimond that she was the child this man spoke of.

"Why didn't you wed her?" she asked. "It sounds as though you loved her."

Tears swam in Lord Gregory's eyes. "I did love her. Deeply. I couldn't imagine a life without her." His voice broke. His hands covered his eyes.

Sir Rodric spoke up. "The baron was already betrothed. Had been for years. He couldn't have wed Lady Celia even if he'd wanted to. And believe me, he did. Legally, though, he already had a wife. The nuptial mass was strictly a formality."

Jessimond's heart ached for this broken man who stood before her and even more for the woman he'd obviously left behind.

The nobleman cleared his throat. "I loved Celia Achard. I abandoned her. 'Tis my biggest regret in life, a sin I can never wash from my soul." He sighed. "I wed as my father expected me to. I tried to be a good husband to Egelina and an even better father to our children."

Her heart skipped a beat. *Children?*

"They know about you," the nobleman said. "My wife died many years ago. I told them then of their half-sister. They've wanted me to fetch you ever since."

He'd *known* where she was all this time? Jessimond couldn't speak. It was as if this man had punched her in the belly and all air fled from her. Anger replaced the sympathy she'd felt for him.

Sir Rodric took up the tale. "After Lady Celia gave birth to you, Lord Gregory charged me to take her from London to her home. Her father and brothers were away that summer. She'd told them she was visiting a friend so no family would be at Sturnwick when we returned."

She wondered how Celia would have explained a baby to her family and decided the young noblewoman would have done what others before her had done, and found a family nearby to take on the babe and raise it as theirs.

"Lady Celia died on the journey home," Sir Rodric continued.

It was another blow to Jessimond. Already, she'd had fantasies of seeking out her birth mother.

"We were near de Montfort lands by that point, still several days away from Sturnwick. I had met Lord Geoffrey and Lady Merryn at court and knew of their reputation of generosity with their people. I thought it best to leave you on Kinwick lands, my lady," the knight said. "I hoped a family there would take you in, especially when they found the amethyst brooch I left wrapped inside your blanket. Lord Gregory had gifted it to Lady Celia. I thought you would fare better there than if I turned up at Sturnwick with the daughter of the house dead and her week-old babe. The servants wouldn't have known what to do."

Jessimond's head reeled with all of this news. Sir Rodric mentioning the brooch let her know beyond a doubt that she was the daughter of this nobleman and Lady Celia.

"I changed after that," Lord Gregory told her. "I quit putting myself first and looked to do for others. I've made a difference at Netherfield, Jess." He paused. "Now, I want to make a difference in your life.

"Come home with me," he pleaded. "Your brother and two sisters long to meet you. If you've left Kinwick and joined this mummers' troupe, it means you were searching for something that you couldn't find there."

She started to speak but Lord Gregory raised his hand. "I know what I did was awful. I know I can never replace the people who took you in. Who loved you. But you have another family, Jess, and they wish to know you. You could live in luxury and be recognized as the lady you are. I will find a husband for you, one nearby so that we can see you often."

He took her hand. "Please. Come home to Netherfield. At least try to get to know us. I beg you."

Jessimond jerked her hand from his. "You know nothing about me, Lord Gregory. Who I am. Who my family is. Even if I come from the place you claim Sir Rodric left me." Rage poured through her. "I don't care who you are or who you think I am. I am not your child and never will be."

She whirled and saw Moss standing nearby, watching over her while she spoke to men he didn't know. He hurried toward her.

"I need Peter," she cried.

"He's back at camp," Moss said.

Jessimond lifted her skirts and ran. She didn't dare look back. Tears of anger streamed down her cheeks. How dare this man appear and claim her as his, especially after what he did to her mother. As she raced away, her anger melted and turned to sorrow for the lost innocence of her young mother at the hands of that knave. Gregory de Challon had plied an inexperienced young woman with sweet words and sweeter kisses, claiming to love her even as he deserted her and made a life on his own. He'd kept his title, gained a wife, and had children—while Celia Achard had died on the road with Jessimond by her side.

She wondered what her mother had named her. Though she wished she could ask Sir Rodric, Jessimond determined never to reveal to him or the baron that she was, indeed, that babe.

Arriving at camp out of breath, she saw Peter entering with a stack of firewood in his arms. One look at her and he dropped it, hurrying toward her.

Her friend didn't ask what was wrong. He merely enfolded her in his arms and held her. Jessimond cried a river of tears for the mother she'd lost and would never know. Finally, her sobs subsided.

"Is it Marcus?" he finally asked.

"Nay. Oh, Peter. 'Twas my father."

"Lord Geoffrey is here? I thought we wouldn't see him until we arrived at Lord Ancel's estate."

Jessimond composed herself. "Not my father. The man . . . the man who . . ." She couldn't continue.

Somehow, Peter understood and wrapped his arms about her again. Jessimond let him rock her. The steady motion calmed her.

"Lord Geoffrey is your father, Jess. Lady Merryn is your mother. The de Montforts are your family," Peter softly insisted. "Nothing—no one—will ever take you away from them. You are a de Montfort daughter as much as Lady Alys and Lady Nan are. No matter who claimed to have fathered you and what woman birthed you, you have been a de Montfort since you were only a few days old. Lord Geoffrey and Lady Merryn and all of your brothers and sisters love you and cherish you.

"Sit," he encouraged. "Tell me everything that happened."

Slowly, Jessimond recounted the entire incident. Peter kept quiet throughout, merely nodding as she spoke.

"I wish never to see him again," she said vehemently. "Not after what he did to her."

Peter said, "I wouldn't judge Lord Gregory too harshly, Jess."

When she began to protest, he silenced her. "He was young himself. Foolhardy. Selfish. And betrothed. It sounds as if he did love Lady Celia and regrets his actions. If you choose to have nothing to do with him or your half-brother and half-sisters, that is up to you. At least you now know your background.

"And if you change your mind, you know where to seek him."

A numbness overtook Jessimond. "I think I will lie down. Could you see to the stew?"

"Of course."

She stumbled to her tent and collapsed upon the pallet. More tears came as she thought over what Peter said.

Her mother and father had been young. Reckless. They hadn't thought through the consequences of their coupling. They'd been caught up in loving one another.

She thought of what might have happened if she and Marcus had continued in their love play. Each time he touched her and brought her to new heights of pleasure, she realized how much control he must have exercised in not taking things further. If he had, Jessimond might have found herself in the same position as her mother. Alone. Unwed. With child.

Sitting up, she scooped water from the small bowl next to her bed and splashed it across her face. She breathed deeply and evenly, until she knew she was in control of her emotions once more. Leaving the tent, Jessimond walked determinedly back toward the faire.

As she hoped, Lord Gregory and Sir Rodric stood near where they'd spoken, as if they'd waited for her to reappear. She approached them, steeling herself.

"I am sorry I fled, my lord," she said to her birth father. "What you revealed took me by surprise."

He gave her a grateful smile. "I knew it would be difficult for you to hear, Jess."

"Jessimond. My name is Jessimond."

"'Tis a lovely name."

"What was my name? Before?" she asked.

"Lady Celia hadn't chosen one yet," Sir Rodric said. "She was waiting to find the exact name that would fit you."

"My sister named me," Jessimond revealed. "Nan was walking with my father when they stumbled across me." She smiled. "She's still very proud of discovering and naming me."

"You've . . . you've had a good life?" Lord Gregory asked hesitantly.

"Aye. A wonderful life with parents and siblings who showered me with love. I have three brothers and two sisters. They've all wed now. I am the youngest."

Still, Jessimond held back. She wasn't ready to tell these men that she was a de Montfort.

"I plan on returning to Kinwick once the mummers conclude their tour," she continued.

"Would you ever consider visiting Netherfield, Jessimond?" the baron asked. "Byrom, Lina, and Lora would be delighted to make your acquaintance."

Her siblings . . .

"Lora is the eldest at eight and ten. Byrom is six and ten. Lina is the youngest at two and ten. My wife, Egelina, died giving birth to Lina."

She wanted to remain loyal to her de Montfort kin, but Jessimond yearned to meet these three.

"I won't make any promises to you, my lord, but I will think on it."

"Would you like me to write to Lord Geoffrey?" he asked. "I know you would need his permission to leave."

"Nay. If the time comes and I am comfortable coming to Netherfield, I will speak to the earl myself."

Jessimond saw so many things in the nobleman's eyes. Hope. Regret. Even love. He had never seen her until today yet she understood that he loved her—because he had loved her mother.

"Celia would be so proud of you, Jessimond," he said. "You favor her so much but you are much more confident. She was shy and always wanted to please others."

Jessimond thought she had more in common with her mother than looks. Before embarking on the tour with the mummers, she had been much quieter, a nurturer who looked to help others before herself.

"Thank you for considering a visit one day," Lord Gregory continued. "I won't bother you anymore. Sir Rodric and I will return to Netherfield. It lies just south of Denwell, not half an hour's ride. I want you to enjoy your time singing and not worry if we are in the crowd."

A deep longing overwhelmed her. Jessimond impulsively embraced him. His arms went about her and held her a long moment before releasing her.

"Thank you for telling me the truth about my origins," she said. "Mayhap we'll meet again one day."

"It will remain my fondest wish," he said.

Turning to Sir Rodric, the baron nodded. Both men walked away. Neither glanced back at her. Jessimond's throat swelled, thick with emotion.

When she'd first had the idea, she hadn't known what touring with the mummers might bring. Now, she'd learned of her birth parents and also fallen in love. She would return to Kinwick a much different person.

Slowly, Jessimond walked back to camp.

CHAPTER 17

MARCUS EAGERLY UNLOADED the mummers' wagons and set up the tents in a circle for the last time. They had arrived at Glenmore, the final stop on their tour, at noon today. Lord Simeon de Grey's estate lay adjacent to Hartefield, though the keeps of the two great estates were well over three hours apart. In fact, de Grey had instructed the Vawdrys to use a field far from the castle grounds. Just the other side of the brook that ran nearby the tents was Hartefield lands and at the edge of Hartefield stood his family's hunting lodge. He planned to take Jess there so they could speak privately.

She had prepared their evening meal early since every belly grumbled loudly after the hard labor of this afternoon. Before they ate, Marcus pulled Rand aside.

"I want you to ride to Harte Castle after eating," he told his friend. "Avoid my father if you can. Find out what has gone on since we left in the spring."

"And if I do run into Lord Charles?" Rand asked.

"Tell him you and I will return at the end of the week."

Rand nodded and they joined the end of the line that had formed. Jess dished up their food and they moved on to where Agatha gave them thick slices from a round of cheese.

Marcus watched Jess and wondered what had changed in her. Ever since they'd been at Denwell, she seemed more reserved. He regretted that they no longer washed the dishes together after the evening meal. When he'd been injured, that task had been assumed by Peter and Agatha. Once Marcus returned to the troupe, the pair continued to handle it. He realized the couple enjoyed their time away from others.

Just as he had. With Jess.

He'd deliberately withdrawn from her since his accident. That was something he would address with her. He scooped the last of the food into his mouth and swallowed whole, ready to set things right with the woman he loved.

Marcus could only admit that to himself. The hurt he'd watched his mother endure and her constant warnings to her son to guard his heart from love rang in his mind. He refused to tell Jess that he'd fallen in love with her. He would convince her to wed him with his actions alone.

Rising, he placed his bowl into a basket at the same time she did.

"Can we go for a walk?" he asked her.

Her brows rose and she pursed her lips. He was afraid she might turn him down.

"There are things I would like to say to you," Marcus said softly.

A look of resignation crossed her face. "If you must."

Marcus indicated the way for them to walk. He was afraid to take her elbow since she seemed jittery.

"Why don't we walk toward the meadow?" she questioned, as he entered the woods.

"I have some place in mind," he replied.

Following him, she said, "You seem to know where you are going."

Marcus halted. "I do."

He took her hand and threaded his fingers through hers. Warmth flooded him. It had been weeks since he'd dared to touch her. When she threatened to pull away, his fingers tightened around hers.

"Come along. It's not far."

He led them to a narrow place that would allow them to cross the brook, though they'd need a running start. Marcus broke out in a run, pulling Jess along, leaping at the last minute when they reached the water. They both sailed across easily and he tugged her up the bank. Within a few minutes, they reached the de Harte hunting lodge.

The structure stood at the far end of Hartefield and hadn't been used much as he grew up. Though the handle turned easily, the door stuck. He threw his shoulder into it, forcing it open, and stepped inside. Marcus allowed Jess to enter and then shut the door behind them.

"Where are we?"

He led her to the stairs and sat on a step, pulling her down beside him.

"We are on my family's lands."

He watched Jess think about that and saw understanding dawn in her face.

Continuing, he said, "We are at Hartefield, home of the Baron of Harteley. De Hartes have lived at Harte Castle for many years."

"And you are a de Harte. The son of the baron."

"Aye, Jess. I am." He brought their joined hands up and pressed a fervent kiss to her knuckles.

She frowned and pulled her hand from his grasp. "I don't understand, Marcus. You have ignored me ever since you were injured. Weeks have gone by and you've barely said two words to me—much less touched me. Now, you bring me here and tell me you are the son of a baron. What do you want from me?"

He cupped her cheeks in his hands. "I want *you*, Jess. All of you. I haven't spoken to you or kissed you because of how much I desire you. Every time I touched you, I tumbled deeper into the abyss. You and I played with fire, sweetheart, and I did not want either of us to be burned.

"We're at my home now. Where I've longed to bring you ever since we met. I want to marry you, Jess. Bury my seed deep within you. I long for you to have my babes—a dozen of them. I need you by my side. In my bed. I want to laugh with you. Share my day with you." He paused. "Even sing with you, if you wish. All I know is that I cannot live unless you are in my life every day. When the mummers disband, I want you to come to Harte Castle so we can wed."

Her eyes filled with tears. "I thought you no longer cared for me," she said, her voice barely a whisper. "You ignored me. I believed you pushed me away because you'd tired of me. Or didn't want to commit to me."

Marcus laughed and kissed her swiftly. "Nay. The opposite, my love. Being near you drove me mad with desire. I couldn't speak to you without wanting to kiss you senseless. I feared if I touched you again, I would tear your clothes from you and take you, wherever we were." His thumbs stroked her cheeks. "I think of you with each breath I take. Every step I make. You are the only woman I want, Jess. No other."

He kissed her deeply, tasting her again after so long a time. As he did, he knew he could no longer wait. Breaking the kiss, he scooped Jess into his arms and ascended the staircase. Marcus brought her to a bedchamber and placed her on the bed.

Kneeling beside her, he said, "My desire for you is strong, love. I know we haven't made our vows yet but more than anything, I long to make you mine." He paused. "We can marry in a week but I need you now. Are you willing to commit your body to mine?"

Jessimond gazed at the face of the man she would always love. She had thought she would wed at Kinwick, her family smiling as she did so. Mayhap, that still might occur. For now, though, she needed Marcus inside her, branding her as his.

She took his face between her hands. "I love you," she said. "Come to me. Make me yours."

He stretched out alongside her. They turned to face one another. He kissed her brow. Her eyelids. Her nose and cheeks. Her lips. His hands roamed from her face, down her neck, and slipped inside her clothing. Her breasts had ached for his touch and now they were rewarded with it, the nipples springing to life as he teased them.

"Enough of this," he proclaimed.

Marcus sat up and pulled them from the bed. Before she could ask why, his fingers found the edge of her tunics and pulled them up, over her head. He tossed them aside and stared at her in wonder.

"You are perfect."

He removed her boots and quickly doffed his own clothing. Standing before her, he looked hewn from rock. Jessimond found she held her breath as she gazed upon him. Then he nudged her back until her legs touched the bed. They fell upon it and Marcus feasted upon her. She felt treasured with each stroke of his hand and tongue. He lovingly tasted every bit of her until she cried out for more.

"Do you want this?" he asked, his smile wicked as he parted her folds and a finger glided inside her.

"Aye," she said breathlessly.

"And this?"

His tongue replaced his finger, darting in and out of her. Jessimond whimpered as his hands clutched her buttocks and his mouth devoured her. The familiar pressure built into a crescendo which erupted with such force that she screamed his name. Her hips bucked as her head whipped from side to side, waves of hot pleasure consuming her until she stilled, limp and unmoving.

Then Marcus hovered over her. He slipped his member inside her, stretching her until she started to protest.

"Nay, you are too large, Marcus," she said, panicking. "I cannot take all of you."

He kissed her. "You are tight because you are a virgin, sweetheart, but your juices flow for me. Your body wants mine. It needs for us to join together. Trust me."

She gazed into the face she loved. "I do. Always."

With that, he thrust once, covering her mouth with his.

Blinding pain struck. She tried to push him off but his hands captured her wrists and raised them above her head. He remained still, only his lips caressing her throat. Gradually, she became used to how he filled her. The pain had receded. Something built within her again. Without thought, Jessimond's hips pushed upward.

Marcus took that as a sign and left her, only to return again. She sucked in a quick breath but found no pain accompanied his movement this time. As he continued to move within her, she tried to bring her hands down to stroke him but he still pinned her wrists above her.

His mouth slipped to her breast, sucking, laving, teasing her while he continued to thrust slowly.

He pushed her wrists together and captured them with one large hand. The other trailed leisurely down her body. As his thrusts grew more rapid, his thumb found the nub that drove her wild. He circled it, pressing harder as his pace increased. Jessimond wriggled underneath him, her whimpers now becoming pants and then moans.

Suddenly, Marcus strained against her as a sea of stars exploded. She cried out and he did the same and they rode an undulating cloud of joy that went on and on. Finally, he collapsed upon her, spent.

"I cannot move," he groaned. "I may never move."

Jessimond pushed against him. "I cannot breathe," she managed to get out.

Quickly, he rolled to his side and caught her against him. She rested her cheek against his chest. Her fingers lightly moved along the scar on his chest, now fading from the angry red it had been.

Marcus kissed the top of her head. "Do you see why I could not wait another moment?" His fingertip traced the outline of her lips.

"I hope I pleased you," she said. "I know you have lain with many women."

He caught her hand and pressed a hot kiss into the palm. "I have forgotten all of those women, Jess. That's how much I care for you."

She noticed he didn't say he loved her. It disappointed her, but Jessimond believed he truly did love her. With every stroke, his body told her so, whether he knew it or not. Once they wed, mayhap he wouldn't be so afraid to say the words she longed to hear.

His fingers entwined with hers and he brought their joined hands to rest between them. "I have never felt this way before," he shared. "Love play has never been more satisfying than with you. I pledge I will never lie with another woman. Only you, sweetheart. Only you."

For now, it would be enough.

"You know how to please me," she began. "I hope you'll show me how I can please you."

Marcus smiled. "Oh, you already do." Then he grinned. "But I can think of a few things to teach you in the years to come."

"Why not start now?" she countered.

Laughing, he did just that.

CHAPTER 18

MARCUS LED JESS back to the mummers' camp. Everything had gone exactly as he'd wished. He would complete his obligation to the Vawdrys and then return to Hartefield with his bride-to-be. He wondered in what condition he would find his father. It had surprised him how the baron had aged while Marcus had been off fighting in the wars with the king.

He'd actually liked his stepmother. He wondered how she'd felt, being meant for one man and then being coerced to marry another more than twice her age. He hoped Lady Ailith and Jess would get along well. He saw no reason why they wouldn't even though Jess wasn't of the nobility. She was beautiful and well-spoken and would make a good future baroness for Hartefield. Once she arrived, Marcus knew what Jess would be drawn to—the newest members of the de Harte family. Already, Marcus could see her with a babe in her arms. His babe.

They leaped over the narrow portion of the brook again. He decided this would be a place to bring his sons in the future. He could teach them to fish. Knowing Jess, she'd want their daughters brought along to learn, as well. He still was uncertain if she'd told him the entire truth about how she'd learned to swing a sword so well but it was definitely something he hoped she kept up. It would be interesting to teach their children to defend themselves with the weapon, especially if they did so side-by-side.

Whatever happened, Marcus knew he would lead a fascinating life with Jess by his side.

Seeing the tents, he steered them in that direction. As he did, Rand hurried toward them.

"Marcus, we must speak." He glanced at Jess. "Alone."

"It's all right. Jess knows who I am. Speak freely."

She squeezed his hand and released it. "Go ahead. I'll give you some privacy."

Marcus watched her move away, the gentle sway of her hips enticing him. He wondered if he could wait a week before engaging her in love play again.

When she was out of hearing distance, Rand said, "Your father is very ill."

"Did you see him?"

"Nay. I spoke at length to Thomas, though. You know he's not one to exaggerate."

Sir Thomas had been the captain of Hartefield's guard for over half a score and was a man Marcus trusted implicitly.

"When I told Thomas that you were nearby, he implored me to bring you home for good. In truth, Marcus, he made it sound as if Lord Charles is near death."

"Then I'll leave at once for Hartefield."

"I'll go with you," Rand volunteered.

"Nay. You should be here for the sword exhibitions. Peter can step in for me as he did before."

"Then I'll tell the Vawdrys on your behalf."

"I'll go speak to Jess and let her know why I'm leaving."

Rand placed a hand on Marcus' shoulder. "Go with God."

Marcus went to Jess' tent. The flap was propped open so he poked his head inside and saw she sat on her pallet talking with Agatha.

"May I see you a moment?"

Jess excused herself and joined him. Marcus led them around to the back of the tents so they would be out of sight.

"I must go to Harte Castle now. My father is gravely ill. I need to see him a last time before he dies."

Concern crossed her brow. "Should I go with you? I might be of some assistance with my herbs."

"Let me see him first. If he looks as if it would be beneficial to bring in a healer, I will come for you myself."

Jess laid a palm against his cheek. "Take care."

"I will."

Marcus bent and kissed her tenderly. He needed this last physical contact with her before he rode into the lion's den.

Jess was the one who broke their kiss. "Go," she urged.

Marcus went to where the horses were hobbled and found that Rand already had Storm saddled and waiting for him. He mounted his horse and set out for Hartefield with mixed emotions. The last few months had been unlike any he'd experienced. All his life, Marcus had trained to be a soldier and then fought in Northern Scotland and Ireland with the king.

Something in him broke, though, when he returned home and learned of his mother's death. When he'd stormed from the keep after his father gave him that news, Marcus hadn't known if or when he'd be back. He only knew if he remained, his father would wind up dead on the floor by his only son's hand. It had taken the child who'd innocently come to Marcus and climbed trustingly into his arms to prevent a bloodbath.

Time away from Hartefield with the mummers had healed his emotional wounds. The life was transient and lighthearted, the people friendly and loyal to one another. Things moved at a different pace and each day proved to be new and different from the one before.

Most important of all, he'd found Jess. By the Christ, this woman was everything to him now. As Marcus rode toward home, he thought long and hard on his mother's words, the ones that warned him never to give his heart to another and if he so foolishly did, never let her know. Margaret de Harte had told him to refuse to utter the words of love that would make him weak.

Had his mother been wrong?

Marcus didn't feel weak loving Jess. In fact, he seemed more powerful for it, as if he could move mountains. Mayhap his mother's bitterness regarding her own situation had colored her view. He had the rest of his life with Jess. Plenty of time to decide if the words recognizing his love for her were important to say aloud.

But his heart told him they were.

It amazed him that Jess had given herself freely to him, knowing she'd said she would only wed a man she loved and one who loved her. He would be ever faithful to Jess, daily showing her how devoted he was to her and any children they might have. His decision regarding future declarations of love could wait for the present. More than anything, he needed to see what awaited him at Hartefield.

Marcus rode through the gates as dusk turned into dark. They were still open, probably at Rand's urging. Sure enough, he spotted Thomas and reined in his horse. Dismounting, he tossed the reins to a stable boy who ran to take them.

Marcus clasped Thomas' hand. "'Tis good to see you, Thomas."

"And you, as well, my lord."

The two men fell into step and headed toward the keep.

"I heard the Irish fight dirty," Thomas said.

Marcus laughed. "I'm sure the men entertained you with all kinds of stories of our years away." Then he grew serious. "How is my father? Rand said he was quite ill."

"Very ill. Lady Ailith, as well, though from what I know, she suffers from a different ailment."

They entered the keep and began up the staircase, passing Sagar, Hartefield's longtime steward. Marcus gave him a brief nod. Sagar turned and followed them to the solar.

When they reached it, the steward told him, "From what I know, Sir Marcus, you'll be our new baron before the week is out. You should know you have my loyalty and that of every soldier and servant at Hartefield. Thomas will confirm that."

Marcus replied, "That means a great deal to me, Sagar."

"We'll wait for you here in case you have need of us," the steward said.

He prepared himself for what he would find and then opened the door.

The first room had been changed from a family room into a sick room. The table and all the various chairs had been pushed to the far side of the chamber. A bed had been brought in. A flushed Ailith de Harte lay in it, coughing harshly despite being asleep. Herleva, the head of Harte Castle's many servants, sat beside her.

She rose. "Greetings, my lord. 'Tis good that you've returned home."

"What's wrong with Lady Ailith?" he asked.

"My lady has both fever and chills," Herleva said. "She's started coughing and has difficulty breathing. I moved her out here so that both she and Lord Charles might be able to rest better apart and not disturb one another."

He studied his stepmother. "Will she live?"

"By God's Grace," the servant replied.

Marcus crossed the room and entered the master bedchamber. Inside, he saw Hartefield's priest and knew that the man of God was present for a good reason. Marcus' eyes were drawn to the shriveled husk in the bed. His father looked nothing like the man he'd seen in early May. Though Charles de Harte had been thin to begin with, he now looked like skin and bones. He'd also lost all of his hair and trembled visibly. He clenched his teeth as if in pain.

Father Pious finished the prayer he intoned over the baron and looked up.

"He hasn't long, my lord. I heard his last confession just moments ago." The priest leaned over the living corpse. "Your son is here, Lord Charles."

His father opened his eyes and sought out Marcus. "You came."

"Aye."

"I'm dying."

"I can see."

The nobleman struggled to breathe. Finally, he said, "You must wed Ailith at once."

His words took Marcus aback. "Lady Ailith is your wife, Father."

"Nay. She never has been. She is yours."

Marcus looked to the priest. "How long has he been confused, Father?"

The priest flushed a dull red. "He's not, my lord. I've seen the betrothal papers. *You* are the one betrothed to Lady Ailith." Father Pious looked back to the baron.

Nausea filled Marcus.

"Tell him," rasped Charles. "I haven't the strength."

"Your confession—"

"Tell him," insisted the baron.

Pious nodded. "Lady Ailith's father brought her to Hartefield only days before your mother's death. He and Lord Charles signed the betrothal papers, legally uniting you and Lady Ailith. She was to remain here and learn about Hartefield while you were away fighting with the king's troops. Lord Charles was most taken with the lady. He waited a month and could no longer fight the demons that made him covet his son's wife-to-be. He . . . he told her that you had been killed in battle. That he would send word to her father and new contracts would be drawn up and signed."

Marcus sucked in a startled breath. "My father *lied* to her? He claimed I was *dead*?"

The priest nodded, shame evident on his face. "He did, Lord Marcus. Your father told the lady he'd received a missive that you'd been killed by the enemy. He then told Lady Ailith that the best solution was for him to wed her to ensure her future and said her father had agreed to new proposed contracts.

"Ones that would make Lord Charles her husband."

Marcus could see how the events played out. A naïve young woman, far from home, trusting the always confident Charles de Harte. A pretense of sending papers back and forth. His father being solicitous and caring, earning Ailith's trust.

"Did they go through a Church ceremony?" he asked the priest.

"Nay. Lord Charles stated the papers sufficed and that made them legally wed. He emphasized to Lady Ailith that he did not want to have a large wedding when he had recently lost his own wife and son, and Lady Ailith had lost the betrothed she'd never seen. The poor lady did not know any better, my lord."

Rage flowed through Marcus. He wheeled toward his father. "So, you seduced an innocent virgin who didn't know how low you would sink. Got her with child since you've wanted more sons ever since I was born. And what did it get you? Two more daughters. Shake any tree around Hartefield and one of my many half-sisters would fall from it." He spat on the floor. "You disgust me."

Charles shrugged feebly. "I always have. You were your mother's child from the beginning. Never mine. Now, though, you must make things right. I don't have long left in this world and I've grown fond of Ailith. You need to protect her and your half-sisters. She was meant for you. Not me. I was nothing more than an old fool. You must do as I say, Marcus. I am Baron of Harteley. I am your father. You will obey me."

His fury boiled over. "Why should I clean up your mistakes?" he seethed. "*You* are the one who's ruined this woman's life. Did you think I'd be eager to take your bloody leftovers? Or even want to raise your bastards by her? No, Father. I refuse to do as you command and wed Lady Ailith. I won't have her and those children foisted upon me. Soon, you will be in your grave and I will be the new Baron of Harteley. I have my own life to live, not one of your making. I will run Hartefield as I see fit, with a wife that I choose by my side."

The baron licked his cracked lips. "I regret taking Ailith to wife under false circumstances. I have confessed to Father Pious. I know I shall burn in the fires of all Eternity for the man I've been." Charles paused. "Be a better man than I was, my son. Take Ailith to wife. I beg you, my son. Now."

"You can plead until no breath is left in you, Father, but I will not wed her. Not now. Not ever."

His father's eyes fluttered shut. Marcus hoped the bastard was dead. He'd been a terrible father and worse husband. The fact Charles de Harte had deceived an innocent such as Lady Ailith only proved what a bastard he truly was. The fires of Hell were too good for him. Marcus hoped God would find an even greater punishment for his father. One where he suffered beyond Eternity.

As his fury cooled, Father Pious placed a hand upon his shoulder. "Lord Marcus, I understand how angry and hurt you are by your father's actions."

"You have no idea, Father. I abhor him and everything he's done."

"I understand, my lord. Time will heal you. Forgiveness will come."

Marcus doubted it ever would but he kept silent.

"You do realize you'll have to do as he requested," the priest continued.

"I will never take Lady Ailith to wife, Father."

Father Pious gazed at him sadly. "You already have."

Marcus paused, going over the conversation in his mind. Realization struck him as a physical blow and he fell to his knees.

Though he hadn't spoken vows in a wedding ceremony, by law he was already a husband to Ailith.

Which meant he couldn't be one to Jess.

CHAPTER 19

MARCUS AWAKENED WITH gritty eyes due to lack of sleep. It had eluded him for most of the night as his mind whirled in circles, all his thoughts centered on Jess. The life he'd planned for them, with their children playing throughout the estate as they worked together for the good of their people.

All gone in an instant.

He worried that she might carry his child. They'd only coupled once but Marcus knew it was a possibility. He couldn't send her away, not when he would want to love the child that resulted from their night of passion. Yet, he didn't believe Jess would stay with him under the present circumstances.

How sick was Ailith? The noblewoman hadn't awakened when he'd come into the solar last night. Marcus had never wished anyone ill but his hopes must be pinned upon his stepmother not surviving whatever illness gripped her body. He would gladly care for Livia and little Mary in the case of Ailith's death and bring them up as daughters of the house. He believed Jess would be generous in her time and affection for these girls, mothering them as her own.

Marcus rose, looking about the familiar bedchamber. Many times, his father had told him that he would one day share it with his brothers. As the years passed, that never occurred, despite his mother's many efforts to provide more sons to her husband.

He returned to the solar. Opening the door, he froze. No one occupied the bed.

Had Lady Ailith died during the night?

Guilt washed over him at his deepest desire already coming to pass.

He sensed a presence behind him and turned. Herleva stood there.

"Where is Lady Ailith?" Marcus demanded.

"I had her moved across the hall," the servant told him as she began stripping the bed and bundling up the bedclothes.

"Why?"

Herleva stopped her task. "She has the measles. The spots appeared late last night. It explains the symptoms she had before. I plan to burn these bedclothes."

Measles were easily spread. Marcus could understand Herleva isolating Ailith from others within the keep.

"What of her children?"

"Lady Livia is fine. I will keep her from her mother." She paused. "Lady Mary, though, has been infected. Lady Ailith nursed the child up until two days ago when she fell ill. The babe is with her mother now. I've found a kitchen girl who contracted measles as a child. She is with them and will handle their care."

Marcus knew once a person survived the disease, they never got it again. He himself had measles as a boy while he was fostering. It spread like wildfire among the pages and squires.

Just under half the boys who came down with the fever and spots had perished within a week.

"Have you seen the baron this morning?" Herleva asked.

"I was about to visit him."

"Don't tell him about the baroness or his daughter," she urged. "It would only hurt him, knowing they suffered."

"I agree." He nodded and entered the bedchamber. Father Pious sat next to the bed where the baron lay, his eyes closed, his face bloodless.

"He's almost gone," the priest said.

Marcus went to stand on the opposite side of the bed. The labored breathing coming from the bed gave him pause. Though his father had never shown him any outward sign of affection, Marcus took his hand, hoping to bring him some small comfort at the end of his life.

"I am here, Father."

Lord Charles struggled to open his eyes. A smile crossed his lips when he caught sight of his son. "Thank you," he wheezed.

Slowly, over the next several minutes, the life ebbed from the baron until his breathing ceased. Marcus released the hand he held and placed it back on the bed.

"I'd like to gather the servants and serfs and have you say mass for him this morning."

Father Pious studied him. "I will do as you wish, my lord. Will you now wed Lady Ailith? Your father would want you to honor his wishes now that he's gone."

"She has the measles. She may not live much longer herself."

"Herleva told me. It matters not. I can marry the two of you now. We'll need witnesses, though."

"I'll find some."

Marcus departed the solar and went downstairs. He sent a servant to find Sagar and Thomas. Within minutes, both men arrived.

"Follow me," he said, leading them upstairs. He paused in front of the bedchamber Lady Ailith now occupied.

"Have either of you contracted measles?"

Neither man had.

"My father requested that I wed Lady Ailith upon his death. Now that he has passed, I wish you to witness the ceremony. Stand at the door but come no closer," he warned.

Father Pious joined them and he and Marcus entered the bedchamber. A servant no more than ten and two sat with the baroness and her babe.

"Have you been here all night?" Marcus asked the girl. When she nodded, he said, "Go. Break your fast and then return."

The girl stood and placed the sleeping babe in her arms next to the baroness and left. Marcus saw how feverish the two were. Bright red spots covered both of them.

The priest shook Lady Ailith's shoulder lightly. "My lady?" he said several times.

The baroness finally opened her eyes. "I'm so parched."

Marcus took a pewter cup sitting next to the table and filled it with ale from a pitcher. He brought it to the noblewoman's parched lips and she drank greedily. He could feel the heat coming off her.

"My lady," he said gently, "I must give you some bad news."

Her eyes, glassy and wide, frightened him. He'd seen men dying on the battlefield who looked no worse. He thought she might pass at any moment.

"Is it my husband?" she asked. "Has he gone to God?"

Marcus seriously doubted God would have anything to do with Charles de Harte but he said, "Aye. Just a few minutes ago."

Ailith sighed. "I'm sorry I could not be with him. He was very good to me. Especially after he received word of your death, my lord. The baron wed me so that I would be under his protection. He dearly loved Livia and Mary, too."

Marcus brushed the hair back from her face. Despite his allegiance to Jess, he couldn't help but have tender feelings for this trusting woman who'd held his father in high regard.

"I plan to take care of you and your daughters now, my lady. Are you ready to wed me as you were supposed to?"

She looked startled. "Now? Shouldn't I mourn for my husband first?"

"'Twas what Lord Charles desired, my lady," Father Pious interjected. "He was thinking of you and your welfare until the very end."

Lady Ailith sighed. "If that is what my husband wanted . . ." Her voice trailed off.

"He did," Marcus assured her, looking to the priest. "Begin the ceremony," he ordered.

Father Pious did as Marcus asked. As they recited their vows, Mary awakened and began to wail. Marcus scooped up the feverish babe and held her close to his chest, quieting her.

Once they finished, the priest told him to kiss his bride. Marcus briefly touched his lips against his new wife's, again feeling the fever's heat radiate from her.

"I promise I will be well soon, my lord."

"Call me Marcus."

She gave him a weak smile. "Marcus," she echoed. "And I am Ailith." Exhausted, her eyes closed.

Marcus returned Mary to the bed, making sure her mother's arm was nestled securely about the babe, and he and the priest left the bedchamber. The servant girl had returned to nurse her mistress and Marcus closed the door.

He looked to the three men. "We'll have a funeral mass for my father this morning. For now, I would ask that you not speak of my marriage to Lady Ailith to anyone."

They agreed to his demand without question. Marcus realized it was because he was now the new, powerful Baron of Harteley.

Within the hour, the estate's servants and workers assembled in the chapel for the mass honoring his father. When it ended, Marcus pulled Sagar and Thomas aside.

"I will be gone part of the day but I'll be back before the evening meal."

He went to the stables and saddled Storm so that he could go to the mummers at Glenmore. He would gather his possessions and return to Hartefield for good. The troupe could do without him for the rest of the week. Peter would be more than an adequate replacement for him.

Marcus also came for Jess. He wanted to see if she could bring any relief to Ailith before death came for the young woman. He also admitted to himself that he couldn't stand to be away from Jess, married or not. He decided not to tell her of his marriage to Ailith, a woman he hadn't even known he was betrothed to. Marcus had done as his father asked and wed the ailing Ailith. He would make certain that Livia and Mary were provided for—if the babe lived. Poor Mary had looked even worse than her mother.

Once Ailith passed, Marcus would wed Jess as he'd planned.

He led Storm from the stables and mounted the horse. Marcus let his mind go blank as he rode toward Glenmore.

Toward Jess.

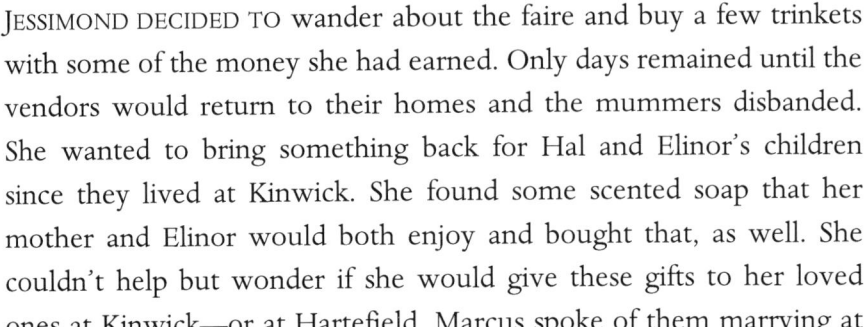

JESSIMOND DECIDED TO wander about the faire and buy a few trinkets with some of the money she had earned. Only days remained until the vendors would return to their homes and the mummers disbanded. She wanted to bring something back for Hal and Elinor's children since they lived at Kinwick. She found some scented soap that her mother and Elinor would both enjoy and bought that, as well. She couldn't help but wonder if she would give these gifts to her loved ones at Kinwick—or at Hartefield. Marcus spoke of them marrying at his family's estate, but she would want all those important to her to be a part of such a special day. It worried her that she hadn't yet told him of her true identity and hoped that, even seeing her with new eyes, he would accept her.

Returning to camp, she placed the purchases inside her tent and then wandered to the stage area. When she arrived, Jessimond saw Marcus had returned and was engaged in conversation with the Vawdrys. Her insides fluttered madly at the sight of him. She found it hard to believe that she had found love on the road. Her parents had always told Jessimond love would find her and that she needn't seek it out. Still, she had acted on her own and joined the mummers, so she felt somewhat responsible for placing herself in proximity with Marcus.

She still had much to learn about him. Now that she knew he was the son of a local baron, Jessimond wondered about his family and what Harte Castle would be like. The place would soon be her new home. She hoped she would grow to love it as much as she did Kinwick.

Marcus spied her coming and rewarded her with a smile that melted her bones. She joined the three men. It didn't go unnoticed that he slipped his arm about her waist and drew her possessively to him.

"Marcus has told us that his family lives nearby," Elias said. "He is leaving the troupe to return to them and he would like you to go with him, Jess."

Before she could reply, Peter strode up. "What's this?" he asked, frowning as he observed how familiar Marcus was being.

"My father passed away this morning," Marcus said. "My stepmother and her daughter are very ill. I want Jess to come with me and help care for them. I fear neither one has long to live and I would see them made as comfortable as possible." He paused. "Jess has little to do now. The costumes are all in fine shape. Bartholomew can sing to the crowds on his own. You can take my place with Rand. But I need your permission, Peter, since you are Jess' brother. May I bring her to Hartefield?"

Peter looked to her and back at Marcus. "Let me speak to Jess. Alone."

He took Jessimond's arm and led her away. "What's going on?"

"I think you know, Peter," she began. "I have fallen in love with Marcus. I thought he was a knight, as Rand is, but he's shared with me that he is the son of the Baron of Harteley." She corrected herself. "Actually, the baron is gone. Marcus is the new baron. He has asked me to marry him."

Her friend broke out in a broad smile and hugged her to him. "'Tis wonderful news, Jess." Then he frowned. "Wait. Marcus still thinks we are brother and sister. That means you haven't told him who you are."

Guilt washed over her. "I plan to. When the troupe disbands, I want you and Agatha to come to Hartefield first. I'll have written a missive to my parents and Ancel by then. You can deliver both and bring my parents to Harte Castle. Marcus wishes us to wed there."

"Not at Kinwick?" Peter frowned. "Lady Merryn will not be pleased."

Jessimond shrugged. "Once I tell Marcus of my background, we may decide to go to Kinwick instead. I'll know more once you arrive at Hartefield." She kissed his cheek. "So be a good brother and grant your permission to Marcus for me to accompany him to his home. I hope I can be of some service to his stepmother and her child."

"As long as you behave yourself," Peter teased.

She didn't make him any promises. The thought of being in a large castle full of rooms made her long to find an empty one and spend time alone with the man she loved.

They returned and found the Vawdrys gone.

Peter said to Marcus, "I will allow Jess to go to Hartefield with you. When our week is up at Glenmore, though, Agatha and I will come to her."

"We will always welcome both of you at Hartefield, Peter. If you decide you would like to remain with us instead of returning to Kinwick, I know it would please Jess. Rand thinks highly of your weapon skills. Mayhap, you would be interested in serving as a soldier in our garrison?"

"I'll think about it." Peter embraced Jessimond. "I will see you within a week. Take care." He kissed her cheek.

"I need to return to my tent," she said. "I want to get my case of herbs and a change of clothing."

"I'll bring your lute and anything else you leave behind," Peter promised.

Marcus escorted Jessimond back to camp, drawing her hand through the crook of his arm.

"I have missed you," he said, his voice rough and low, sending a thrill through her.

"No more than I have you."

She gathered her things and they returned to where Storm stood with the other horses. Rand greeted them.

"Jess and I are returning to Hartefield," Marcus told his friend. "My father died early this morning. According to Sagar, I have much to do since Father had been ill all summer and many things have been left undone."

"I see Jess is going with you," Rand noted.

"Aye. Lady Ailith and her babe are gravely ill. I'm hoping Jess can ease their suffering. When you return to Hartefield, Peter and Agatha will accompany you."

Rand nodded sagely. "So, that's how it is?"

Jessimond felt her cheeks heat as the knight studied them.

"Jess and I will wed soon," Marcus shared.

The knight looked at her. "Lady Margaret would be most pleased with your choice in a wife, my lord."

"My mother," prompted Marcus. "She passed on a couple of years ago."

"Lady Margaret was beloved by her people," Rand said. Smiling, he added, "I'm sure Lady Jess will also find she is loved. You've made Marcus happy. 'Twill be enough for them."

Marcus slipped her clothing into a satchel attached to Storm's pommel and then tied her case on, as well. Mounting the horse, he leaned down and lifted Jessimond so that she sat in front of him.

"See you soon," he called to Rand, who waved goodbye to them.

As they cantered away, Marcus' arm tightened about her waist, drawing her into his chest. He nuzzled her ear.

"It won't take long to reach the castle grounds."

Feeling secure in his arms, Jessimond said, "I don't care if it takes all night. As long as we are together."

CHAPTER 20

Jessimond noticed that Marcus slowed the horse. She looked ahead and didn't see their destination, though they had ridden for some time. Before she could ask, he turned the mount and entered the forest running alongside the road. He threw his leg over and came to the ground. Grinning, he clasped her waist and pulled her down next to him.

Marcus' fingers tightened on her waist as he leisurely explored her mouth. Her arms went about him. Jessimond gave herself over to the kiss, reveling in every stroke of his tongue against hers. He pulled away, leaving her breathless.

"I couldn't wait," he admitted. "I also know I'll be busy and we won't see each other much once we arrive at Harte Castle."

"We won't?" she asked, disappointed.

"I needed you nearby, Jess. Under the same roof. I would have been miserable being apart from you. I do have many new responsibilities, though. I'll need to throw myself into the affairs of the estate and make sure the fall harvest is going as planned."

"What of our wedding?"

"It must wait," he said firmly. "As long as Lady Ailith and little Mary are ill, they need to be our chief concern, though Livia, who's two, is in good health."

"What's wrong with them? Are they ill with what your father had?"

"Nay. He had withered away since last I saw him in May, as if something inside had eaten him up. My stepmother and half-sister have the measles."

Jessimond sighed. "I can give Lady Ailith something for her fever and a headache if she has one but measles must run their course." She paused. "Marcus, measles are very serious. You've mentioned a two-year-old girl and a babe. If Lady Ailith has given birth twice so quickly, her body already is in a weakened state. 'Twill be hard for her to fight through it, and even harder for a babe since she won't be able to drink from a bowl as her mother can."

He cupped her face tenderly. "That's why I thought you might ease their pain. I understand that they probably will not survive this crisis, Jess."

"I have not had the measles," she revealed.

"Then I want you nowhere near them. I have a servant tending to their needs now. You are to stay far away from the bedchamber they lie in, but you can pass along any herbs and instructions." He kissed her. "I don't want you catching this, sweetheart. Promise me you'll stay away from them."

"All right," Jessimond said reluctantly. It pained her that she would not be able to speak to her patients in person, but she knew how easily it would be for her to come down with the dreaded red spots if she didn't keep her distance.

She decided now was the time to reveal her identity to Marcus, before they reached Hartefield. Jessimond opened her mouth to speak but he kissed her again, greedily drinking her in. By the time he finished, her head swam. Marcus set her atop Storm and joined her, clicking his tongue. The horse took off at a gallop. Conversation would be impossible, especially for telling Marcus such unexpected news. She decided to wait until they had time alone before she bared her soul to him.

He stopped the horse again. "What do you think?"

She heard obvious pride in his voice and gazed in front of her. A lush valley stood beneath them, wheat fields golden with their abundant crops. Small cottages dotted the landscape. In the center of it all, tall, stone walls surrounded Harte Castle. From their vantage point, she could see both the outer and inner baileys and the keep itself.

"It's beautiful."

"I think so, too."

Jessimond marveled at how this estate would be her new home. She couldn't wait to explore it.

Marcus nudged Storm and the horse began cantering along again. Soon, they reached the gates and gained admittance. Marcus steered the horse to the stables and handed him off to a young boy. He untied her case and the satchel and told the boy to be generous with Storm's oats. They crossed the inner bailey, which appeared deserted.

"We're in time for the evening meal," he told her, leading her inside the keep and into the great hall.

Well over a hundred people had gathered to eat. Marcus led Jessimond to the dais. He set the satchel and case down and then lifted her onto the dais before seating her. A servant quickly appeared.

"Are you hungry, my lord?"

"Very hungry and even more thirsty."

"Be right back, my lord." The woman bobbed and disappeared.

Jessimond looked out over the crowd and noticed many people eyed her with interest. She glanced about, seeing the tapestries hanging on the walls were numerous and the rushes on the floor fragrant. The smell of roasted chicken wafted up, causing her stomach to gurgle noisily. Despite the fact that the lady of the castle lay ill, the servants had continued to complete their tasks. She thought it an excellent sign since it spoke highly of them.

The servant returned and she and Marcus ate their fill with what the girl brought to them.

"It's nice to eat someone else's cooking for a change," she remarked.

He took her hand under the table and squeezed it. "You were a much better cook than Agatha ever could be." He paused. "Will you want her and Peter to stay with us or do you think the Earl of Kinwick will be happy to have them return to his estate?"

Though Jessimond would enjoy having Agatha at Hartefield, she knew Peter would wish to remain with his family at Kinwick. One day, he would succeed his father as head blacksmith at the castle.

"I think that is a decision best made by the two of them together," she said. "Selfishly, I would like them here, but it is something they must weigh and consider."

Marcus sliced a bite of cheese and handed it to her. Jessimond sank her teeth into it.

"Oh, I am going to enjoy Hartefield's cheese. This is so rich and creamy."

"You'll have plenty of time to explore the keep while I'm away. For now, though, I wish to keep our marriage plans a secret."

"Why?" She was ready to shout the news from the treetops and was concerned that Marcus didn't feel the same way.

"My father only passed this morning. With Lady Ailith and Mary fighting for their lives, I think it appropriate to wait before we announce our intentions."

"Of course," she said. She understood he needed time to mourn and that they must do what they could to help those who were ill. Jessimond was determined to do everything she could to ensure that Lady Ailith and her child lived.

"You can help care for Livia if you'd like," he suggested. "She'll be missing her mother. Herleva, who is in charge of our servants, has made sure to keep the child away so she won't become ill."

"I'd enjoy that," Jessimond said. "I adore children."

He smiled. "I know you have experience raising them. You must be quite good at it since the earl and countess entrusted you with their grandchildren."

Jessimond felt guilty hearing the lie she'd told him come from his own lips.

"My lord? Could we spend some time discussing the estate?"

"Of course, Sagar. We can meet in the records room." Marcus turned to her. "Jess, this is Sagar, who has served the de Hartes for many years as our steward."

A woman came to stand next to Sagar. Marcus continued, "And this is Herleva, whom I spoke to you about. This is Jess Gilpin. She is a healer who has come to do what she can for my stepmother and the babe. Jess will also help care for Lady Livia."

With that, he handed her items to Herleva and helped Jessimond from the dais. "I'll leave you in Herleva's hands." He looked to the servant. "Find a bedchamber for Jess and under no circumstances is she to enter Lady Ailith's room. I don't want her exposed to the measles."

Marcus left with Sagar. Jessimond took her case from Herleva. "I can carry this. Would you take me to see Lady Ailith and her daughter now?"

"But Lord Marcus said—"

"He has warned me not to enter their chamber. I can stand in the doorway, though, and see how they are. It will help me decide what herbs to grind and prepare. The baron told me they both burned with fever."

The servant pursed her lips a moment, contemplating what to do. "Come along then."

She led Jessimond up the stairs and along a long corridor. Halting before a door, she said, "This is where Lady Livia is sleeping. Would you like to see her now?"

She smiled. "I would. And since I will help care for her, might I sleep in this chamber?"

Herleva returned her smile. "Of course. Come inside." She opened the door.

Jessimond stepped in and saw a lone candle burned next to the bed. She crossed the room and set her case down so she could sit on the bed. A child with a mass of dark ringlets slept, her breath soft and even. Jessimond brushed back the curls and saw how beautiful the little girl was. Her skin was very fair and long lashes swept across her cheeks.

This child would be an orphan unless she could do something to heal Lady Ailith. A deep longing rose within her as she watched this little one sleep. Either Jessimond would be able to save Livia's mother—or she would need to become a mother to this child. She brushed a kiss against the girl's forehead and rose.

Herleva had placed the satchel in a chair. Jessimond retrieved her herb case and the two women left the bedchamber. They walked past three more doors before the servant paused.

"Remember your promise and keep your distance," Herleva warned before opening the door.

Jessimond saw a woman younger than she was propped up against pillows. Her face, even more beautiful than her daughter's, held the spots of measles upon it. Seated in a chair was a young girl who rocked a babe. The infant also had angry red dots on her.

"Who are you?" Lady Ailith called out weakly.

"Lord Marcus brought Jess to help you," Herleva said. "She's a healer."

"See to Mary first," pleaded the noblewoman.

"I will help you both the best I can," promised Jess. To the servant, she asked, "Has the babe been feeding?"

"Nay. Lady Ailith's milk dried up. Lady Mary has had nothing for a day. Mayhap longer."

"What is your name?" Jessimond asked.

"Bea."

"All right, Bea. I will have Herleva find a nursing mother to express a small amount of milk into a bowl. You will take a small square of linen and dip it into the bowl and then hold it to Lady Mary's mouth. We want her to try and suck on the cloth. If she can get some nourishment that way, we'll also have her drink some of the water I steep herbs in the same way."

Jessimond looked to the mother in the bed. "You, my lady, also will need to drink. That will help you make milk for your babe. I will return soon with something for you to drink. It will have herbs to fight your fever and something to help you sleep. Sleep is a good tonic and will help you recover more quickly. I'll be back shortly."

She accompanied Herleva downstairs and told the servant, "I'll go to the kitchen and boil some water and grind my herbs there. Please find a nursing mother so we have some milk that we can try to give Lady Mary."

Half an hour later, Jessimond returned to the sickroom with two bowls. She set them on the floor and had Bea retrieve them.

"Lady Ailith is probably too weak to hold the bowl. You'll need to do that for her. Have her drink all but a small bit of the contents before you try to feed the babe."

She watched as the noblewoman drank the herbs steeped in water and then collapsed against the pillows again. Bea did as instructed and dipped the square into the milk before brushing it against Lady Mary's lips. She tried numerous times but the babe never attempted to suck on the cloth.

"What should I do?" wailed Bea.

"Remain calm," Jessimond said. "Try again every few minutes. Either she will or she won't. You cannot force her. I'll return after Lady Ailith has slept and see if what I gave her is working to break her fever."

"I'll try," Bea said, a dubious look on her face.

She returned to the sleeping Livia and climbed into bed next to her. The child nestled against Jessimond and gave a contented sigh. She closed her own eyes, sending a prayer to the Virgin Mary to guide her efforts to restore both of her patients to good health.

Hours later, Jessimond awakened. She slipped from the bed carefully so as not to wake Livia and returned to Lady Ailith's bedchamber. Opening the door, she heard soft weeping. The noblewoman slept so Jessimond knew the tears came from Bea.

The servant cradled Lady Mary in her arms. "I have tried, Jess. Many times. She cannot drink. She is barely breathing now." Bea stood. "Would you bring Father Pious? He should be here."

"You've done your best, Bea," Jessimond reassured the servant. "I knew there was but a slim chance that the babe would suck. I'll return with the priest."

She hurried downstairs and left the keep. They had passed a small chapel on their way in last night. She entered it now and saw a man kneeling near the altar, his head bowed. She went to him and touched his shoulder gently. He glanced up, looking perturbed at the interruption.

"I am sorry to disturb your prayers, Father, but Lady Mary may not be long for this world. Would you please come?"

Rising, he said, "Of course. Who are you?"

As they returned to the keep, Jessimond introduced herself and explained why she'd come to Hartefield.

"Lady Mary never had a chance," the priest said mournfully. "I only pray that Lady Ailith can recover."

They started down the long hallway. Jessimond saw Marcus emerge from what she thought would be the solar. He made his way toward them. She quickly explained the situation and he accompanied them to the sickroom. Both Marcus and Father Pious entered, leaving Jessimond hovering in the doorway.

Bea still shed tears and Jessimond saw that Lady Ailith was awake and also wept as she held her daughter in her arms.

"Do something," she said as the men approached her. "Please. Husband. Do something. Save her. Save my babe."

Jessimond shook her head. Poor Lady Ailith was delirious. Jessimond guessed that Marcus must favor his father and, in her feverish state, Lady Ailith confused the two. The noblewoman might not have been informed of her husband's death yesterday, due to her illness. Sorrow filled her, knowing that the woman had lost her husband and now her child.

The priest took the babe from her mother and began prayers for her. Marcus stood beside the bed and held his stepmother's hand. Jessimond thought how incongruous it was for a stepmother to be even younger than her stepson. From what little Marcus had said, his mother had only died a few years ago. The baron must have remarried very quickly in order to have fathered two daughters in such a short time.

"She is gone," Father Pious said softly. "Lady Mary is with her earthly father and her Heavenly Father."

Lady Ailith wailed mournfully. Marcus put his arms around her as she sobbed. Bea looked utterly lost.

"I'll will take Lady Mary to the chapel," the priest said. "Bea, come along and help me prepare her for burial."

Jessimond stepped aside as the two left the room, the bundled infant in Father Pious' arms, and closed the door behind them. Hopefully, Marcus could offer some comfort to Lady Ailith. Jessimond would see to choosing some new herbs that might help break the fever raging through the noblewoman's body.

First, though, she decided to check on Livia. Entering their shared bedchamber, she saw the child sitting up, rubbing the sleep from her eyes.

"Who are you?" the tiny voice asked.

"I'm Jess," she said as she sat on the bed. "I'm going to help take care of you."

"I want Mother," the girl said stubbornly and then thrust her thumb into her mouth. A loud sucking noise followed.

Jessimond pulled Livia into her lap and smoothed her curls. "Your mother is very sick. But she's going to get better."

Livia removed her thumb, her eyes wide and hopeful. "Soon?"

"Aye. Very soon, my little lady."

If it were the last thing she did, Jessimond would nurse Ailith de Harte back to full health.

CHAPTER 21

WHY HADN'T HE stayed with Jess at the mummers' camp?
Marcus cursed again, knowing he was backed into a corner. Time had run out. Within an hour or two, Rand would arrive with Peter and Agatha in tow.

And Ailith de Harte would live. He was trapped. For life.

"God's Blood and Bones!" he cried out, frustration seeping into every pore.

He sat alone in the records room at Harte Castle, ledgers scattered haphazardly across the desk in front of him. For the past week, some of his time had been spent here while the rest had been out on horseback checking on the estate or working with his soldiers in the training yard. Very little of it had been with Jess.

Why hadn't he left her with the Vawdrys? It would only have been for a handful of days.

Marcus was angry with himself for heeding Rand's urgent words and traveling to Hartefield in the first place. If he'd stayed with the troupe and finished out his last week in the Vawdrys' employ before they disbanded, he would have arrived to the news that his father was gone. A dead Charles de Harte wouldn't have been able to tell Marcus of his betrayal—much less share that his son was betrothed to Lady Ailith. Marcus would have assumed his role as the new Baron of Harteley and wed Jess.

Ailith, too, would certainly have been dead by today without Jess nursing her back to health. Though the baroness was still as weak as a newborn, Jess had beamed with pride when she told Marcus that his stepmother would make a full recovery. He could still hear Jess' words, telling him how relieved she was to have saved Lady Ailith's life since Marcus had already undergone so much loss recently.

The biggest loss would now be Jess.

If only he'd left her with the mummers and had Rand escort her when he returned to Hartefield today. Marcus could have spent the last waning days comforting his dying new wife and then buried her with no one other than Father Pious and two witnesses the wiser that the marriage had occurred. Instead, he'd been selfish and wanted the woman he loved nearby. Jess, being the good soul she was, had toiled day and night, concocting new brews for Ailith to drink until her high fever subsided and her cough was brought under control. She also created scented, soothing mixtures to bathe Ailith with to help ease the terrible itching from the rash that covered her entire body.

Ailith would live, thanks to Jess. The woman who meant everything to him had unwittingly chained him to a stranger and dashed any hopes of them ever joining together as man and wife.

Now, Marcus would have to tell Jess the truth—and watch the light go out of her eyes.

He rose, knowing what lay ahead was more difficult than any battle he'd ever fought. Dread coursed through him. Marcus didn't know how he would be able to survive without Jess in his life.

And what if his babe grew within her?

Reluctantly, he mounted the stairs, knowing he would find her sitting in the doorway of Ailith's bedchamber. Jess had spent countless hours there watching over her patient and many others keeping Livia entertained. He ventured down the corridor and saw the empty chair at the chamber's entrance. He wondered where Jess might be and decided to ask Ailith.

As Marcus came to the doorway, he glanced inside and saw Jess sitting next to Ailith's bed. Anger filled him. He had cautioned her not to enter the sickroom. Jess probably had decided Ailith was no longer contagious at this point but she shouldn't have made that choice without speaking to him.

He marched to the bed and heard Ailith say, "Nay, Jess, I know my first husband is dead. Marcus is my new husband."

Jess jumped to her feet, her body stiff as a board. She wheeled around and saw him. Those beautiful amethyst eyes were wide in horror as her jaw hung open.

"Jess, let me explain."

She pushed past him and fled the room. Marcus turned to follow.

From the bed, Ailith rasped, "What's wrong?"

He ignored his wife and ran after the love of his life.

Marcus caught up with her and grabbed her elbow. Jess spun and faced him, her eyes now dark and filled with tears that began to spill down her cheeks. He latched on to her other elbow, holding her in place, not knowing how to begin. She stared at him in silence.

"Jess, I was coming to tell you."

Her mouth trembled. "Now. You were coming to tell me now. That you are wed. To Lady Ailith."

"Aye," he said softly, dropping his head in shame.

"You *knew* you were wed to another and yet you dallied with me."

He raised his head as she squeezed her eyes shut, as if she couldn't stand the sight of him.

"All those times we talked. Laughed. Flirted. The times you kissed me. When you told me you cared for me." Her head fell. "When I gave you my virginity."

Her voice was so low he strained to hear those last words. As he did, it was like a knife to his heart.

"Jess. Look at me."

She shook her head.

"Please." His voice broke.

Slowly, she lifted her head. Her eyes streamed tears of anger and shame and sorrow.

"What I feel for you is real. Every moment spent in your company was an honest one. I didn't know I was betrothed to Ailith. Not even when I returned from two years of combat." He swallowed. "I arrived and found her in my father's bed. I called her his whore, not knowing that my mother had died. He told me Mother was gone. I realized, seeing the two little girls, just how fast he had remarried. I left Hartefield before I killed him."

Marcus paused and gathered his thoughts. "When I returned a week ago and found him dying, Father told me Ailith had been my intended bride. A surprise for me when I returned from battle. He'd served as my proxy and signed the betrothal contracts in my name. When Mother passed suddenly, his lust overcame his good sense. He told Ailith I'd been killed in combat and then pretended to wed her. Ailith has no idea they were never truly married. Livia and Mary are Father's bastards."

Jess' eyes grew wide.

"Father's dying request—no, demand—was for me to marry Ailith and take those girls under my protection. Ailith's fever raged out of control. Everyone told me she would be dead within days, if not hours. So I did the noble thing and wed her. She was already my wife by law. And I pitied her, for everything she had gone through. 'Tis why I brought you here, to help ease her suffering before she passed."

Dully, Jess said, "And I saved her instead."

"You did. Every day, I hated myself for I wished her to die. Every day, you worked another miracle and helped Ailith to grow stronger. Now, she will live."

"My actions have torn us apart," Jess said softly. Her tears flowed freely now. "I have become my mother. She loved a man betrothed to another." She paused. "I must leave. At once. Nay, Peter is on his way. I will wait for him and Agatha."

Marcus gripped her tightly. "I forbid it. You cannot leave me, Jess. I will wither and die without your touch."

Shock crossed her face. "You are *married*, Marcus. Married! I cannot stay at Hartefield another day." Her lips trembled. "I cannot watch you with your wife. See the children you two share play at your feet. Have my heart shattered into a thousand pieces every minute of the day. Nay, I will leave as soon as Peter comes."

"Jess," he pleaded. "Don't go." His own tears blinded him. "I love you. I've always loved you. I don't know why I couldn't say the words before but know they are true."

She recoiled as if scalded. "You cannot say them now," she hissed. "You can never say them to me again." Jess stiffened. "Release me, Marcus."

Reluctantly, he loosened his fingers and let his hands drop to his sides.

Jess gave him a wistful smile. "I suppose I should find comfort in knowing you truly loved me, but for your sake and Lady Ailith's, you must now let me go. You need to lead your life here—with your wife."

She turned and hurried down the corridor.

His heart rent in two as he watched each step take her further away from him.

Marcus had to say it once more. "I love you, Jess."

She glanced over her shoulder as she reached her bedchamber's door. "I know."

JESSIMOND FELL ACROSS the bed and wept. Sobs racked her entire body. Nausea overtook her and she stumbled to a basin and vomited. Too weak to walk, she leaned against the wall and slid down it until she hit the ground.

Marcus was married. To Lady Ailith. Bitterness filled Jessimond. She had prayed for hours to the Virgin Mary to intervene and save the noblewoman's life, especially after Ailith lost little Mary. She'd tried everything she knew to break the raging fever and calm the deep cough. She'd sat watching, instructing Bea to bathe Ailith's limbs over and over. And all the while, Jessimond worked to heal the wife of the man who held her heart and soul.

She dragged her feet closer and dropped her head against her knees. Wrapping her arms around her legs, she cried until no more tears came. Spent, she pushed herself to her feet and bathed her face in water before gathering her few possessions. The minute Peter arrived, they would leave. She didn't want to see or speak to Marcus or Ailith or Herleva or Livia or anyone she'd come to know during her stay at Hartefield. More than anything, she needed her family now. Thankfully, Ancel and Margery were not far away. They would have to cross Hartefield and then go the length of Sir Simeon de Grey's property, but after leaving Glenmore, they would be on Bexley lands.

Jessimond realized they would be walking so that their journey would take longer. It didn't matter, though. Nothing mattered anymore. She'd left Kinwick an innocent girl and would return a woman, somewhat wiser for having been foolish enough to fall in love with the wrong man. Her head told her that her heart would mend one day but, at this point, Jessimond thought she would be an old woman and still burn for Marcus de Harte's touch.

A knock sounded at the door. She threw back her shoulders and held her head high as she answered. Herleva stood there.

"I'm to tell you that Peter and Agatha are here," the servant said, looking at Jessimond with questioning eyes but wisely saying no more.

"Thank you."

She picked up the satchel and her herb case and followed Herleva downstairs. Peter and Agatha stood close together, both their brows knitted together in confusion. Rand came into view, his face betraying his knowledge of the impossible situation.

Suddenly, Livia toddled in from the great hall as Jessimond reached the bottom of the stairs. The girl threw her arms around Jessimond's legs and buried her head against Jessimond's knee.

Peter reached and took her things so that she could lift the child in her arms.

"You leave?" Livia asked, her mouth turning down in a frown.

"I am. Your mother is all better now. I told you she would be." Jessimond swallowed, blinking back tears.

Livia smiled. "I love you, Jess."

"I love you, too."

She kissed Livia's brow and set her on the ground. The girl ran off, giggling.

Rand stepped forward. Quietly, he said, "Marcus knows you do not wish to see him. He's asked that I lead a guard to escort you safely back to Kinwick."

Jessimond shook her head. "I want to see no one from Hartefield." She placed a hand on his forearm. "I need a clean break, Rand."

"He won't be happy," the knight said.

"Neither will I," she replied. "Just let us leave quietly."

"You don't even have horses, Jess. Can I at least provide you with a better horse and wagon than the one I bought from Elias? It barely got Peter and Agatha here. I'm afraid it will fall apart on the road to Kinwick."

"Nay. We will walk home if need be."

Rand enfolded her in his arms and held her tightly against him. Jessimond looked up and said, "Take care of him for me."

"I will."

With that promise, Rand released her. Jessimond nodded to Peter and he and Agatha accompanied her from the keep. A dilapidated wagon awaited them. She saw her lute in the back and climbed up into the wagon's bed. She claimed the lute, locking her arms possessively around it as Peter assisted Agatha. The girl came and sat next to Jessimond. She slipped her hand through Jessimond's arm and held it firmly.

Herleva ran out, a basket in her hand. She gave it to Peter and then hurried back inside the keep, her eyes avoiding Jessimond.

Peter set her things in the back and then climbed into the driver's seat. They passed through the gates of Hartefield and continued down the road. When they reached the end of it, Peter looked over his shoulder for instructions.

"Bexley. We go to Bexley," Jessimond confirmed.

CHAPTER 22

JESSIMOND DELIBERATELY KEPT her mind a blank. If she thought about the situation, she would collapse in grief. Peter kept the horse at a walk so the cart wouldn't fall apart from the vibrations. She wondered how far the vehicle would make it before disintegrating.

Finally, they crossed from Hartefield to Glenmore. She waited until she thought they were halfway across Lord Simeon's estate and called out to Peter to pull off the road. He did as she asked and assisted her and Agatha from the wagon. Jessimond indicated the basket and he lifted it. They walked a few paces and sat on the ground. Without a word, Peter opened the basket and distributed the legs of chicken and gave Jessimond the loaf of bread to divide. He began slicing cheese.

"There are things you need to know, Agatha," Jessimond began.

"About Kinwick?" Agatha asked. "Or why you parted on poor terms with Marcus."

"He's not Marcus. He's Lord Marcus de Harte, the Baron of Harteley. His father passed last week and as the only de Harte son, Marcus inherited the title," she explained.

Agatha face crumpled. "Since he's a lord now, he doesn't want you anymore, Jess?"

"Nay, Agatha. Lord Marcus already has a wife."

Her talkative friend only stared at her, dumfounded. Peter sprang to his feet. Jessimond feared he might take off running to Hartefield and pummel Marcus to a bloody lump.

She held a hand up. "Wait, Peter."

He froze. "Why should I?" he said, his tone surly.

"Lord Marcus did not know he was betrothed when he joined the mummers. His father handled the betrothal contracts and acted as his proxy while he was away fighting with the king."

Peter thought a moment and then argued, "But he returned to Hartefield. Saw his father. And he still came back for you, Jess." His fists began to flex.

"His wife was a few heartbeats from death." She paused to let that sink in.

"Lord Marcus has a tender heart," Agatha pointed out. "That's why he came for Jess. He wanted her to ease the baroness' suffering."

"Aye," Jessimond agreed. "Only my mother taught me too well, I suppose. Lady Ailith is still ill but she will recover. Lord Marcus must remain true to his vows with her."

Pain crossed Peter's face. "I am so sorry, Jess." He came and sat next to her, putting his arm about her shoulder and drawing her close. "I would not have understood before now. I know Lord Marcus loves you as much as I love Agatha. If I had to give her up now, I would be lost."

She took comfort in Peter's presence but pressed on. "Agatha, there is more to my story. Just as Marcus is Lord Marcus, I am also of the nobility. I am Lady Jessimond de Montfort, youngest daughter of the Earl and Countess of Kinwick."

Agatha couldn't hide her astonishment. She looked from Jessimond to Peter. "So . . . you aren't brother and sister?"

"Nay. Peter is the son of our blacksmith and is a fine one in his own right. We grew up playing together since I am the youngest of six and my siblings are much older than I am. Peter and I are only a year apart."

Agatha thought things over. "I like your name. Jessimond. It suits you."

"Sometimes my family does call me Jess."

Agatha frowned. "Why were you with the mummers? I don't understand."

"You don't have to understand everything now," Jessimond reassured her. "Just know that you have a place at Kinwick, whether it is helping inside the keep or merely taking care of Peter."

"This is so much to take in."

"There's more, I'm afraid. We aren't going to Kinwick first. The next estate after Glenmore belongs to my oldest brother, Ancel. He is the Earl of Mauntell. We will remain at Bexley and send word to Kinwick. My parents will come once they receive my missive and then escort us home."

"My lady? Does Lord Marcus know you are a daughter of Kinwick and not a mere servant there?" Peter asked.

She shook her head. "I was going to tell him but I never found time alone with him. He was consumed with his new responsibilities at Hartefield while I spent my time nursing Lady Ailith or caring for Livia, her child."

"Whose child is Lady Livia?" Agatha asked.

"That is where things become complicated," Jessimond said. "For now, you know all you need to know. I would ask that neither of you speak of my special friendship with Marcus. My feelings are still raw since I only learned of his marriage today. In time, I might be able to discuss it. For now? I want to enjoy my time with Ancel and Margery and close the door on the last few months."

"If that's what you wish, we will respect that," Peter said.

Jessimond stood. "Good. Let's continue on to Bexley."

Peter assisted them into the cart's bed again and after three hours, they arrived. Driving through the gates, the two rear wheels on the vehicle collapsed and one side fell to the ground. She and Agatha gingerly climbed from the wagon while Peter removed their possessions and placed them on the ground.

"Free the horse and take him to the stables," Jessimond instructed Peter. "I'll have someone come for our things. Mayhap the wood from the wagon can be chopped and used as firewood. Agatha, come with me to the keep."

As they started off, her friend said, "I hope I will remember to call you Lady Jessimond from now on."

"If you forget, it's not a problem," she assured Agatha, leading her through the bailey.

When they reached the keep, Jessimond's heart began pounding with the familiar faces she saw awaiting her.

"Jess!" Nan cried. She moved toward Jessimond and immediately, Jessimond saw that her sister was again with child. Looking at Nan's slighted rounded belly, she believed the child would come next February or March.

They embraced and she said, "I see I am to be an aunt again. Since you already have a boy and a girl, what do wish for this time?"

Nan laughed, her hands going to her belly and rubbing it affectionately. "Tristan says as long as the babe is healthy, we should be happy with whatever comes out." Nan hugged her again. "Oh, it's so good to see you, Jess."

By now, Margery and Elysande had joined them. Jessimond embraced her cousin. Elysande had taught her to ride and then much about horses. She had fond memories of time spent at Sandbourne and in its stables.

"What are you doing here?" she asked.

"Nan and Tristan came on their annual pilgrimage to purchase some Sandbourne horses," Elysande revealed. "Michael and I decided to accompany them back to Leventhorpe and make sure the horses were settled in."

Margery held out her arms and Jessimond went to her brother's wife.

"Fortunately, they all decided to stop for a brief visit at Bexley on their way to Leventhorpe," Margery said. "When I told them you were due to arrive, they wanted to wait and see you."

"Oh!" Jessimond realized she'd forgotten all about Agatha. She turned and saw the young woman hanging back. She waved her forward and noticed Peter coming toward their group. "This is Agatha. She will be coming to Kinwick when I return. She and Peter plan to wed."

"Congratulations," the three women said in unison and laughed.

"Nice to meet you, Agatha," Nan said. As Peter arrived, she greeted him. "Well done, Peter. She's lovely."

"Thank you, Lady Nan. 'Tis good to see you."

"Let's return to the keep," Margery suggested. "The men will be through in the training yard soon. I'll need to arrange a place for Agatha and Peter to stay."

"I can sleep in the stables tonight, my lady, since I'll leave at first light for Kinwick," Peter said. He looked to Jessimond. "Will you have written a missive for me to deliver to Lord Geoffrey and Lady Merryn by then?"

Jessimond thought of the message she had written in her mind several times this past week, the one telling her parents that she had fallen in love with Marcus de Harte and would wed him. Words that would never be written, much less delivered.

"Nay, Peter. Simply tell my parents that I arrived safely at Bexley and am eager to see them," she replied.

"Very good, my lady."

Margery led them back to the keep and handed Agatha off to a servant. She also asked that the evening meal be brought to the solar so that the family could enjoy private time together. The women had only talked for a few minutes when Ancel, Michael, and Tristan entered and three servants brought huge platters of food.

She embraced Michael and Tristan and then let Ancel pick her up and swing her around. He set her down and frowned.

"What's wrong, Jessimond?" he asked, drawing her away from the others.

"Nothing," she quickly assured him. "I'm merely worn out after months of travel on the road."

His palm cradled her face. "You know I would do anything for you."

She covered his hand with hers. "I know you would slay dragons for me, Ancel. If I see any, I will certainly call you," she said teasingly.

He kissed her forehead and then looked to the others. Jessimond saw the table now laden with food as everyone began seating themselves.

"I am so hungry," she proclaimed. "Let's eat."

She and Ancel took a place at the table as the group began filling their trenchers. She saw venison with frumenty and inhaled its heavy spices, and looked forward to eating the blackmanger she spied, as well.

"I want to hear about your time with the mummers," Tristan said.

Jessimond told them of King Ralph's talent and how the others vied for various roles. She recalled funny stories involving Jopp and shared how the Vawdrys ran the troupe, as well as the various places they'd journeyed.

"What were you involved with?" asked Michael.

"My chief task was mending costumes that had been damaged and sewing new ones for upcoming plays. I also cooked many of the troupe's evening meals. Probably my favorite thing was serving as a troubadour during a part of every day."

She related how Bartholomew had fallen ill and how she'd stepped into his shoes for a few performances.

"Once he returned, Elias and Moss asked if I would join Bartholomew on stage before each play began. The crowds seemed to enjoy that. We sang some songs together and performed a solo each time."

"I've always enjoyed when you and Beatrice sing together in Kinwick's great hall," Margery said.

"You and Beatrice harmonize beautifully," Elysande added. "I'm sure your voice also blended nicely with Bartholomew's." She sighed. "I wish I had such a talent and could sing."

Tristan laughed. "Your talent is knowing horses, Elysande."

Michael slipped an arm about his wife's waist. "And keeping me happy." He growled and kissed her cheek.

A wave of sadness swept through Jessimond at the sweet, familiar gesture. Marcus would be doing the same kind of things to Ailith once she healed, while Jessimond would spend the rest of her life alone. She glanced up and saw Nan studying her with interest.

To place the focus on others in their group, Jessimond said, "I have been dominating the conversation tonight. I need you to tell me what's been happening with your families since the last time I saw you."

Talk turned to their children and estates. Jessimond sat back and listened quietly, no longer adding anything to the conversation.

Finally, the hour grew late and Margery said, "Let me take you to your bedchamber, Jessimond."

"I can do that," Nan volunteered. She stood and waited for Jessimond to do the same and then linked their arms. Looking to Tristan, she said, "Would you check on the children? I won't be long."

Nan led her down the corridor and opened a chamber door. Ushering her inside, she closed it behind her and then released Jessimond's arm.

"I know you better than anyone, Jess. You're hiding something from me. From us all. Please, tell me what's wrong. Let me help you. Whatever it is, I want to make things right for you."

Jessimond burst into tears and fell into her sister's arms.

CHAPTER 23

JESSIMOND SWUNG HER sword. It met Nan's and the clang of steel sounded. Her arms reverberated with the contact. She'd been reluctant to spar with her sister, due to her delicate condition, but Nan insisted.

"I'm always sick most of the morning during the first few months but as I enter my fourth month, it never fails. I get a burst of energy and feel as if I can conquer the world," Nan had shared.

The way her sister moved gracefully now verified her words. With that reassurance, Jessimond had agreed to duel with Nan. Her advice to Jessimond had been to keep busy each day until Geoffrey and Merryn arrived. Consequently, Jessimond's hours had been filled from mass shortly after dawn each morning until bedtime. She'd taken long, daily rides with Elysande and even helped her cousin tend to a lame horse in the Bexley stables. With Margery, Jessimond had worked in the gardens, baked bread, and made candles. Though Ancel's three children were away fostering, she'd been able to spend many hours playing with Nan's two little ones. Her niece was two and her nephew five. Both were adorable and inquisitive.

She did fall into bed at night exhausted from all of the day's activities—but sleep took its time coming. Despite knowing it would bring her nothing but misery, Jessimond lay awake and thought about Marcus. She recalled the first time she'd caught sight of him that day in June. Remembered watching him duel with Rand and his few turns as an actor when called upon. She could see him unloading the wagons and pitching the mummers' tents at each stop, and thought back to how he helped her carry the dishes to a stream to be cleaned.

And their kisses. Those many, drugging kisses.

Jessimond tried her best to remember each occasion they kissed. The sensations she'd felt. The feel of his sleek muscles bunching beneath her fingers. His scent. His taste. Over and over, she relived their time alone in the cottage, when she'd given everything of herself to him. Coming together, their bodies as one. Love for him would surge through her at these memories.

Then the tears would begin to flow. She knew it was wrong to wallow in such memories but she couldn't help herself. Marcus had come so suddenly in her life and then left it even more abruptly. She would do everything in her power to remember everything about him and never forget.

For memories would be all she would ever possess of him. He belonged to another now. It mattered not—Jessimond would love Marcus de Harte for the remainder of her life.

The sound of a sword slicing through the air had her dance back just in time.

"That was much too close," Nan admonished, giving her a long look. "Don't let your mind wander."

"I'm sorry."

They continued for several minutes until Nan called a halt to their swordplay.

"I'm getting hungry," she explained.

"You stay hungry," Jessimond teased.

Nan laughed. "I'm simply making up for the weeks I couldn't keep my morning meal down." She rubbed her belly with both hands. "I need to make sure this little one grows strong. Who knows? I might even carry two babes inside me, like Alys and Ancel. That would certainly surprise Tristan."

Her sister linked an arm through Jessimond's. "Let's go inside."

Suddenly, Margery appeared. "They're here. The de Montfort banner has been sighted from the wall walk." She frowned at them and Jessimond was aware of how disheveled they appeared after their bout. "You have time to change your clothing if you hurry."

Jessimond and Nan rushed into the keep and parted, each seeking their separate bedchamber. Jessimond stripped off her tunic and pants and washed her hands and face before donning one of the smocks and cotehardies Margery had loaned her. She went into the corridor and saw Nan emerging from her room, closing the door behind her.

"Are the children still napping?" she asked.

"Aye. Like sleeping angels. Let's go greet Mother and Father."

They joined Margery, who now stood with Ancel, at the entrance to the keep. Michael, Elysande, and Tristan had joined them. Jessimond heard the sound of hoof beats growing closer and then spied her family's banner as the riders entered the inner bailey. Her throat grew thick with emotion as she caught sight of her parents. Love blossomed in her heart for these two wonderful people who had taken in a babe of unknown origin and loved her as one of their own. She broke away from the group and ran toward them.

Her father pulled on his reins and leaped from his horse. He gathered her up and Jessimond relaxed for the first time since she'd arrived at Bexley. Being in Geoffrey de Montfort's arms brought a sense of security. It was the beginning of her healing.

He released her. "I know it's only been a few months, Jessimond, but I have missed you so much, my sweet girl." He brushed a tender kiss against her brow. Jessimond felt truly treasured.

Her mother appeared and wrapped Jessimond in a tight embrace. No words were needed as they clung to one another.

Merryn finally relaxed her grip and looked at Jessimond. "You grow more beautiful every day. I hope you found what you were looking for on the road."

Tears welled in her eyes. "I have much to share with you and Father. In private."

Merryn nodded. "Let me greet the others. Then we will talk."

After many hugs and kisses, Jessimond saw her mother whisper something to Margery. Immediately, her sister-in-law said, "Why don't you three go to the solar for a more private reunion? I know Jessimond must have so much to tell you about her travels."

"We'll return to the training yard for now," Ancel said, leading Michael and Tristan away.

The three women escorted them upstairs as they discussed the child Nan carried. As Jessimond thought, Nan said the babe would be due come February.

"I'll have food and drink brought to you," Margery said. "You must be famished after your journey."

"Wine is all we need now, Margery," Merryn told her.

Margery poured it for them. "We will see you later."

Merryn smiled at her daughter. "I cannot wait to see my grandchildren."

"They'll be awake and ready to talk your ear off," Nan promised.

Once the others left, Merryn seated herself and turned to Jessimond. She didn't speak but gave her an encouraging look.

Jessimond said, "I am torn. I have two important things to tell you. It's hard to know where to begin." She took a seat opposite her mother and her father remained standing. Geoffrey always had trouble sitting for long spells, especially after riding a great distance.

"Open your heart," he told Jessimond. "Speak of what matters most, first."

"Very well." She clasped her hands tightly in her lap. "I fell in love this summer." She paused to let her words sink in.

Neither of her parents said anything. They merely waited for her to continue.

"I am sure you can tell by my face that it did not end well. Nan and the others have done their best to help me keep my mind off Marcus, but he's all I want—and someone I can never have."

The tears came freely now. Her father knelt beside her and took her hands, warming them in his. She hadn't realized how cold they were until he did so. Her mother moved to sit next to her. Her physical presence comforted Jessimond as Merryn's arms went about her. They made no demands upon her. Slowly, Jessimond's sobs subsided and she gained control of her emotions.

Merryn stroked her hair. "Tell us about Marcus. Where you met."

Jessimond took a deep breath and let it out slowly. "He was a knight traveling with the mummers this season," she began.

Gradually, her story—their story—unfolded. Jessimond told her parents as much as they needed to know, though she left out her one coupling with Marcus. Some things should remain forever in her heart.

Once she finished, she looked at them expectantly. "I love him. I will always love him. Though he is bound to another, I feel as if our souls are linked as one. I may or may not wed one day. Who knows what my future may bring? But I will hold this love in my heart for Marcus until my dying day."

"I understand, Jessimond," her mother said. "When your father was gone for those seven years, my feelings for him never lessened. I knew the king would marry me off at some point but my heart told me I would always belong to Geoffrey de Montfort, both in this life and in any to come."

Her father squeezed Jessimond's hands. "'Twas the same for me." He gave his wife a long look that spoke of his devotion to her even now. "Loving your mother was what got me through my lonely years of imprisonment. When I was finally released and able to come back to her, we knew in an instant that the love still ran deep between us."

Geoffrey paused. "Those first weeks together were hard. Far from perfect. We had grown to be very different people in those years apart. But love for one another was entrenched in our cores." He kissed her cheek. "So we understand how strong your feelings run for this nobleman."

Merryn added, "You know you always have a home with us, Jessimond. If you choose not to wed, we will understand. If you decide to marry, though, we hope you will do your best to make you and your husband happy." She stroked Jessimond's hair again. "You are such a nurturing soul, my dearest one. I do hope one day you will be able to find room in your heart for another man. To wed him and give him children."

"That is far in my future, Mother." Jessimond paused. "There is more. Much more. I also discovered where I came from this summer," she confided.

Merryn's sharp intake of breath gave Jessimond pause. Geoffrey's grip on her hands tightened.

"Mayhap this isn't something you wish to hear."

"Nay," Merryn assured her. "We were curious in the beginning. Looked high and low to see if anyone would claim you."

"And secretly prayed that no one would step forward," Geoffrey added. "It would have killed all of us—Nan, in particular—if someone had taken you from us. You became a part of our family from the start."

"Tell us how this came about," Merryn urged.

"It happened while I was singing." Seeing her parents' astonished faces, she realized they knew nothing of her life with the mummers' troupe these past few months.

"Besides sewing and cooking, I joined the Vawdrys' troubadour, Bartholomew, before each play. We performed a half-dozen songs for the crowd."

"You've always been shy about your singing, though you have a lovely voice," Merryn said. "I've always enjoyed when you and Beatrice have sung for us, especially at Christmastime."

"I've learned a great deal about myself," Jessimond said. "Grown in confidence. I'm not who I was when I left Kinwick in June."

"Go on," Geoffrey encouraged.

Jessimond explained about the man who'd stared at her and how the knight approached her after her performance, questioning her and telling her he'd return with his liege lord to hear her sing.

"They did and Lord Gregory, who is the Baron of Netherfield, revealed to me the story buried in his past. Of how he'd been betrothed to one woman and had fallen in love with another."

She saw in her mother's eyes that Merryn didn't miss the fact that history had repeated itself.

"Lord Gregory told of entrusting Sir Rodric, the knight who first approached me, and charging him to bring my mother and me to her family's home."

"Did you learn her name?" Geoffrey asked.

"Celia. Lady Celia Achard. She was weakened from childbirth and died on the journey to her home. Sir Rodric was familiar with you and mother. He'd met you both at court previously and respected you. He decided it was better to leave me on Kinwick lands and give me a chance at a good life, rather than take me to my mother's home and have her family give away her bastard child."

Jessimond sighed. "I knew for certain I was this child when Sir Rodric told of the amethyst brooch he'd left with me, hoping something that valuable would convince a tenant of Kinwick to take me in."

"Little knowing Nan and I would find you and bring you to the castle," Geoffrey noted.

"Aye. Lord Gregory verified that he'd given the brooch to my mother because it matched her amethyst-colored eyes. He told me I look exactly as Celia did. That was how he and Sir Rodric recognized me in the first place."

Jessimond finally took a long drink from her goblet. "I told them very little about myself. They knew I'd been adopted by a family at Kinwick but not which one. I didn't explain to them why I traveled with the mummers' troupe. Lord Gregory did invite me to visit him at Netherfield if I ever felt comfortable doing so."

"What would his lady wife say to the arrival of her husband's lovechild after so many years?" Merryn asked.

"She died years ago. The baron told his son and two daughters about me after she was gone. They've encouraged him to seek me out."

Her father gazed lovingly at her and asked, "Would you like to visit this birth father, Jessimond? Meet your half-siblings?"

She shrugged. "I hadn't thought I would. I was reluctant to even tell you and Mother about this encounter and what I'd learned."

"Why?" they both asked at the same time.

"I didn't want to hurt you," she admitted. "I thought you might think I loved you less for seeking them out."

"Nay," Geoffrey said vehemently. "Family is important. If this man and his children desire to know you, you should give them every chance to do so. All of your lives will be richer for coming together."

He lifted her hands and kissed them tenderly. "You will always be ours, Jessimond. You will forever be a de Montfort. But if you wish to know these blood relatives, I encourage you to visit them." He smiled at her fondly. "A heart has a great capacity for love. I know yours has room for us and this new family, as well."

"Thank you," Jessimond said, overcome with emotion.

"You don't have to decide now," Merryn said. "Think on it."

"I don't have to, Mother." She looked at them hopefully. "Could we call at Netherfield on our way home to Kinwick?"

"Consider it done," Geoffrey said.

CHAPTER 24

JESSIMOND TRIED TO quell her nerves as they drew closer to the cutoff point to Netherfield. Ancel had been familiar with where the estate lay and had given them good directions. Fortunately, their party would pass fairly near Netherfield on their way home to Kinwick since the baron's land sat a few leagues from the road they now traveled. Her father had told Jessimond at any point if she decided to abstain from visiting Gregory de Challon to let him know. They would continue home and never speak of it again.

Geoffrey turned his mount from where he led the escort party and approached Jessimond and her mother. They rode in the center of the ten knights escorting them. Two others had been left behind with Peter and Agatha, who would travel by cart and go straightaway to Kinwick.

"Have you changed your mind?" he asked, those familiar, patient eyes searching her own.

"Nay, Father," she replied. "It may not work out to my liking. We may leave after only a few minutes. But I don't want to hold on to a lifetime of regret simply because I didn't have the courage to face this situation."

His smile was reward enough. "That's my girl." He spurred on his horse and returned to the front of their group.

Jessimond wondered what kind of reception they would receive when they reached Netherfield unannounced. Since she hadn't known if they would stop or not, no messenger had been sent ahead to inform the baron of their impending stop. Even now, she noticed that her father did not motion for a rider to peel away from the group. Their visit truly would be one of surprise.

Would it be one of acceptance?

She remembered how Peter had encouraged her not to sit in judgment of Gregory de Challon and his actions from almost a score ago. Since she now found herself in similar circumstances to Celia Achard, Jessimond was much more understanding toward her birth parents. Celia had loved Gregory, despite the fact that he was betrothed and sent her away after she'd given birth to his child. Jessimond still loved Marcus, even though he was husband to another woman. He would hold her heart even beyond the grave.

She was certain he felt the same about her.

Circumstances, though, had torn them apart. Marcus would make a new life with Ailith and become father to her young daughter, Livia. Jessimond would also need to move forward and forge her own way. Taking this step by going to Netherfield was the first of many in a life without Marcus. She was glad she had the support of her parents in this unusual endeavor. If she was welcomed by Lord Gregory, she would remain at Netherfield for a visit. If the nobleman no longer wished to know her because of the harsh way they'd parted, she would return to Kinwick without regret, knowing she had given Lord Gregory the opportunity to learn more about her.

They arrived at the locked gates and their party waited. Merryn reached out and touched Jessimond's shoulder. She gave her mother a tight smile, trying to keep a firm rein on her emotions as the gatekeeper admitted them to the castle grounds. They trotted through the baileys as workers paused and openly studied them, interested in the new arrivals. Before they reached the keep, she spied Lord Gregory as he hurried toward them.

From the look of it, the baron came straight from the training yard, where he must have been hard at work with his soldiers. His dark blond hair was damp with sweat and his face red from exertion. He still carried a sword in his hand.

Her mother said, "He doesn't look anything like you. Are you sure—"

"I am." Jessimond slipped from her horse and went to meet the nobleman.

Lord Gregory halted in his tracks. He looked from her to Geoffrey de Montfort and back.

"You had Lord Geoffrey escort you here?" he asked in surprise. Then he threw his arms about her. "I am so glad you came, Jessimond." He held her to him a long moment and then pulled away.

Still gripping her shoulders, he said, "I didn't think you would ever come. You seemed so adamant when I last saw you. I never thought I would lay eyes upon you again."

"I'm sorry. Meeting you—and hearing what you had to say—shocked me. It took time for me to digest what you revealed."

The baron kissed her cheek and released her. He turned to her father, who had dismounted, as had all of their party. Her mother had come to stand next to her husband.

Jessimond took a deep breath and said, "Lord Gregory, I would like to introduce you to my parents, Lord Geoffrey and Lady Merryn de Montfort."

The baron's jaw dropped and his eyes widened. "By the Christ! The earl and countess are the ones who took you in?"

Tears began to stream down his face as he moved toward her parents, his hand thrust out. Geoffrey took it and then Lord Gregory accepted Merryn's offered hand and kissed it.

"I cannot begin to tell you how grateful I am to you for raising Jessimond." His voice cracked as he said her name. "I don't know what she's told you but my prayers were answered far beyond what I asked of the Holy Father."

"It was a privilege to add Jessimond into our fold," Merryn said. "She is the youngest of our six children."

"And the one with the sweetest temperament," Geoffrey added.

Lord Gregory looked at them hesitantly. "Would you ... would you like to come inside the keep? We could ... talk for a while."

Jessimond spoke up. "We would like to stay a bit, my lord. At least, I was hoping that I might visit for a few weeks if you are receptive to the idea."

Relief—then joy—broke out across de Challon's face. "I would be honored." He looked to Geoffrey. "Mayhap you and Lady Merryn would care to stay a few days before leaving Jessimond in my care? I want to prove myself worthy to you." His face darkened. "I was immature and self-absorbed in my youth. I know now I should have cared better for Celia and for Jessimond. That experience changed me for the better."

"We would be delighted to accept your hospitality," Geoffrey said.

Lord Gregory had the de Montfort men take their horses to his stables and told them they would be welcomed at the evening meal and could stay in his soldiers' quarters during their visit. He also offered them the use of his training yard and expressed his hope that they would spar with the Netherfield soldiers. Then he led the others into the keep.

After speaking to a servant, he led them upstairs to the solar.

"Food and drink will arrive shortly. I thought it best to take our evening meal together in private."

He ushered them inside and continued. "My son, Byrom, is not home at present. He is fostering in the north. I will send word to him that his half-sister has visited Netherfield." He looked at Jessimond. "I hope that you will agree to come back another time so that you might meet Byrom."

"How old is your boy?" Merryn asked.

"Ten and six, my lady. He is already taller than I am and wields a sword with confidence."

"You mentioned that I also have two half-sisters," Jessimond said.

"Aye. They will be here momentarily."

As the baron finished speaking, the door to the solar swung open.

"Where is she?" a young girl cried as she raced into the room, followed by a more sedate one near Jessimond's age.

Both stopped, the younger one gawking at Jessimond as the older offered her a shy smile.

Lord Gregory said, "This is my daughter, Lora, who is ten and eight, and my youngest child, Lina."

"I'm ten and two," Lina said. "And very curious about you. Father didn't think you would come to visit." She studied Jessimond with interest. "You are quite beautiful but you don't look like a de Challon at all. Are you certain this Jessimond is your daughter, Father?"

Jessimond noticed the indulgent smile the baron gave her as he said, "I am. Just as Byrom resembles me strongly, Jessimond is the image of Celia Achard. In fact, I called her by Celia's name when I first laid eyes upon her. The likeness was that strong. I have no doubt she is our child." He turned to Jessimond. "When I first caught sight of you, it was like seeing your mother all over again after being parted from her by twenty years. And death," he added quietly.

"My grandmother always said that Lora and I favor our mother. She's also dead," Lina said matter-of-factly.

Jessimond wondered about the raven hair both Lora and Lina possessed, and had guessed it came from their mother.

"Both my daughters take after Egelina in their looks and height," Lord Gregory said. "Lora is reserved, though, while you can see Lina is more outgoing."

"And what is Byrom like?" Jessimond asked.

"Byrom is wonderful," proclaimed Lina. "The best brother there ever was."

Lora stepped forward and dropped a curtsey to Jessimond's parents, urging Lina to do the same. "I am sorry my sister burst into the room and we haven't been properly introduced to one another. You know I am Lora de Challon and Lina is my younger sister. May I inquire who you might be?"

Jessimond stepped forward to make the introduction. "These are my parents, Lord Geoffrey and Lady Merryn de Montfort. They are the Earl and Countess of Kinwick."

"Your parents?" Lina asked, her shock obvious. "Father said that you'd been left at Kinwick and that serfs must have taken you in." She frowned. "So, why were you traveling with a mummers' troupe if you are part of the nobility? Was it to escape your parents? Do they treat you less than their own children?"

Horrified by the girl's indiscreet questions, Jessimond started to reply—but Lina looked to Merryn and boldly asked, "Is it hard loving someone who isn't truly your child? Do you make Jessimond clean the keep and wait on your children like a servant?"

"Lina!" her father roared, his face darkening in anger.

The girl shrugged. "I'm merely curious, Father. I cannot imagine finding a babe and bringing it home, only to treat it like a family member."

"That's exactly who Jessimond is to us, Lina," Merryn said firmly, her tone indicating she would tolerate no nonsense from the youngest de Challon. "From the moment Geoffrey and Nan brought Jessimond home, she became an integral part of our family. I can't think of her as anything *but* a de Montfort. Sometimes, I think she is the most loved of all of our children because she is the youngest of six and no more came after her."

Lina looked amazed hearing such a revelation. "Even though she didn't grow in your belly, you really think of her as your own? You truly love her as much as one of your other children?"

"Aye," Geoffrey said, his voice strong, brokering no doubt. "Jessimond is a de Montfort, through and through. I love Jessimond no less—and no more—than her other siblings. Merryn and I do love each of our children in different ways, though. Sometimes, one child needs more attention lavished upon them than another one, but our hearts have room to love them all."

Jessimond finally spoke up. "I already have a family—but I came to Netherfield in order to have the opportunity to spend time with my birth father and my half-siblings. To get to know you. You may not ever love me but I hope we can at least become friends."

"I would like that," Lora said, her eyes brimming with tears. She reached and took Jessimond's hand and squeezed it.

Not to be outdone, Lina latched on to the other one. "Would you like to see the keep, Jessimond?"

Before she could reply, three servants arrived with trays of food.

"Let's enjoy our meal first," Lord Gregory recommended. "Jessimond and her parents have been traveling and could use some food and drink."

As they sat, her half-sisters on each side of her, Jessimond hoped that these girls would accept her as readily as all the de Montforts had done on that day almost a score ago.

CHAPTER 25

JESSIMOND WATCHED LORA twirl about, a sweet smile on her face.

"It's lovely, Jessimond. I can't imagine anyone having a finer bridal gown. You have crafted a work of art with your needle," Lora exclaimed.

"I was happy to do this for you," she said. "Hopefully, Richmond will like it as much as you do."

Her half-sister glowed as she smoothed the blue silk skirts. "I had the same thought," she confided. "I'm very happy that the betrothal contracts were signed while you are at Netherfield and that you can attend the nuptial mass."

Jessimond had enjoyed the past three weeks at Netherfield, though she'd been very tired of late. She supposed all that time on the road with the mummers had finally caught up to her. Her appetite, too, had suffered since she'd arrived. The rich sauces and heavy spicing had not been to her liking. She longed for what she'd grown accustomed to, the simpler fare she'd prepared for the mummers.

"Have you decided about the trim we discussed earlier?" she asked.

"I think you should sew it on," Lina voiced. "On both the hem and the sleeves."

Jessimond hid a smile. Lina had to be the most opinionated person she'd ever met. When it was her time to wed, Jessimond only hoped Lina's husband would be able to handle his bride.

"I did like it," Lora said, hesitating. "Would you have time to add it to the hem, Jessimond?"

"Of course," she assured Lora. "The wedding is not for another two days. I can easily finish up tomorrow."

A servant entered the bedchamber. "My lady, Lord Gregory would like to speak to you in the solar."

"Thank you," Jessimond told her. To Lina, she said, "Help your sister remove her gown. Spread it across the chest so as not to wrinkle it. I'll claim it in the morning."

She hurried from the girls' chamber and went to her own. That queasiness had struck her again. Jessimond did not want to be ill for the wedding nor did she want to bring sickness to Lora. She reached her chamber and rushed inside, closing the door, and then moved to the basin. No sooner had she leaned over it than what little she'd eaten earlier came back up. She rinsed the awful taste from her mouth and wiped it with a cloth. Touching her forehead, she felt no sign of fever. She wished she could shake off the dull nausea.

Not wanting to keep Lord Gregory waiting, she made her way to the solar and knocked. He bid her to enter and Jessimond joined him at the table where he sat. She noticed he'd set up the chessboard again. It had become their habit to play a game or two while they conversed.

"How was your day?" he asked.

"Very good. Lora and I visited a few of the tenants and took them some food. I also worked on her wedding gown. It's almost complete except for a trim along the hem that I'll add."

"Lora told me how pleased she is with it. It was very good of you to take on such an elaborate project."

Jessimond moved her first piece along the board. "I enjoy sewing and am happy to contribute to such a happy occasion."

The baron moved his chess piece. "Richmond will be a good match for Lora. He's an earnest, steady fellow. I think they'll suit one another well." He paused. "My offer still stands. If you wish for me to look for a husband for you, I am willing to do so."

"Nay, but I thank you," she said politely, once more shutting the door to that topic.

Jessimond had explained previously that she wasn't betrothed and that none of the de Montfort children had been. Lora and Lina had thought her mad when she told them that de Montforts all married for love. The two sisters had argued back and forth about it. Jessimond had caught her birth father staring at her wistfully and knew that he understand exactly what she spoke of. He had loved at one time in his life but had been unable to wed that love. She neglected to tell him that she, too, loved another though she could never become his wife.

As they played their game, Jessimond asked questions about Celia Achard. Her curiosity about her birth mother only grew the more she found out about Celia.

"Did you ever meet any of her family? What were they like?"

Lord Gregory sighed. "Her father, Lord Americ, was Baron of Sturnwick. He was an adviser to the king and did not make much time for Celia. He brought her to court to find her a husband but then neglected to do so. Celia was left on her own most of the day. With her sweet disposition and beauty, she was envied—and ignored—by most of the ladies at court."

"And her mother?"

"The baroness died when Celia's younger brother was born. She rarely spoke of her mother. From what little she said, her two brothers had little to do with her when they were home from fostering."

Jessimond thought how different her life had been and said a swift prayer to the Virgin, thanking Her for the large, loving family she'd been raised in. "She must have been so lonely."

"Aye, she was." Lord Gregory frowned. "Seeing that loneliness drew me to her. I wanted to comfort her."

"You did love her, didn't you, my lord?"

He took a long pull from his wine goblet. "I did. I didn't want to. I even tried to stay away from her. In the end, I couldn't."

Jessimond recalled how Marcus had also avoided her, only to be drawn back to her. Her throat thickened with emotion.

"How did you learn of her death?" she finally asked.

"Through Sir Rodric. You've met him. He was the knight I designated to escort Celia and you to her home. He's a man I have always trusted, from the time I was a young boy. Sir Rodric continued on his journey in order to take Celia's body home. That way, she could be buried next to her mother."

"Have you ever visited her grave?"

"Nay. It wasn't my place to do so. I was not her husband. I was Egelina's. After Sir Rodric informed me of Celia's tragic passing, it shook me to my core. I vowed to God Himself that from that moment on, I would be a better man than the one I'd been up until then. I swore to be faithful to my wife and be a good father to my children." He gave her a steady look. "All of them. I'm grateful that we have finally found one another, Jessimond."

"I have enjoyed getting to know you, my lord."

The baron winced. "I hate how formal that sounds. I realize that Geoffrey de Montfort raised you and he alone should be called *Father* by you. I only wish you could call me something other than Lord Gregory."

Jessimond thought a moment. "What if I refer to you as Uncle Gregory?" she mused. "'Tis not as formal and still conveys a family relationship."

He smiled. "I would very much like that, Jessimond."

They continued their game in silence until its completion. As usual, she emerged as the victor. When they'd first starting playing against one another, she thought he allowed her to win but he shared that he'd never been much of a chess player. His smile each time she defeated him told Jessimond of his pride in her.

"I think I will retire for the evening," she said. "The hour grows late. I find I am tired."

"Thank you for spending this past hour with me, Jessimond. I look forward to our conversations. Once Lora is wed and leaves Netherfield, mayhap you will have more time available for me."

She laughed. "I fear Lina will demand even more of it with her sister gone." Standing, she brushed a kiss on his cheek for the first time. "Good night, Uncle Gregory."

"Good night," he echoed.

Jessimond turned as he brushed a tear away and left the solar.

Jessimond went to help Lora dress for her wedding. She found her half-sister pacing the bedchamber she shared with Lina.

"What's wrong?" Jessimond asked as she closed the door.

"I don't know what to do tonight," Lora moaned, wringing her hands. "I was so young when Mother died so she never told me anything. I'm so frightened." She threw herself onto the bed and buried her face.

Lina, sitting in a nearby chair, shrugged. "The servants say it hurts."

Lora's head popped up. "It *hurts*? Why did they tell you and not me?"

"Because I asked about it," Lina retorted. "I saw a groom and a serving wench coupling in the stables. They were both moaning and then she shrieked something awful. I couldn't very well ask them so I spoke to several of our servants."

"When was this?" Lora asked, her eyes welling with tears. "You never told me about the incident."

"I was seven or eight, I think." Lina began pacing the room now. "They all repeated the same thing. That it's a duty you must do, whether you like it or not. If you lie still and keep quiet, it passes quickly."

Jessimond decided to take the situation in hand. "Both of you. Sit. Now."

Lina returned to the chair. Lora pushed herself up and glanced hopefully at Jessimond, who took a seat next to her on the bed.

"I will tell you what I know," she confided, and proceeded to describe love play as Merryn had, adding in a little of her own experience from her single coupling with Marcus.

"It sounds like it hurts only a little," Lora said. "I hate pain, though."

"It won't last but a moment," Jessimond assured her. "Love play will bring a couple closer together. Remember, you and Richmond will act in unison in all matters once you are married."

Lora bit her lip. "What . . . what if I don't please him?" she whispered.

"You should be worried about him pleasing you," Jessimond retorted.

For a moment, a shocked silence filled the room, and then Lora and Lina erupted in laughter.

Lora hugged her. "You are so different from all the women I know, Jessimond. I am proud to call you sister."

Lina wiggled between them and also hugged Jessimond. "I call you sister, as well. And I want only you to sew my bridal gown when I wed. It will be even fancier than Lora's. I think green. Or mayhap yellow. Father always says he likes me in yellow."

"You have a few years to decide," Jessimond said. "It's time now to ready your sister for her special day."

She brushed Lora's hair until it shone and then braided it intricately, pinning it up and intertwining the braids as she did so. Lina handed her the crown of flowers the two of them had woven together yesterday afternoon and Jessimond placed it atop Lora's head. She helped the bride step into her wedding finery and then surveyed her handiwork.

"You look like a princess!" exclaimed Lina.

A light tap sounded at the door and then Lord Gregory poked his head in. A brilliant smile broke out on his face as he entered.

"I came looking for my daughter but only see a princess," he said.

"Oh, Father, do I really look like a princess?" Lora asked. "Both you and Lina think so."

"You do, my dearest. So does that make me a king?" he teased.

All three of them laughed at his wit.

"It's time to go," he told them, holding out his arm.

Lora took it and they proceeded to the Netherfield chapel, where a large crowd had gathered. Lord Gregory escorted Lora to the front steps, where Richmond waited with the Netherfield priest. Jessimond and Lina stopped a few paces away and Lina reached for Jessimond's hand, holding it tightly.

As the ceremony proceeded, Jessimond's thoughts rambled far away to other happy times in her family, and other weddings she'd witnessed. Her parents were the picture of wedded bliss after decades of marriage, and each of her five siblings had been blessed to find their soul mate. Jessimond struggled with being the only unwed de Montfort, knowing she'd found love and lost it so cruelly.

The assembled group moved inside for the mass. As the priest droned on, her belly knotted painfully. Her head hurt. Her heart ached. In that moment, Jessimond had never been more miserable. She dreaded what a future without Marcus held and wondered what she should do with her life.

Once more, the people moved from the chapel to the bailey and into the keep. Jessimond found herself swept up in the crowd as everyone journeyed to the feast awaiting them in the great hall. She went to take her place on the dais with the other family members. Lora and Richmond sat in the center. Before Jessimond could take a seat, the smell of venison assaulted her nose. Her stomach lurched uncomfortably and she had to swallow hard to keep the bile from coming up.

Without warning, she felt as if she'd been punched in the gut. A sudden clarity descended upon her. With that understanding came fear.

She was with child.

CHAPTER 26

September, 1396

MARCUS PULLED ON the reins and brought Storm to a halt. He stared at the castle in the distance.

Kinwick. Where Jess lived.

He closed his eyes and could see her image even now. The porcelain skin and thick, golden blond hair. Her tiny waist and enticing curves. Those large, amethyst eyes that he could get lost in. A lump formed in his throat.

It had been a year since he'd seen her. Touched her. Tasted her. A year of abject misery—though he hadn't let anyone see it. Marcus had been what he hoped was the most industrious baron Hartefield had ever known. He knew every tenant and servant by name. Trained daily with his soldiers. Kept meticulous records of the harvest and livestock. Played with Livia and told her stories as he put her to bed each night, making sure she knew she was well loved.

Then spent his sleepless nights thinking of Jess and how much he'd hurt her. Would she take him back—now that he was free?

He would soon find out.

Marcus opened his eyes and tamped down the fear that raced through him. What if she refused to come with him? Or the earl said Jess must remain at Kinwick?

Then what?

He couldn't think of any outcome other than one which consisted of Jess in his arms within the next hour. Marcus would tell her over and over how much he still loved her between passionate kisses. He sent another silent prayer to the Virgin, pleading for Her intercession. Though he'd never been much for prayers, Marcus had kept up a constant conversation with the Holy Mother for days, hoping she would take pity on him.

Nudging Storm's flanks, the horse continued on the last league of their journey. He arrived at the gates of Kinwick after passing workers harvesting grain in the fields and identified himself, expressing his interest in speaking with the earl on urgent business. Granted entrance, he was directed to the stables, where he left Storm before starting out for the keep.

Marcus crossed the bailey and paused a moment when he saw a familiar couple at a well. Peter glistened with the sweat of hard labor as Agatha, her belly swollen with a coming child, held the ladle to his lips. He approached them, uncertain of the reception he would receive.

Agatha spied him first and gasped, dropping the ladle. "Marcus! I mean, my lord."

Peter wheeled to face Marcus, his hands bunching into fists. He took two steps forward and slammed one of them into Marcus' nose. Marcus stumbled back from the powerful blow but did nothing to defend himself.

When Peter's arm went back again, Agatha jumped and pulled it down.

"Nay. Stop, Peter," she begged.

He glared at Marcus. "Why are you here?"

"I've come for Jess." He paused and wiped a dribble of blood from under his nose. "I will speak to your father, of course, but I know I must also talk with the earl and compensate him for the loss of a valuable servant."

"Good luck with that." Peter spat on the ground, his eyes narrowing as he gazed at Marcus with contempt.

"Lord Geoffrey should be finishing up in the training yard this time of day," Agatha volunteered. "You can find him there." She looked at Peter. "I'll go to the keep and tell the countess they have a guest." She lifted her skirts and raced off.

After she left, Marcus said, "I am sorry, Peter. For everything."

"You'll get no forgiveness from me."

"I admire your loyalty to your sister. Somehow, I will make it up to her. And you. My offer still stands. You and Agatha are welcome to come live at Hartefield. You can serve in whatever capacity you choose."

Peter walked off without another word. Marcus watched him go to a nearby blacksmith's shed. He lifted a hammer and began pounding it against an empty anvil. He supposed Peter imagined Marcus' head on the block.

Turning, he headed toward the training yard. As he neared it, soldiers began streaming past him, the end of their day done. Marcus waited patiently and finally saw an imposing man with dark hair now streaked with gray was the last to leave the field. Though close to three score, he looked as if he could take on a man a third his age—and be victorious in their encounter.

"Lord Geoffrey?" he asked.

"Aye? Who might you be, my lord?"

"I am Marcus de Harte, Baron of Harteley. I have an urgent matter to discuss with you."

The nobleman's demeanor changed in an instant. A scowl darkened his still handsome face. "Haven't you already done enough harm? Leave my estate. Now," the earl commanded.

"I cannot, my lord," Marcus insisted. "I need to speak to you. About Jess."

"Why would you come here after so long a time and stir up trouble, man? Have you no sense of decency?" Waves of anger poured off the earl.

"I am here for Jess, my lord. If she'll have me, I wish to wed her."

Astonishment filled the older man's face. He took a long breath and exhaled. "Come to my solar. I make all important decisions with my wife."

With that, Lord Geoffrey strode away. Marcus followed him, keeping a short distance between them. They passed Peter again, who continued slamming his hammer down with purpose.

Arriving at the keep, the two men mounted the stairs leading up to it. Lord Geoffrey pushed open the door, Marcus trailing behind him. Once in the hallway outside the great hall, he saw Agatha rush down a staircase that he assumed led to the bedchambers and solar.

"My lord, Lady Merryn awaits you and Lord Marcus in the solar."

"Thank you, Agatha."

Geoffrey de Montfort mounted the stairs, Marcus keeping pace. The earl ventured down a long hallway until he reached its end and pushed the door open. Entering behind Lord Geoffrey, Marcus saw a striking, older woman with incredibly blue eyes, sitting as regally as any queen ever had. She must have been the great beauty of her day for she still was impressive even now.

Marcus crossed the large room to where she sat and took her hand.

"My lady." He kissed her fingers. "I am Marcus de Harte, Baron of Harteley." He released her hand and stepped back.

Lord Geoffrey had gone to stand behind his wife and put a hand on her shoulder. Lady Merryn reached up and took it as she assessed Marcus.

"Have a seat, my lord."

He took a chair opposite the couple. "I have come to Kinwick to ask your permission for Jess Gilpin, one of your valued servants, to leave your property. I know she looks after your grandchildren and will be hard to replace. I will amply compensate you for her absence from Kinwick and even pay for her replacement. If you agree, my lord, I will seek out her father and ask his permission for her hand in marriage."

The couple glanced at one another and back at him.

"It is my understanding that you are already wed, Lord Marcus," Lady Merryn began.

"I was, my lady. My wife—Lady Ailith—passed away several days ago."

"And you came straight here?" Lord Geoffrey asked.

"I did." Marcus swallowed. "I fell in love with Jess last summer when we both toured with the mummers. I had no idea my father had betrothed me to another woman. I did my duty and wed Lady Ailith, but I never lay with her. That would have been the worst betrayal to Jess."

"Your wife accepted that arrangement?" the noblewoman inquired.

"Aye. I shared with her how much I loved Jess. Lady Ailith knew Jess since she had tended to her when she had the measles, though Ailith never truly recovered from that illness. I was informed that, often, those who survive bouts of it go blind or have a weakened heart. My wife's heart was severely affected by the high fever she'd experienced. Ailith kept to her bed this past year and had little strength. She finally slipped away. Her last words thanked me for caring for her daughter and urged me to go to Jess."

Marcus stood. "I know I broke Jess' heart for my own has been torn in two ever since we parted. I have done my duty to my family and my people, but every breath I take has been one of sorrow and pain. My lord, my lady, if I do not have Jess in my life, I'm not sure I can go on living. I'll do anything you ask but I must have her. I want to make her happy once again. Give her children of her own.

"I promise to spend the rest of my life making up to her all the wrongs I've done. Jess will be the most treasured wife in all of England. Nay, the entire world," he said with vehemence.

Lady Merryn gasped. She looked to her husband. "Geoffrey?"

Lord Geoffrey smiled. "Jessimond will make her own decision. 'Tis not one we can make for her, my love."

He turned to Marcus. "My daughter is in our bedchamber." He waved a hand toward an open door.

Marcus took a few steps before stopping in his tracks. "Your . . . daughter?" he asked hoarsely, looking from Lord Geoffrey to Lady Merryn and back.

"Aye," the earl replied. "Jessimond is our youngest child."

"Jess is . . . a de Montfort," he said, trying to comprehend the words. "The daughter of one of England's most powerful families."

"She is. A strong woman with a mind of her own," Lady Merryn said with a smile. "I know—because I raised her that way."

Marcus looked hopefully to the door Lord Geoffrey had indicated. Jess—nay, Jessimond—was inside that chamber. With the door ajar, she must have heard their entire conversation.

And yet she'd remained hidden.

That didn't bode well. Still, Marcus hadn't come all this way to face defeat. He straightened his shoulders, determined that she would be his. Whatever it took.

"If you will excuse me," he told the couple and strode across the room, pausing in the doorway.

Jess sat in a chair beside the door, a babe in her arms. Marcus' first thought was that she looked lovelier than the Madonna holding the Christ child. He gathered up every ounce of courage he had and stepped through the archway and closed the door behind him. Their conversation would be for them alone.

She looked up at him, those amethyst eyes swimming with tears.

Marcus had practiced what he would say to her throughout the entire ride to Kinwick but now seeing her, every word fled. Finally, he asked, "Which de Montfort grandchild is this?"

"The newest one," she replied, her gaze locked on his. "Mine. This babe is mine. I'm a de Montfort and so is Margaret. I named her after your mother."

He heard what she said but merely stood there, looking from her to the babe and back.

"You . . . had a child? Our child?"

Jess nodded and smiled down at the sleeping girl. "Isn't she beautiful?"

Marcus fell to his knees, great sobs escaping his chest. His head rested in her lap. His hands clutched the material of her cotehardie. Vaguely, he heard the door open as he wept.

"I'll take her," Lady Merryn said.

Jess handed the infant over and the noblewoman left the room.

Marcus felt Jess' hands as they began lightly stroking his hair. Her gentle touch made him cry all the harder.

Raising his tearstained face, he said, "How can I ever make it up to you?"

"By loving me," she said simply. "I have never stopped loving you."

Jess leaned toward him and pressed a soft kiss to his lips.

The heavy burden Marcus had carried for a year floated away like a cloud. He came to his feet, bringing Jess with him. His arms came about her as he teased her lips apart. Their tongues met. Marcus poured everything of himself into the kiss as their passion flared. He wanted the kiss to tell her how sorry he was. How much he needed her forgiveness. How he'd longed for her day and night. It went on and on. Time ceased to exist. Only he and Jess existed in this world of two.

Nay, three. The babe made them three.

Marcus broke the kiss and rested his brow against hers, reluctant to part from her.

"Can you ever forgive me?" he asked hoarsely.

"There's nothing to forgive, my love," she replied.

He cradled her face tenderly. "I abandoned you. You gave birth to our child alone. I should have been there."

She brushed her lips against his. "You will be there for the rest, Marcus. I'm sure we will have many more babes. After all, I will need to provide an heir to Hartefield, won't I?"

He kissed her again and again, one kiss melting into the next.

Breaking away so they could catch their breaths, he asked, "What am I to call you? Jess? Jessimond?"

She gave him a radiant smile. "I rather like Wife," she declared.

Marcus beamed at her. "I shall call you all three, my love. And I will be at your side each time you give birth. We will never be parted again, I swear. My life is yours, Jessimond. My precious, precious love."

He kissed her deeply, reveling in her taste and the feel of her in his arms. Finally, he pulled back. "I would like to hold our daughter now."

Jessimond took his hand and led him from the bedchamber. Her parents sat in the next room, Lady Merryn cradling her youngest granddaughter.

Marcus released Jessimond's hand and asked, "May I hold her?"

"Of course," the noblewoman replied. "She is the sweetest tempered babe in our family. Just as her mother was."

He took the sleeping bundle and drew her to his chest. Suddenly, the babe's eyes opened and stared at him with interest.

"'Tis your father, Margaret," he choked out, his eyes blurring with tears. "I've come to claim you and your mother and bring you home."

Marcus began walking around the solar with the babe as she cooed at him. His heart swelled with love and spilled over. Jessimond came and joined him, slipping her hand through the crook of his arm and leaning her head against him.

"Isn't she lovely?" she asked.

"She is the most perfect babe ever," he said.

A knock sounded on the chamber door and Lord Geoffrey bade them to enter.

A servant stepped in and said, "Lady Jessimond's father is here. Shall I bring him up?"

Marcus' jaw dropped as Lady Merryn instructed the servant to send him up. "I thought Lord Geoffrey was your father."

Jessimond grinned. "Oh, you have much to catch up on, Marcus."

He kissed the tip of Margaret's nose. "I will enjoy every moment of it. Because I will be with the two women I love now and forever."

CHAPTER 27

Marcus dressed in the wedding finery Jessimond had sewn for him, first putting on the new gypon and cotehardie and then topping them off with a formal houppelande. She'd heavily embroidered the high neck of this rust-colored outer garment, which struck the floor. It had full, flaring sleeves and hung in large folds that Jessimond had lined with fur. Marcus had never possessed such fine garb and thought his outfit a work of art.

He combed his dark hair and calmed the nerves skittering through him. They weren't doubts regarding his upcoming marriage, but rather his wish to please and impress the hordes of de Montforts and their many relatives, who had descended upon Kinwick over the past week. Just when he thought he had remembered the right names and titles and could associate them with the correct individuals, someone new would arrive and confuse him all over again. Still, he'd enjoyed getting to know Jess' large, extended family and couldn't wait to add to their own.

Little Margaret already had him dancing to her tune. At three months, she was beginning to smile often and blow bubbles, which entertained her—and him—to no end. Marcus already thought her the most clever child in the world. He and Jessimond had discussed how they wanted to add to their brood. That would start after their wedding feast ended.

Mayhap even before.

Since he'd arrived at Kinwick two weeks ago, Marcus had refrained from touching Jess beyond holding her hand and stealing a few heated kisses. He'd spent countless nights over the past year recalling every curve of her lush body. His fingers ached to skim that satin skin once again.

Tonight, his longings would become reality.

Exiting the bedchamber, he found three very imposing men awaiting him in the corridor. Jessimond's three brothers all were tall and broad-shouldered. Ancel, Earl of Mauntell, was the eldest male. Hal, captain of Kinwick's guard, was the middle son. Edward, Baron of Shallowheart, was the youngest and closest male to Jessimond in age.

"Father would like a word with you," Ancel said. His tone let Marcus know this was more an order than a request.

He followed the three men downstairs, remembering that a bevy of women had taken over the solar to help prepare Jessimond for the nuptial mass. They led him into the great hall, where he saw Geoffrey de Montfort standing near the fire. With him, he recognized Nan's husband, Tristan, Earl of Leventhorpe, and Alys' husband, Kit, Baron of Brentley. Marcus realized this group composed all of the husbands that were de Montforts or had married one.

"Welcome, Marcus," Geoffrey greeted him as the four men joined the ranks of those standing with him. The earl handed Marcus a wine goblet and then passed one to each nobleman gathered in their circle.

"We've brought you here to toast you and Jessimond," Geoffrey continued.

"And to recognize the remarkable women in this family," Kit said. He gestured to Tristan. "Both Tristan and I feel blessed to have married into such a strong, loving family."

"One of *very* strong-willed women," Tristan added, and they all chuckled.

"We are fortunate that the women we've brought into the de Montfort family have also been resolute," Ancel said.

"Yet, they are tenderhearted and faithful, as well," Edward said.

"And every man standing here, be they de Montforts by blood or through marriage, have learned that love is the key to everything," Hal said. "We are richer men for allowing the love in our hearts to guide us, no matter what we do or where we go."

Geoffrey raised his pewter cup. "Here's to Jessimond and Marcus—and to every couple represented here, man and woman alike—especially my dearest Merryn, the woman who has believed in me and showered me with love for decades. May we continue to live long and love well with our wives ever by our sides and forever in our hearts.

"To love!" Geoffrey declared.

"To love!" every man echoed.

Marcus swallowed the sweet, rich wine, enjoying the warmth it brought. He lowered the cup and said, "My family was not a loving one and I had been taught from an early age to beware of love. I am beyond grateful that Jessimond came into my life and opened my eyes to the truth. I know now that a life filled with love is an abundant one. Loving Jess has fulfilled me in ways I never knew existed. From now on, all de Harte sons and daughters will be raised in love and know how powerful a force it can be.

"To love!" Marcus proclaimed again and his new brothers-in-arms cheered.

JESSIMOND NURSED MARGARET while Nan sat beside her with her seven-month-old babe, doing the same. Alys and her cousin, Avelyn, continued intricately braiding Jessimond's hair in preparation for the upcoming nuptial mass.

"If you'd like, you can feed Margaret after the feast and then let Tristan and me keep her overnight. I know you and Marcus would enjoy time alone after spending the last few days with so many relatives. If she gets hungry during the night, I will nurse her."

Jessimond gave her sister a grateful smile. "I appreciate your thoughtfulness, Nan. So will Marcus."

She had tried not to think of Marcus during the year they were apart. Many days, she had worked until the brink of exhaustion, hoping her sleep would be dreamless. Yet, even after giving birth to Marcus' child and knowing he was wed to another woman, Jessimond had daydreamed about her lover's touch. She eagerly awaited tonight, the first in which they would sleep side by side as man and wife.

Chuckling, she thought, mayhap, not much sleep would occur.

Margaret finished feeding and Jessimond burped the babe before handing her to Agatha. She knew from her friend that Marcus had once more extended his offer for Peter and Agatha to come live at Hartefield, with Peter serving either as a soldier or blacksmith. The couple was still considering what they would do. Selfishly, Jessimond hoped they would choose Harte Castle so their first babes could grow up together, playing as she and Peter had so long ago.

Knowing it was time to dress, she stood as Elinor and Rosalyne brought the layers of clothing she'd sewn and helped her into them. She'd chosen to wear shades of blue interspersed with gold. As she smoothed the folds of the rich silk, Elysande handed her a mirror to admire herself. The image reflected spoke of a woman deeply in love. One eager to start the rest of her life with the man she loved by her side.

Beatrice bent and pinned Jessimond's amethyst brooch to her breast as a finishing touch and then suggested, "Let's give Jessimond a few moments alone to reflect." Beatrice herded the group of women from the solar.

Only her mother remained behind. As Jessimond went to her, they clasped hands. Merryn's eyes were bright with unshed tears.

"The happiest day of my life was when Geoffrey returned to me after being gone for so many years," Merryn began. "The second happiest was when he and Nan brought you home to us. You were the sweetest of all of my babes." She paused. "And today is the third happiest day I have experienced, for the last of my children will unite in marriage with the man she loves."

Merryn kissed both her cheeks. Jessimond repeated the gesture.

"I can't thank you and Father enough for taking me in," she began. "You changed the course of my life. You raised me as one of your own, with no difference between me and my siblings. You and Father are good people, Mother. The absolute best. I am proud of you and all my brothers and sisters. I was raised in love. I will continue to live in love and hope I can be half the mother you are to my own children."

They embraced as a quick knock sounded. Geoffrey de Montfort entered the solar. He held her to him for a long moment.

"The last of our children to leave the nest," he said. "You have added great riches to our lives, Jessimond. I thank the Virgin and Christ Almighty for bringing Marcus back to you—and Margaret." He pressed a kiss upon her brow. "You look so very beautiful, Daughter. Are you ready?"

"I am, Father."

The trio left the solar and headed to Kinwick's chapel. Flowers had been strewn along the path and a band of musicians played as they made their way to the entrance, where Marcus and the priest stood awaiting them. She spied Uncle Gregory standing with Lina and Byrom on one side and Lora and Richmond on the other. He blew her a kiss as she passed. She and Geoffrey arrived at the steps to the chapel. Jessimond took a sleeping Margaret from Agatha's arms and kissed the babe. She allowed Marcus to do the same and then handed their child to Merryn.

Marcus threaded his fingers through hers and the ceremony began. As they spoke their vows, Jessimond marveled at everything that had occurred during the last year. She'd joined the mummers' troupe and made countless friends during her travels. Learned the story of her birth and grown close to her birth father and his children. Fallen deeply in love with Marcus and brought little Margaret into the world. Now, here she stood, uniting with this man in holy matrimony. From an unclaimed orphan to a noblewoman marrying for love, Jessimond knew she'd already lived a wonderful life.

And the best was yet to come.

EPILOGUE

April, 1406

JESSIMOND GAZED AT the portrait hanging on the wall. Rosalyne had painted it as a wedding gift half a score ago. Jessimond smiled at the painting of her and Marcus. She decided it was time to ask her sister-in-law to do another one. Marcus had been handsome ten years ago but now that a tinge of silver touched his temples, she thought him even more attractive.

At that moment, her husband raced through the door and across the room. He fell to his knees and took Jessimond's hand.

"I'm not too late?" he asked.

"Nay, Husband. I'd say you were right on time." She bit her lip as another labor pain hit.

He brushed the damp hair from her brow and cradled her cheek with his palm. The look of love in his eyes still caused Jessimond's heart to flutter, even after a decade together.

"My lord!" the new midwife admonished. "You mustn't be in here. Lady Jessimond will give birth at any moment."

A slow smile turned the corners of his mouth up and he said, "I know. I look forward to that moment."

"But... but... you cannot be present," the midwife sputtered. "'Tis not the done way. I will make sure the babe is cleaned up and the baroness presentable. Only then can you see her and the child."

Marcus leaned in and brushed his lips against Jessimond's, bringing her warmth and comfort. "My wife is always presentable. In fact, she glows with eternal beauty as each new babe is born. And I assist in those births. I missed out the first time with Margaret. I swore I would never do so again." He grinned as he gazed at her. "So far, I have seen another daughter and two sons come into this world."

Jessimond heard the midwife's gasp. "It's true. Lord Marcus always attends the births of our children. He has massaged my belly to urge them to come forth and even caught one—nay, two—as they made their appearance in the world. He will stay."

"I will stay," reaffirmed Marcus, his eyes never leaving hers.

She sucked in a quick breath and winced, squeezing his hand tightly as her toes curled into the mattress.

"Is the pain bad, my love?"

"No worse than usual." Jessimond gasped again. "Oh, this one wants out quickly, I fear." She cried out as the contractions increased. At the same time, the unbearable urge to push overwhelmed her.

"'Tis time," she managed to say.

Her husband lifted the bedclothes and then met her eyes. "I see the head crowning. Push, Jess. Now. As hard as you can," he commanded.

She bore down, concentrating on nothing but that sensation. Vaguely, she heard words of encouragement coming from both Marcus and the midwife as she focused all of her energy into bringing this new life into the world. Gritting her teeth as another labor pain came, she rode the wave of agony and then forced the child from her with one last, lengthy push.

Falling back against the pillows, she heard Marcus' delighted laugh. "We have another son!" he proclaimed.

Jessimond slowed her breathing, relieved the birth had ended. She was marginally aware of the bustling about as the babe was cleaned and bundled and the afterbirth expelled. A servant wiped Jessimond's face with a clean cloth and helped her to sit up as she was dressed in a new smock and the bedclothes were changed. Sinking back into the pillows behind her, Marcus suddenly loomed over her, their newborn cuddled against his chest. He lowered the babe to her and Jessimond accepted him.

Peering into the face of the newest de Harte, she smiled. "He's perfect," she declared.

Her husband slid in beside her, his arm going around her, and they admired the latest addition to their ever-growing family, as those who had assisted with the birth left the room. The welcomed silence would not last but she reveled in it all the same. She had a new child to love in her arms and a husband who was her very life beside her.

Their son began to mewl softly and then his cries increased in volume. Jessimond guided him to her breast and he latched on, greedily sucking the nourishing milk from her.

"We have been blessed beyond measure," Marcus finally said as the babe stopped nursing. He offered his son a finger. Immediately, the newborn wrapped his own fingers around it.

"He's a strong one," Marcus noted. "He'll need a name to reflect that strength. Have you thought of what you might wish to call him, Wife? If not, I have a suggestion."

Eager to hear what name he was considering after all the ones they'd mentioned as a possibility, Jessimond said, "Share your thoughts with me, Husband."

Marcus said, "I want to call him Geoffrey. After your father. He was the strongest and yet most vulnerable man I have known. I would be proud for our son to bear his grandfather's name and always carry a part of the de Montfort legacy within him."

Tears sprang to her eyes. Geoffrey de Montfort had recently been laid to rest, living three score and ten years. His death had been sudden and Jessimond was too heavy with child to make the journey to Kinwick for his burial.

"Father would have been proud to know we named our boy after him."

Marcus brushed a tender kiss against her temple. "He knows, Jess. Geoffrey de Montfort is watching over us all from Heaven above. One life might have been extinguished but another has come to light and will bring us great joy in the years to come."

Jessimond de Harte believed her husband's words rang with truth. She would love this new Geoffrey as she had the children who'd come before him and the others that would follow, just as she'd loved her father. She brought the now-sleeping babe close and kissed him and then nestled the littlest de Harte against her side as she wrapped her arms around Marcus.

This man, the greatest love of all, would be by her side—now and until the end of time.

Jessimond kissed him and knew in that moment that life was good. Oh, so very good.

Knights of Honor Series by Alexa Aston
Word of Honor
Marked by Honor
Code of Honor
Journey to Honor
Heart of Honor
Bold in Honor
Love and Honor
Gift of Honor
Path to Honor
Return to Honor

About the Author

As a child, Alexa Aston gathered her neighborhood friends together and made up stories for them to act out, her first venture into creating memorable characters. Following her passion for history and love of learning, she became a teacher who began writing on the side to maintain her sanity in a sea of teenage hormones.

Alexa's historical romances use history as a backdrop to place her characters in extraordinary circumstances, where their intense desire for one another grows into the treasured gift of love.

She is the author of *The Knights of Honor*, a medieval romance series that takes place in 14th century England during the reign of Edward III and centers on the de Montfort family. Each romance focuses on the code of chivalry that bound knights of this era.

A native Texan, Alexa lives with her husband in a Dallas suburb, where she eats her fair share of dark chocolate and plots out stories while she walks every morning. She enjoys reading, watching movies and sports, and can't get enough of *Fixer Upper* or *Game of Thrones*. Alexa also writes romantic suspense, western historicals, and standalone medieval novels as Lauren Linwood.

Alexa loves to hear from her readers. You can connect with her through FB, Twitter, and her website: alexaaston.com.

Facebook:
facebook.com/authoralexaaston

Twitter:
twitter.com/AlexaAston

BookBub Follow:
bookbub.com/authors/alexa-aston

Newsletter sign-up:
madmimi.com/signups/422152/join

Amazon Page:
amazon.com/author/alexaaston

Made in the USA
Middletown, DE
17 November 2018